The Flaws of Gravity

Stephanie Caye

Edited by Julie Kay-Wallace

Cover Design by Danielle Fine

1

I CURSED ALOUD WHEN I fumbled my key in the lock, then risked a glance up and down the hallway. Still empty. Maybe the fancy condo owners were used to jittery, dishevelled women swearing at doors after midnight when they couldn't figure out how keys worked. Probably everybody just had good sound-proofing.

Glaring at my traitorous, shaking hand, I took more care to fit the key into its hole. The tension left my shoulders when the deadbolt shot back and I slipped into the apartment.

"Jude." Aubrie appeared in the kitchen doorway as I brushed the snow out of my hair. He had the sleeves of his sweater pushed to the elbow and a kitchen towel draped over one shoulder. In the harsh overhead lights, the grey in his thick blond hair was more apparent than usual.

"I've asked you to only use that key if I'm not here," he chided. A sink full of dishes sat behind him. He'd definitely cooked something earlier. Two wine glasses sat on the counter.

"I knocked."

"You didn't."

"I thought you'd want this ASAP." I pulled the chilly laptop from my under secondhand coat and shoved it at him. Slim and expensive, the thing didn't weigh much, but handing it off still let me breathe easier.

"What is it?" Aubrie accepted it on the tips of his fingers like I'd just handed him a grenade, eyeing the smear of blood across the top.

"What you asked for. Codes, or whatever." I headed into the apartment's expansive living room, scanning the room for a leftover wine bottle or preferably something stronger. "Do you have anything to drink? I'll settle for wine if that's what's open."

"Is he alive?"

My knuckles itched. Was there still blood on them? I wiped them on my jeans. A minute ago it had seemed like I'd never be warm again, but now I felt flushed. "I didn't check. I was in a hurry."

"You didn't *check*?" Aubrie caught my arm, forcing me to lift my chin and meet his eyes.

I hissed in pain when his fingers dug into my skin. "I'm sorry!"

"Sorry won't fix it." He let me go and tossed the laptop onto a sofa cushion, striding back into the kitchen.

Outrage fused through me seeing the computer cast aside so carelessly after what I'd done to get it. I swallowed the objection, rubbing my bruised arm as I followed him. Dread coiled in my stomach at what 'fix it' might entail.

Aubrie rifled through a drawer, then snatched the towel from his shoulder and used it to withdraw something from the back. He held it with the fabric like it might scald his bare hand.

I stumbled back when he surged forward and swung his fist at my chest. He still managed to bury something sharp in my shoulder. Searing agony spiked through my arm.

Before I could move, he grabbed the front of my shirt and flung me to the side with the full force of his strength.

I rolled to a stop against an outdoor railing, six stories above the street. A deafening crash rang in my ears. When I sucked in a shocked breath, the freezing air stung my lungs as much as the glass shards speckling my skin. It took a moment to register that I'd gone straight through the sliding balcony door, shattering it.

Aubrie had *thrown* me through it.

My shoulder throbbed hard enough to make me see dark spots, half-obscuring his back-lit form in the ruined door frame. I had to get up, run, before he got to me. The fire radiating from whatever he'd buried beside my collarbone made it hard to move fast.

When I closed my free hand around it to pull it out, the metal burned my fingers like a hot stove.

Iron.

I tightened my grip and yanked anyway, gagging on a scream when the metal tore through muscle. It came halfway out, letting me see what looked like the top of an arty corkscrew slick with blood.

Aubrie strode three steps across the balcony and hauled me to my feet like a limp, broken doll. The hard look on his face froze me harder than the snowy air. That expression of disgust had always been reserved for other people—lesser people.

Before I could manage a word, I was airborne, falling fast through the cold.

I shifted gravity on instinct, spinning the world around me sideways so that 'down' slammed my body into the building wall. The impact sent me bouncing off the bricks like a ping-pong ball. The iron corkscrew in my shoulder weighted me, siding with the earth's gravity over my own to tug me toward the street below.

Using my power to veer dizzily into the wall again slowed my descent but didn't stop it. I rolled down the rough bricks like they were a steep hill, my scrabbling fingers raking air.

Breath left my lungs when I hit the ground. Pain radiated through my body, a roiling mass without origin. The lights of the building blurred, dimmed and seeped away.

2

I FLOATED, DRIFTING SIDEWAYS. Distant noises vied for my attention—voices without words, sounds without context. Footsteps, dishes clattering, doors closing, persistent electronic beeping. Light grew brighter until it stung my eyelids and forced them open.

My surroundings came in fuzzy as I blinked awake. Propped half-upright in a bed, I rested against a pillow that felt like a sack of shredded newspaper. A TV hung in the corner of the room, commercials chattering away on low volume. Machines hummed on the wall beside my bed.

A hospital room. I hadn't been in a hospital room in . . . maybe ever? If I had, I'd been too young to remember. Turned out they looked pretty much the same as on TV, only smaller and not as well-lit.

What was I doing in this one? My stomach lurched at a jolt of memory—Aubrie's furious face, the wind rushing against me as I fell, the iron in my shoulder weighing me down like an anchor. I breathed in through my nose to fight the surge of nausea, then pulled the hospital gown off my shoulder. Where there should have been a nasty, discoloured wound, only a small scar marked my skin.

Had any of that even happened? Why would Aubrie have had an iron corkscrew in his kitchen? Nobody with Faerie blood would willingly keep that shit around. Plus I didn't have scabs on my hands or arms from going through the glass door. I should be in pain if I'd fallen as far as I thought. I tested my muscles, pointing my toes under the starchy sheets, stretching my spine and making fists with both hands. Everything worked.

A red spot on the back of my hand twinged and I rubbed what seemed to be tape adhesive from the skin around it. Weren't hospital patients on TV always hooked to an IV that they pulled along with them as they walked? Where was mine? I didn't know what any of the machines around me were.

The door to the room stood open. Muffled noises echoed from outside, voices and footsteps down the hall, laughter and something moving on squeaky wheels. None of the sounds approached my room.

My *private* room.

I sat up to take in the whole space. No other beds, no curtained-off sections. Just me. A private room wasn't standard—public health insurance never covered bells and whistles. I only knew a couple of people who could shell out cash to wrangle this.

Since one of those people had just hurled me out a sixth story window, he probably wasn't footing my bills.

I fought to swallow around the lump that formed in my throat, then shoved the blankets off my legs. I swung them over the side of the bed to get to my feet. Wobbly, but my muscles held. The edges of my thoughts still felt fuzzy, like I'd woken up disoriented in the middle of a dream.

It hadn't been a dream, though. Aubrie, Spencer Aubrie—my closest friend and literal partner in crime—had poisoned me with iron and tossed me into the air like a fucking Frisbee. My eyes burned, chest tight like a giant fist had squeezed the air out of me. I caught myself on the rail at the end of the bed when my legs went rubbery.

Why? I'd brought him the goddamn codes he'd asked for—he should have been proud of me, relieved that he wouldn't have to call in whatever other shitty hired guns he'd had on deck.

I dug my fingernails into the hard plastic. On the TV, commercials gave way to a local news channel. An anchorwoman's soothing cadence helped clear my head. "Due to a leak in the school's gym," she was saying, "the graduation ceremony is being postponed to this Saturday, June twentieth—"

"Saturday *what*?" The words slipped out aloud before I could stop them. My voice in the empty room made me jump. I looked to the open door to be sure I hadn't drawn any attention, then whipped back to face the TV. I searched the text scroll at the bottom for a date and found it along with the time in the lower right-hand corner.

6:46 p.m., June 17. At least the year was familiar.

But *June*?

I almost tripped over my own feet getting to the window. In the bright sunlight, full, green trees dotted the streets below. No bare branches, no snow.

Summer.

No wonder nothing hurt. I'd had three months in a hospital bed to heal up. I searched for landmarks to gauge where I was. None of the buildings looked familiar and I couldn't see the downtown Toronto skyline.

I caught the dim ghost of my own reflection in the glass. My hair hung greasy and tangled around my face, and dark circles ringed my eyes to match its colour. It curled past my shoulders, longer than I remembered. I'd missed my birthday in April. Twenty-five now.

My nose looked crooked, so I touched it to confirm. My fingers slid over the new bump where it must have been broken and reset. A narrow scar ran down the side of my left cheek, dark and puckered. Seeing the evidence of my injuries, I felt Aubrie's hand tightening on my arm, the fire in my shoulder before I was airborne, and—

Nope.

I couldn't think about Aubrie yet, try to figure out what had happened, why he'd attacked me. Every nerve in my body screamed to get somewhere safe—but where was

6

safe now? His place was supposed to be my refuge, the only spot in the whole city where I could breathe easy.

Not anymore. The thought sent a pang through me. *Stop. Can't lose it. Need to get out of here.*

I still had a few friends in the city—probably downgraded to acquaintances at this point, since I hadn't seen them in forever. I'd had a drink with my old roommate Lilah maybe . . . eight months ago? Maybe she'd let me crash on her couch for a few nights.

It was as good a first stop as any. Nobody in my current life would know her, would expect me to go there.

Couldn't leave in a hospital gown, though.

Before slipping out of the room, I went through the drawers in the particle board bedside table, looking for my phone, my wallet. Nothing. That was a worry for future-Jude. I eased out the door and walked down the hallway with my spine straight, gaze forward to tell anyone nearby that I had every reason in the world to leave. Maybe no one would recognize me awake.

I followed a nurse into the locker room and slid into a bathroom stall while her back was turned. Holding my breath, I waited for the slam of a locker and the door swinging closed again. Silence. I crept out to look for new clothes. A couple of lockers without padlocks yielded a pair of black jeans and a tank top. I rifled through a few more near the showers and scored a pair of black boots, fake leather, flat-heels. My style. A size too big, but I pulled them on anyway.

Behind me, the locker room door clicked shut. I spun away from the locker I'd just closed, expecting to be chided by a nurse, or worse, security.

The woman shutting the door looked like a mannequin from an expensive store window. From beneath short red hair shot through with grey, she fixed me with eyes that glowed green under the harsh fluorescents.

My skin hummed with uncomfortable electric goosebumps in what I'd come to recognize as a magical early warning system.

7

I darted for the far wall. Gravity spun around me with reassuring ease and I scrambled straight up. I fought to keep from panting at the exertion as I crawled onto the ceiling. The magic in my blood let my centre of gravity shift to hold me there, extending to my clothing. My hair had even settled on my shoulders like I was upright.

"That's not necessary, Judith." The newcomer eyed me, unimpressed.

"It's Jude." No one I knew used my full name, not even my mother. "If you came to smother me with a pillow, you're late."

Her mouth quirked in a half-smile. "I haven't."

Crouching on the ceiling, safely upside down and out of the intruder's reach, I winced at the sponginess of the wide tiles under my hands and knees. It felt like heavy cardboard. Ceilings weren't made to hold weight like floors were. I had to brace the pull of my gravity against the regular world's to keep myself from getting too heavy.

The Faerie below watched with a knowing expression, like she was aware of the tense high-wire act that kept me from crashing through the tiles into whatever mess of pipes and ducts ran above me.

"Who are you?" I asked her.

"Miranda."

"Don't know a Miranda. Are you with the Consilium?"

"I am not." The iciness in her tone told me what she thought of that guess.

I should have known better. The strength of the tingle in my skin meant she was a full-blood Faerie. Real Faeries didn't work for the Consilium. They stayed loyal to their own world.

"You need to get out of here," she said.

"Four out of five doctors probably disagree," I shot back.

"The police would too, I'm sure, if they knew your location." Miranda paused to let that sink in, then inclined her head toward the door. "The glamour's wearing off.

Someone will remember you exist soon and come to check on you."

"You *glamoured* me?" I lowered my chin to take a look at my body as if it might show signs. That would explain my easy sneak into the locker room. Here I'd thought it was skill.

"Only for the last few hours, while you've been coming to."

"Why?" Even if she knew I was no longer Consilium—and she probably did, given everybody but me had had three months to get up to speed—there was no reason she should want to help me.

Her cool expression didn't change but her tone turned dry. "To reduce the number of annoying questions I would have to answer. We have a house nearby. A safehouse. You're welcome there."

When I still didn't move, she said, "Jude, if I wanted you dead, I had only to allow this hospital to give you a human blood transfusion. You have nothing to fear from me." She put a hand on the door. "Are you coming down or not?"

My heart raced. She knew I couldn't have a normal—human—amount of iron in my veins and survive. She'd probably saved my life.

I let myself drop back onto the floor, straightening up to face her. It wouldn't take long for the cops to arrive once that glamour wore off and everybody human realized I was awake. I'd already obliterated my ties to the Consilium three times over and gotten myself cast out of Aubrie's good graces somehow. Bunking with Lilah wouldn't last long. Couldn't hurt to see what the Faeries had to offer.

Yes, it could. It could hurt a lot. Faeries lie. Aubrie and the Consilium had held that little nugget of warning in common.

Miranda pushed the locker room door open to reveal a space different from the hospital hallway that had been outside a minute ago. She stepped inside, turning to wait for me.

I moved closer without crossing the threshold. It looked like the foyer of a small house. Stairs disappeared into the shadow of a second floor. The faded yellow wallpaper studded with lines of tiny green trees didn't brighten the room.

"We have really different definitions of *nearby*," I said.

3

A VOICE ROSE FROM the airport bathroom stall, just barely audible above the music in Spencer Aubrie's earbuds. *Noise-cancelling, my ass.* He glared at the doors behind him in the men's room mirror as the unwelcome orator broke into song. *Never go with wireless.*

The expensive earbuds hadn't worked to block out the crying baby across the aisle on his two-hour flight either—who the hell flew business class with a baby? Aubrie waved his hands under the automatic faucet, impatient to rinse the soap off and move away from this latest annoyance, which had increased in volume.

Routine airport aggravation wasn't the only thing vexing him. He'd felt uneasy even before boarding the plane in Toronto. Anticipation rather than anxiety, but it was still a feeling he wasn't accustomed to, and one he didn't like. It stretched too far beyond his control.

The song around him turned strange. The melody seemed to float on the air, hovering like a physical presence. Sounds that couldn't be made by human vocal chords slipped around the stall door. The notes took on a lilting, choral tone, as if two voices had begun to blend together.

Muscles tightened in Aubrie's shoulders but he managed to clap his wet hands over his ears. He pressed the earbuds in deeper with his palms to drown the song under the tinny music playing from the phone in his back pocket.

Keeping his hands tight to his head, he inspected the stalls behind him in the mirror. Several were closed, lock tags turned to red. The twinned voices bouncing off the tiled walls made it impossible to pinpoint the singer's location.

The melody wormed its way into the rest of his muscles, stiffening them. *Relax*, it whispered. *Yield. Wait for me.*

Aubrie reached into his back pocket for his phone, sending the volume soaring to a painful level. Then he let his carry-on shoulder bag slump to the floor in a show of following the song's command.

Once he'd remained frozen at the sink for a full minute, a door behind him opened and a blond man walked out. He had no tell-tale signs to mark him as anything otherworldly except his lips moving in the offending song.

Aubrie spun around and caught him by the throat, cutting off the song mid-syllable.

"The Mab's sent you alone?" he asked, modulating his voice when he realized he was shouting over the recorded music in his ears. "No army?"

The other creature looked surprised, but no fear touched his pale eyes.

"You're not worth an army," he spat. He wrapped his hands around Aubrie's wrist, face growing red as he struggled to loosen the unnaturally strong grip on his windpipe.

Aubrie started to squeeze harder, but the man's body melted in his fingers. What had been a man of his own height morphed and reformed into a smaller, lighter woman, as if an invisible wind had blown the original form away like sand.

The difference in weight threw Aubrie off-balance, pitching him forward. In the same movement, the newly-formed woman tightened her grip on his wrist, holding onto it to steady herself as she jumped. Her feet slammed into Aubrie's middle and the impact forced him to loosen his hand.

He fell back and caught himself against the sink as she wrenched away.

She tumbled to the floor, gasping for breath. Wheezing, she turned onto her back, then propped herself up on her elbows to glare at him. Rather than try again, she pulled herself upright and fled. She nearly collided with another man entering the bathroom.

A shocked laugh bubbled in Aubrie's chest, but he held it in. Wiping his still-damp hands on his slacks as if nothing had happened, he headed for the door, ignoring the startled look the other man gave him. His stomach ached where the woman's feet had connected. At least she'd only used enough force to free herself.

Despite the pain, there would be no lasting injury. He didn't see her outside the bathroom, but he wasn't looking for a rematch. He made for the exit at a brisk walk, pulling out his phone to turn down his music to a less-than-deafening level.

It buzzed in his hand with a message: *At Arrivals, but not for long according to these airport traffic cops. ETA?*

He smiled despite himself, imagining the message delivered in Mei's bracing deadpan, then texted back, *5 min.*

Six minutes later, he slid into the passenger seat of the sleek, black sedan that awaited him in the Arrivals section. He tossed his shoulder bag into the backseat and leaned over to kiss Mei.

"How was the flight?" she asked.

Before Aubrie could answer, a voice came from outside the car. A traffic guard in a neon vest gestured to Mei.

"Yeah, yeah, get moving," she muttered, raising a hand to the guard and pulling into the slow traffic that edged out of Arrivals.

Aubrie watched the neon-clad woman bark at another car and gesture as they passed. All this ridiculous security theatre around simple airplanes while humans had no idea what was really out there, beyond their line of sight, waiting to pounce.

He answered Mei's question: "The flight was tiresome. Then the Mab sent a small but annoying welcoming committee."

"I thought no one knew you were coming. You only informed *me* five hours ago."

"And I appreciate the last-minute favour." Aubrie tried to assuage the accusing tone that had crept into her voice. "It's good to see you."

She cast him a dubious sidelong glance. "Spence, I don't believe for a minute that you're here to see me."

"I can multi-task."

"How romantic."

"Isn't that the definition of romantic to an accountant?"

"Chief Financial Officer." Mei stressed each word with a sharpness that warned him the joke had been a step too far.

"I'm sorry," he said.

"Multitasking's never exactly been your strong suit." Her grudging tone indicated she'd accepted the apology.

"Have dinner with me. I'll show you otherwise."

"I can't. I'm meeting with clients tonight."

"Clients who have nothing to do with us."

"Yes, Spence, people in the *real* world." Mei steered onto the freeway ramp. "Are you going to tell me why you've really come?"

He suppressed a swell of triumph. She didn't like his forays into magic because it took his attention away from her, but her withering tone held a note of real concern. She *was* interested in his plans.

"The Mab's messenger's here," he said.

"What else could possibly draw you out to the city where I live but hunting down pieces of your puzzle?"

"Mei—"

"I know. This is an unparalleled opportunity to seize our birthright. The time is right to take hold of the magic we've been denied for so long, caught between the human and Faerie worlds but accepted by neither. We've burned down the old orders and it's up to us to manage what grows anew. We need to focus on the future and the future is us." She paused. "Did I miss anything?"

"No." Aubrie couldn't help but smile. Her sarcastic read of the situation stirred such a swell of affection in him that he nearly forgot they'd been on their way to an argument. He put a hand over hers on the steering wheel. "Tell me I don't sound like that."

She didn't glance at him as she accelerated onto the freeway, but the corners of her lips turned up in a smile. "I may have exaggerated a bit for effect. What's a Court agent doing in Montreal? Jazz Fest or F1?"

"Imprisoned in a Consilium facility."

Mei's hands tightened on the wheel. "I didn't think there were any *Consilium* facilities left."

"This one was off the grid," Aubrie said. "A warehouse reinforced in iron. Daniel's using it as a base of operations for . . . whatever he's playing at now." When Mei said nothing, he added, "We don't have to worry about it tonight. I haven't gotten everyone here yet and Pru and Jasper have another assignment. I thought we'd have dinner, spend the night—"

"Then you should have given me more than five hour's notice." Her voice turned sour. "And *deigned* to stay with me."

"Don't be like that. I don't want the Court to know where you live. Clearly I'm under surveillance somehow." He hadn't expected so fast or so precise an intercept from his enemies. If not for the damned earbuds, that siren would have hooked him.

He hadn't made a considerable effort to hide, since the Mab didn't have as many resources as she would have in times past, but he'd have to be more careful. He'd already sacrificed so much. He couldn't afford mistakes now.

15

4

I PEERED INTO THE house Miranda had revealed, waiting for the scene to melt away and change into something scarier. Magical houses were not standard issue outside Toronto hospital locker rooms—or anywhere.

Before I could decide whether or not to step inside, a hand pressed into my back. Miranda gave me a shove that sent me stumbling forward. In the instant it took to regain my balance, she'd shut the door behind us.

I whipped around to fight my way back out, but a new voice from behind made me bounce back on my heel.

"Well, hell, somebody rubbed *you* raw." A man who'd appeared from a brighter room at the end of the hallway tipped a ten-gallon cowboy hat back on his head, sizing me up. "You look like a boiled lobster."

I moved to put a wall at my back so I could see them both coming, but neither moved toward me. I couldn't help scanning my arms for a sunburn or rash, but the genes from my Turkish grandmother had ensured I usually tanned rather than burned. Three months in a hospital bed hadn't left any new colour in my skin. "You need to get your eyes checked, Tex."

"I'm not from Texas." The cowboy spoke in a drawl to match his outfit: faded jeans and a button-down shirt with a diamond pattern. "Wyoming." He came closer and extended a hand. "Abe."

American. Well, that fit the look and the accent. I glanced down at his hand but didn't shake it.

"Empathic Faeries typically come from further away than the States," I pointed out, taking a guess to try and keep what I hoped was the upper hand. "And aren't you supposed to *feel* what I feel?"

"Some feel 'em. I see 'em." He confirmed my suspicion, then added: "Human quirk, maybe."

"You're human?" The mild humming in my skin had already clued me in that he wasn't—at least, not fully.

"One quarter," he confirmed. "Feel better?"

"Not really."

"I know." Abe smiled, clearly still reading whatever pictures my emotions were painting on me. "You're savvier than I expected. Pegged me right off." He nodded to himself. "Hungry?"

My stomach answered for me, but I ignored it. "No."

"Shame. I'm making flapjacks."

This had been a mistake. Chalk it up to the head injury. Outrunning cops or the Consilium would be saner than accepting the ridiculous offer of *flapjacks* with Faeries. At least it would have been more predictable.

"Thanks but no thanks." I darted past Miranda and grabbed the front door knob. Yanking it open revealed a blinding white void. I had to turn my head against the light as a rush filled my ears and sucked the breath from my lungs.

Not an exit.

I shut the door, blinking away the wavering dots that lingered in my vision.

Behind me, neither Miranda nor Abe had moved. I did catch a knowing look that Miranda cast the cowboy.

"How do I get back to Toronto?" I snapped.

"In good time." Abe turned toward the doorway at the end of the hall.

The casual dismissal tightened my jaw. I stalked into the closest room off the foyer: a living room with a big fireplace on one side and a picture window on the other. Outside, a suburban street glowed in the pink light of sunset.

That stopped me short. It had been at least two hours from sunset when Miranda had pushed me in a couple of minutes ago.

I couldn't let Faerie tricks derail me. I grabbed the nearest heavy object—a ceramic vase full of plastic flowers—and heaved it at the window glass.

The vase shattered but the window remained intact. Not heavy enough.

Before I could seize a better weapon, Miranda said, "No need to destroy the decor. It's not locked."

Her wry tone already told me it wouldn't be an exit, but I couldn't help undoing the lock and shoving the window wide open.

Outside, the same blinding nothingness. The suburban street seemed to be projected onto the glass panes, though it looked unnervingly real, even with the window open. A car drove down the street, moving through each angled pane in turn and disappearing from sight. I peered down over the windowsill and my stomach dropped when there was no down. No up. Nothing.

My muscles shook like over-stretched wires and dizziness leached into the edges of my brain. I needed a chair.

When I turned, Miranda gestured in the direction Abe had gone. As much as I wanted to refuse and plant myself on the dusty carpet in here, it looked like the fastest way of getting the hell out of the Faerie dollhouse was to see what they had to say.

I followed her into a kitchen at the back of the house so sparkling clean it looked fake, like a movie set. Abe had batter already mixed and a skillet on the stove. A couple of browned sausage links rested on a plate beside it. They smelled amazing, all spice and smoke. I held my breath to keep my stomach from giving me away again, swallowing hard and feigning calm rather than showing that my legs were about to give out as I pulled a chair away the table.

Abe had plucked his hat off, tossing it aside on the counter as he moved in front of the stove. Underneath, he was completely bald, his head smooth in contrast to his craggy face. I'd expected tentacles, maybe a second face—at least a badass tattoo. The Faeries who ran around in our world could only take human-ish form through glamour. Easier to operate here if you looked like a human being as opposed to, say, a giant snake.

The cowboy dished three large pancakes onto a plate with the sausage links, then set it on the table in front of me. He started to offer me a fork, then paused. "Gotta promise you won't stab me with it."

"I don't make deals with Faeries."

He returned the fork to the drawer and set a spoon beside my plate instead.

It took all of my resolve not to swing it at him. Miranda's presence in the chair to my right stopped me. It was a Consilium rule that nobody took on a Faerie solo, much less with worse odds. Seemed kind of useless to start following Consilium rules now, but two-on-one with my stomach growling and muscles aching wasn't going to go in my favour.

Abe picked up a second plate from the counter, then looked to Miranda in a wordless offer. When she shook her head, he settled down at the table with it himself.

"What do you want?" I asked, hating the exhaustion that crept into my voice.

He cut into his pancakes. "We keeping you from some other important plans?"

"Yes. The plan of getting the hell out of here and finding a warm beach to lounge on indefinitely." Couldn't stay in Toronto without Aubrie's protection, might as well dream big. "Rio's supposed to be nice, right?"

"With no money, no passport?"

"I'm resourceful." I glanced down at my stolen boots. "And not in the mood for riddles. If you're offering money and a passport to do some Faerie dirty work, just get to it so I can say no."

"Need your help with an old contact," Abe said. "Daniel Cain."

My throat closed, heart making a racket against my ribs. Contact. Surely they knew better and were being polite.

"He's alive?" I hated the relief that flooded me. I didn't deserve to feel it. I'd beaten Daniel unconscious. I hadn't even checked his pulse before fleeing.

"And in possession of a spell we'd like," Abe agreed.

A bitter bark of a laugh escaped me without permission. "What the hell do you think *I* can do? I killed his father, I stole codes for Aubrie, I might have *blinded* him—"

"You didn't." The exhale as Miranda said the words came out as a disappointed sigh.

"Doesn't matter." The thought of looking Daniel in the eye again made me feel like I had a panicked bird loose underneath my ribs. "The Consilium's probably got way better security on any spell you want by now."

"The Consilium's gone," Miranda said.

I blinked at her. The words didn't make sense together. "What do you mean *gone*?"

Abe took that one: "Court wiped 'em out."

That made no sense. The Consilium must have been at least three hundred people in Toronto—more in the rest of the world. They couldn't be *gone*. And why would the Faerie Court have chosen now, of any time in the last thousand years of rivalry, to make a real move?

Something twisted in my stomach like a letter opener with a white bone handle.

"Is that why you guys are glamouring hospitals? Did Faeries invade the world?" I hadn't seen anything magically weird from the hospital window, but the one in the living room had looked normal at first too.

"Nah." Abe frowned. "Consilium gave the Court as good as they got. They took each other out."

I gaped at him, waiting for a grin to split that weathered face as he confessed that he was *pulling my leg* or some other folksy euphemism for an inappropriate joke about the demise of both the major players in the clandestine, supernatural cold war that had given me job security for the last three years.

When he didn't, a cool relief made its way up through my shock.

"That's a hell of a Get Out of Jail Free card," I muttered.

"Guess you can go relax on your beach," Abe agreed, "and let Spencer Aubrie get away with tossing you off a balcony."

I dropped the spoon I hadn't realized I was holding. It clattered against the plate but I barely heard it, snared again in the memory of the vise-grip on my arm, the burning iron in my skin, the sudden pain of smashing through the sliding glass door.

Having someone outside my head know what Aubrie had done made it worse, more real. It was harder to think of a rational explanation, an excuse to override the cold contempt on his face when he'd dropped me six stories.

A spark of fury nestled into the ache squeezing my lungs. "What's he got to do with your spell?"

"He wants it too."

"Why? What's it do?"

"It's a . . ." Abe paused, as if deciding on the best explanation. *Or the best lie.* "Short version is, it'll help him get across into the Faerie realm."

"There's no spell to get into the Faerie realm. We *looked.*" Anyone with human blood going through a portal would always be met with armed guards or worse—nightmare things with teeth and claws. They always saw us coming. "What's the long version?"

"Complicated."

"That's convenient."

"Just thought you might want to get to the spell before he does."

"And bring it back to you like a good retriever?"

Abe smiled. "Nobody's asking you to bring it back for a milk bone, darlin'. You bring us the spell, we'll pay you and get you whatever travel docs you need to head on out to your next adventure. And, as a bonus, it'll piss off the asshole who pitched you off a building."

My shoulders tensed at the pointed reminder. I fought my immediate refusal. "Pay me how much?"

"Twenty thousand."

"Dollars? Not, like, magic beans?"

"Whatever currency you like, we'll make it happen."

Twenty thousand dollars and a passport would be a great start to getting me far away from this whole mess. I had nothing now, not even my driver's license—no way to prove I even existed on paper, outside of a police file.

But it seemed too easy. *Faeries lie.*

I rested my elbows on the table. "So that's all? I get this spell from Daniel, you give me twenty thousand bucks and a valid passport and I get to fuck off in peace?"

"Yes," Abe said.

"Sorry, Cowboy, I want *her* to answer." I thrust my chin toward Miranda. "Actually, no, I want her *word*."

Faeries were bound by their word. According to the Consilium, breaking an explicit promise meant nasty consequences for their magic. I'd never tried it out before, but Miranda's slow smile told me that the rumour was true. The disdain in her eyes reminded me I had nothing to bargain with.

"You have my word that if you bring me the spell, you'll be financially compensated to the degree Abe has indicated," she said.

I shook my head. "That's not enough."

"I believe it's quite generous," Miranda said. "Given my *not insignificant* investment in you. But if you insist on negotiating . . ."

A flip response died on my lips when she reached across to the nearest drawer and withdrew something, setting it on the table. Inside what looked like a plastic evidence bag sat a letter opener with a white bone handle, the blade still stained rusty red.

5

THE SHOWER SPRAY STUNG like needles. I combed my fingers through my hair, slicking it back against my skull. Already hot, I turned the water hotter. I ached to hit something and loathed myself for it in the same instant.

I should have run from the hospital. Shouldn't have followed Miranda. First instincts were always right.

Almost always.

After Miranda had made me the offer I couldn't refuse with the letter opener, Abe-in-Good-Cop-mode had taken pity on me and suggested I clean up. A hot shower had been the only thing so far that sounded good, and time away from the Faeries to think sounded even better.

None of the scenarios I'd concocted for running as soon they let me out of the house to go after their spell worked easily without cash, papers or a clean police record.

Plus if Aubrie really did want this spell, getting my hands on it would be a good opener for confronting him about the decision process that had led to him tossing me off the fucking balcony. Because then I could tear it to pieces if I didn't like his answer.

My stomach twisted, the mix of fury and pain making me suck in a breath of steam.

Or maybe I'd just pass the spell off to the Faeries as promised and make them give me a passport in the new name of somebody who'd never heard of Spencer Aubrie or the Consilium, somebody who believed Faeries were cute little winged creatures in kids' books.

Either way, I had to get the thing first. But how hard could that be? Just ask Daniel to turn it over, and hit him a few more times if he said no.

Had he known, that last week we were together March, that I'd been the one who killed Alan with that letter opener? Daniel and his father hadn't been anything near close—like, I preferred to keep my distance from my own mother in the hundreds of kilometres, but I'd never called her by her first name with the casual, detached tone he had always used for Alan—as if they were strangers who'd roomed together for a few years.

Still, Danny wasn't callous enough to fuck his father's murderer, or stupid enough to let her sleep beside him for a week—not deliberately, anyway.

I grabbed a bar of soap sitting on the shelf. It dissolved into suds and lather that covered me from head to toe as I scrubbed away the hospital and the sting in my eyes. Steam filled the bathroom and the water maintained a steady scalding temperature. I wrapped my fingers around the handle, intending on turning it even hotter, but I was out of soap and starting to feel lightheaded again.

When I pushed the curtain back, my stolen threads were gone. A stack of clean clothing sat on the counter, along with a plate of pancakes and sausage and a fork. I hadn't heard the door open.

My stomach wouldn't let me turn down the food this time, especially after the dizzying heat of the shower. I wolfed down the pancakes and sausage, finishing with a long drink from the faucet before getting dressed.

The new pair of jeans, black t-shirt, underwear and socks fit like they'd been made for me. My boots looked exactly the same as when I'd taken them off, except they'd somehow shrunk to my size too.

I couldn't ignore a nagging unease—despite my own powers, I'd never been very comfortable with outright magic, like boots spontaneously resizing to fit me or houses hovering in shiny, blank space. You couldn't trust it.

But if the clothes disappeared once I got outside and I showed up naked to see Daniel, at least that'd be an ice-breaker.

I slipped my boots back on and headed downstairs.

Abe stood at the sink doing dishes. He glanced over his shoulder when he heard me. "Clothes fit?"

"Oh, that was you sneaking into the bathroom like a creep?" I snagged a cold pancake from a plate on the counter.

"Wasn't meant to be creepy." He turned back to the sink. "Can't function in boots that're too big, myself."

I stopped myself before asking how he'd known, or how he'd changed them. Turning to the window and running a hand back through the wet curls that left damp patches on my shoulders, I asked, "Where's Miranda?"

"She had an errand."

An errand. As if blackmailing me was just a daily task to be checked off her list before she ran to the grocery store.

"Thought she'd stick around and tell me how to find Daniel."

"She left you an address." Abe nodded to a folded piece of paper tucked beneath the plate of pancakes. "He's in Montreal."

"That's not helpful." I took the paper and another pancake. "It's a big city and I don't speak French."

"Imagine you'll get by."

I made a face at his back. "How do I get out of here?"

"Tell the door where you want to go."

"Tell the what *what*?"

"House exists on a separate plane between the spheres," Abe said. "You can exit anywhere in the—our—world."

That weird white space. Did that mean . . . were we just floating somewhere between dimensions? I craned my neck to peer out the window over the kitchen sink again. It showed a neat, fenced-in backyard long with shadows in the falling twilight.

I walked to the back door and put my ear against it. It didn't seem special, but I'd seen the blinding emptiness outside the front. "Can I just walk into Faerieland from here too?"

"Nope."

Of course I couldn't, not with human blood in my veins.

"So I just . . . tell it where I want to go?" It couldn't be that easy. Why hadn't I tried something like that earlier?

"Well," Abe said, "you'll also need to paint a sigil with the blood of a blue-throated hummingbird and knock four times."

I opened my mouth to protest, then snapped it shut when I saw his grin. Jackass.

With a sigh, I put a hand on the knob and recited the address from the paper to the door. Pulling it open revealed a city street, full of long shadows under the street lights. It was fully dark outside, in contrast to the sunset beyond the kitchen window.

"Shouldn't I be outside an apartment or something?" I asked, peeking out the door.

"It's not quite that precise," Abe answered. "But you're probably within a block."

I half-expected to fall through space or pass through a shimmery veil, but I just stepped onto the sidewalk. The door fell shut behind me and I turned to find only the smooth brick side of a building. The Faeries hadn't told me how to get back once I had their spell.

Not exactly my biggest concern right now, though. I took a deep breath of the humid summer air. It reminded me how much time had gone by without me in it. A yawning void stretched out behind me, filled with weeks and months I hadn't lived, though the rest of the world had marched on around me and winter had turned to spring and then into summer.

By fall I'd be out of this country and out of this life, relaxing somewhere warm, far from the snowy Toronto winter where everything had gone off the rails.

I started checking addresses on the nearby buildings.

6

DANIEL'S PHONE RANG ON the second flight of stairs to his third-story walk-up. His adrenaline spiked when he saw the name on the screen. "What's wrong?"

"Nothing's wrong." His sister's voice, more chipper than usual for the time of the evening and for somebody who had a two-year-old kid. "Why does something have to be wrong?"

"You said 'text only' after eight." He relaxed and continued up the stairs.

"I said *you* should text so the phone ringing didn't wake Riley," Gracie returned. "Ears like a bat, that kid. Even with the white-noise machine going."

As if to demonstrate her relationship to said kid, she picked up on the noise of his key in the lock as he reached his front door. "Are you just getting home? At least tell me you were somewhere fun."

In the privacy of his apartment, it was safe to reply with deadpan honesty. "Fun like hours of detailed planning to pin down the best way to boost a magical artifact from a tiny museum that shouldn't have it in the first place?"

"No. Normal-people fun."

Daniel laughed. "Like you've got a clue what normal people do."

"Hey, I went to toddler yoga today."

"I stand corrected." He locked the door and slipped his shoes off but didn't turn on the light, not intending to stay long. The apartment felt stuffy, even now that the sun had gone down. The stagnant, humid air had a musty scent, old wood with a hint of ant spray. The building was more rundown that anywhere he'd lived before, but comfort hadn't really been on his mind when he'd rented the place.

"You're right, the museum sounds more fun," Gracie said. "Everything on schedule?"

"Everything except a way around those motion sensors in the storage room."

"Can't Fabiola do something about them?"

"Too risky. She doesn't normally have access to the alarm system, and she's already got to be the one to catch us on the way out. If somebody put the two together—"

"Sounds like Fabiola's problem."

"You never were any good at team sports." Daniel couldn't help but smile at his sister's blunt assessment. He went to the bedroom and unlocked the window to shove it open. The sliding door in the front room that led to the tiny balcony would air the place out better, but the bedroom window seemed safer—it had nothing beneath it but a three-story drop into the alley.

"Teams aside," Gracie's voice turned breezy in the way that said he wouldn't like what she had to add, "you wouldn't have to mess with the sensors at all if you get somebody who can just shimmy up the wall and walk across the ceiling."

"Somebody—" He realized with a jolt who she meant. "No. Fuck no."

Shimmy up the wall. The too whimsical description made him regret opening the window. He tried to shove it closed again, but the old wood stuck.

"It just seems fortuitous that Jude bounces out of a coma right when we need somebody for O'Meara," Gracie said. "Hear me out. We can *use* her—"

"There's no *we*. You're not going, *I* am. And there's no way I'm taking her." Daniel used both hands to try and force the window closed. It refused to budge. He rested his forehead against the glass and reminded his sister, "She's probably still working for Aubrie."

Gracie snorted. "I'd be pretty pissed at somebody who tried to kill me."

"Guess we have that in common."

"I know it's not an ideal solution—"

"Not a solution at all." Daniel left the bedroom, closing the door tightly behind him, then tapped the phone into speaker mode so he could carry it around the corner into the kitchenette and set it on the counter.

"When you and Olivier are sitting in jail because somebody tripped a motion sensor—"

"I would be better off." He pulled a nearly-empty bottle of vodka from the freezer.

"And I'm sure Aubrie would agree." Gracie seized on that as if it were the opening she'd been waiting for. "Because then he could just grab the cross from the O'Meara himself."

"He doesn't know about the cross. If he did, he'd have gone after it by now."

"So every minute you waste trying to find some better way inside the goddamn museum is more time he's got to find out, then sweep in and take it easier than we can." Gracie paused. "I don't like it, but Jude's just the most efficient option."

"Your *most efficient option* stabbed our father to death and put me in the fucking hospital." Daniel couldn't believe he had to say the words aloud.

"Alan had it coming."

"And what did I do?"

That silenced her.

"I sound like a heartless asshole," she finally said. "I get it." Without giving him time to agree, she added, "But if you remember, I'm the one who wanted to kill Jude in her sleep. *You're* the one who said no."

"I said she wasn't worth the effort with our limited resources. I didn't say let's go ask her for *help*."

"Well, we need the help. The enemy of my enemy—"

"—is an unpredictable psychopath."

"Who can *walk up walls*," Gracie pressed. "And even psychopaths have buttons to push. You must know some of hers."

"Now you sound like Alan."

"Fuck you."

The sharpness in the words told Daniel that he'd hit the nerve he'd intended. In the silence that followed, he imagined her pinching the bridge of her nose between two fingers the way she always did when forced to rethink her position.

"I hear it," she finally said. "I *am* a heartless asshole, but, hell, I obviously come by it honestly." She gave something between a groan and a sigh. "I accept the veto. This shit's just bringing out the worst in me. I'm feeling, I don't know, outmatched these days."

"Can't imagine why."

"Don't be a pessimist."

If there had ever been a time in their lives for pessimism, it was now. But admitting that wouldn't do either of them any good. Daniel changed the subject. "Any optimistic leads on your side?"

"Yes, actually!" Gracie perked up. "The shaman—I'm not kidding, that's what the charlatan called himself, a *shaman*—was a total bust, but another source came up with the title of a book, which I'm pretty sure has the . . . Oh, hang on—" The line went silent for a moment, then she returned with: "Rye's awake. He's being all squirrely tonight with Ted gone. I've gotta go. Talk tomorrow?"

"Sure."

"Great." Gracie hung up first.

Daniel tapped the phone off and unscrewed the cap on the vodka bottle, still fixed on his sister's suggestion. She was right. Getting Jude would be a thousand times easier than anything they'd come up with for the museum. Jude could just pull herself up to the ceiling, never even trigger the motion sensors. She could be careful and precise with her power when she wanted to be.

The thought stirred nausea in the pit of his stomach. He left the vodka bottle untouched, shoved his cell phone into his back pocket, then returned to the closed bedroom.

Devoid of even a shade, the window gaped like a wide-open eye. A hammer against the sash might work to slam it shut again, but he didn't have tools here.

No, he had one.

He retrieved the heavy, iron fireplace poker from the corner beside the bed where he'd left it propped. The apartment didn't have a fireplace, but few other tools were made in pure iron anymore. There was nothing better for repelling supernatural threats.

Using both hands, he tried to jam the window down with the force of the metal rod. The glass shook and the sash gave a screech against the frame, but it still didn't move.

He lifted the poker to try again, then stopped, certain he'd heard a noise from the dark living room. It sounded like a footstep on the old wood floorboards.

Getting a better grip on the weapon, he turned, prepared to swing it at the level of a person's head—assuming whatever was out there was human.

After a moment, a calm voice called in, "Are you armed?"

Relief fused through him, but not enough to make him set the fireplace poker aside. He lowered it, waiting through the footsteps in the living room.

A shadow appeared in the doorway.

"You're here." Mei's eyes went to the iron weapon. "I didn't expect you to be home so early."

"Didn't mean to interrupt your burglary." Daniel crossed the room to turn on the lamp beside the bed. "How did you get in? Scaled the balcony?"

"Not in these heels." She extended a toe to examine her presumably expensive footwear. "I came up the back stairs and melted the lock on your kitchen door."

"Inconspicuous." Daniel kept his tone dry to hide his surprise. She'd have to have shape-shifted to use that kind of power.

"I honestly expected something difficult like cast-iron deadbolts. You ought to upgrade." Mei glanced to the open window. "And that. Really? Even on the third floor, you're practically inviting the monsters in."

"It's a little late to worry about that."

7

I FOUND THE ADDRESS listed on the paper Miranda had given me. Like most of the buildings on the Montreal street, the steep metal stairs to the second story of the triplex were exterior—this particular set in a chipped white paint that shone under the streetlights, matching the colour of the balcony railings on the second and third floors.

I took the stairs to the two doors on the second floor landing. Both had three small, rectangular windows in them like they hadn't been renovated since the '70s. Since the windows were dark, I took a chance and cupped my hands against the one under the correct address, then peered in.

Inside, I could just make out a second set of interior stairs leading up to another door that had to be the third-floor apartment. Now what? I couldn't buzz my way up on the ancient intercom. No way would Daniel open the door to me. I could shift my gravity, give myself enough heft to kick in this first door, but by the time I got up those stairs, he'd have heard the noise and he'd probably be armed. The narrow stairway wouldn't offer me many options to fight back from any angle.

The duplex next door presented itself as a good choice for recon. I returned to the street, crossed the narrow alley full of garbage cans and picked a dark corner of the neighbouring building, where nobody would pass by close enough to see me. Then I turned gravity to walk up the wall to the roof.

I stayed low and picked my way around discarded cans and cigarette butts from some recent roof party to reach the opposite edge, facing Daniel's building. Crouching, I looked across the alley right into the bedroom window of the third-floor apartment.

An Asian woman stood beside the bed, looking out of place against the sparse IKEA-type furniture in a pair of pristine black slacks and a soft blue blouse. She reached up to tuck her long hair behind her ear, saying something.

Daniel faced away, concerned with a table beside the bed. He wore jeans and a t-shirt in contrast to whatever occasion his guest had dressed up for. When he turned back to her, I caught my breath, not ready for the face I recognized too readily. His dark hair looked a little shorter than I remembered, and he hadn't shaved in a few days. No glasses. My fist cracking the frame and putting the lens through his eyelid had probably prompted a trip for laser correction, since he hated contacts.

The familiarity of that thought made me tense.

He handed the woman a folded piece of paper, which must have been what he'd been digging out of the drawer. She said something else, straightening her shirt collar. Her eyes caught the light and gleamed yellow.

Golden, like a cat's. No way she was entirely human. *I guess you have a type, Danny.*

After another minute of conversation, she slipped out of the bedroom. Daniel waited, listening for her. I craned my neck but didn't see her silhouette leave by the exterior stairs out front. Still, Daniel relaxed like he'd heard her leave. He sat down on the bed, then fell backwards to lay on the mattress, rubbing his eyes with one hand.

Now or never.

I moved to the side to keep from being seen through the window where I'd been spying, then slid over the edge of the duplex roof. Gravity spun around me, dropping me across the alley onto the wall of the opposite building.

I hit with my palms, bending my elbows and tucking my head to somersault onto my knees. Then I crept down the bricks, back to Daniel's open bedroom window. I grabbed the top frame and swung inside upside-down. Twisting to land on my feet, I slapped one hand on the floor to steady myself.

Daniel bolted upright, going for the bedside table.

Without giving him a chance to grab whatever weapon he had stashed there, I shot to the ceiling, used it to propel myself across the room and dropped, landing squarely on top of his legs. I grabbed his wrist with one hand, shifting my gravity to be heavier and press him down against the mattress. A warm wave of déjà vu swept through me straddling him. It turned sour when I saw the new scar below his left eyebrow.

Something slammed into my hip, hard enough to knock me off the bed.

I landed on my back on the hardwood floor, throbbing pain racing up my side. Propping myself on my elbows, I found the tip of what looked like an iron fireplace poker at my throat.

"Okay," I said, holding as still as I could. "I deserved that."

Daniel gaped at me, somewhere between amazed and furious, like he wasn't sure I was real but the very thought of me pissed him off anyway. His surprise seeped away and deepened into a glare.

"What the hell are you doing here?" he asked.

Should have planned this better. "I need your help."

"You think I'm that stupid?"

"I think you haven't stabbed me yet."

A muscle in his jaw twitched as he reconsidered that oversight, but he pulled the iron point from my throat to my stomach.

It made me pick a hasty starting point. "I woke up from a coma today, in Toronto."

His expression didn't change. Of course he already knew that. If I were him, I'd be keeping tabs on me too.

"A Faerie named Miranda scooped me out of there and to a safehouse," I said. "You've got a spell she wants. She sent me."

"Sent you to what?" His hand tightened on the poker.

"To *ask*." My other more violent options were too dependent on him not jamming the iron tip through me. "Look, I thought it was a stupid plan too, but she offered me tw—ten thousand bucks. I'll split it with you if you just tell me—"

A sound like the front door slamming open in the next room cut me off. I threw up a placating hand. "I came here alone—I swear!"

Despite how little he probably believed those last two words, my confusion at the noise must have been convincing. He shifted his weight and lifted the poker away from me, toward the doorway.

I scooted backwards then lifted myself up to put some distance between us. Moving my leg made me wince at what would definitely be a bruise on my hip.

No footsteps came into the apartment. Something struck the wall in the other room with a splat, making us both jump. A second one followed on the other side of the room. Then a third.

Daniel met my eyes and inclined his head toward the door. Apparently, I was supposed to be the one to look out into the dark room and possibly get my head blown off.

"No way!" I hissed. But damn it, he did have good reason to think this was something I was in on.

I gave in and crept to the door, tilting my head to peer out into the main room.

Something flew past me. As I jerked back, it hit the bedroom floor and splattered, leaving a puddle of liquid and pieces of coloured rubber. Another rolled in past it, intact. A childlike giggle came from the front room.

"A water balloon?" I exclaimed, swinging around the doorway.

"That's not—"

I stepped into the front room in time for a glass bottle to fly through the open front door. It shattered against the hardwood floor.

Fire flared up, illuminating the front room as I spun on my heel and charged back into the bedroom. The heat seared me even as I left the doorway. The sweet, acrid smell was unmistakable. "Molotov cocktail!"

"And gasoline." Daniel skirted the broken balloon that had flown into the bedroom, studying it with a hint of disbelief. "Sloppy."

"Maybe critique your attempted murder later." The smoke alarm above the bedroom door finally sensed the sour black cloud rising from the floor and went off with a shriek. I already knew the window I'd come through didn't have a fire escape, so I bee-lined for the closed window on the back wall, jerking the lock open and shoving the casing up to stick my head out.

Score. A narrow back balcony sat underneath the window, more easily accessible by a door to my left, which probably led to the kitchen. Another metal staircase sprouted off the balcony, spiralling down to the backyard.

With the pulsing whine of the alarm bleating in my ears, I crawled out the window onto the balcony. I ducked to look back through the window and found that Daniel hadn't followed.

He'd moved closer to the bedroom door, as if intending to make a run for it through the main room. That direction held no exit. Whoever'd tossed the balloons would be there waiting.

"Hey!" I raised my voice over the alarm to get his attention and gestured to the window.

The instant of reluctance across his features reminded me that the rickety-looking bare metal staircase spiralling three stories down might not be the first choice of somebody who hated heights. Or maybe he just didn't want to follow me.

With greasy black smoke making the room hazy and the alarm blaring, it was still the best option, and a second later he knew it. He climbed through the window after me, still brandishing the iron poker in front of him like I might choose this moment to attack.

I pounded down the spiral stairs to the tiny backyard, where a child's picnic table sat in the grass among several abandoned soccer balls. As I reached the yard, a shiver of electricity danced across my skin, freezing me before I could leave the bottom stair. A Faerie watched us from nearby in the dark. I held my breath, scanning the shadows as I tried to anticipate the attack.

Nothing came.

Daniel shouldered past me without noticing, as if he'd forced himself down those steep stairs as quickly as possible. Then he seemed to come back to his senses and lifted the poker, turning his head to study the dark yard.

A voice from a neighbouring window called out to us in French, but I didn't understand it and Daniel ignored it. People had gathered on the backyard-facing balconies of the buildings around us to watch the flames from the third story.

When nothing pounced out of the dark around us, Daniel took off for the back gate.

I hurried after him, casting a glance over my shoulder to see if any shadows followed. We slipped into a wider alley, this one apparently meant for cars, with garages behind some of the buildings. My goosebumps faded. Whatever'd been waiting there in the backyard hadn't tailed us. Maybe they'd intended to grab Daniel when he fled and hadn't anticipated him being armed with iron. Or hadn't banked on my presence.

Daniel took a sudden right, turning down a walkway between the buildings.

"Hell of an entrance," he said over his shoulder.

"What?" His tone snapped me back to our present situation. "I didn't do this! It's way too complicated! Water balloons full of gasoline? Who thinks that shit up? Besides, why would I get somebody to torch your apartment with *me* in it?"

He stopped. "I'm not speculating on your motives. Run back to Aubrie."

That hit like a knife in my stomach. "He threw me off a balcony."

"That's the story."

"You don't believe it? Why else would I come to you for *help*?"

He laughed. "Same reason you came to me the first time."

"That's not true."

"Not much is with you."

An argument welled up in my throat but I couldn't spit it out. Not like I could blame him for retconning our past in light of what I'd done, but it still burned me. *I didn't sleep with you because Aubrie told me to. I just almost beat you to death a few months later to get something he wanted.*

Yeah, there was no good way to spin that.

Daniel stood between me and the street. The brick walls stretching up on either side of the narrow walkway meant he'd have a clear shot to heave the poker at me for a good few seconds if I turned and ran or if I shifted gravity and fled toward the roof.

Even if I made it unscathed, I'd be on my own. I'd be adding that weird Faerie faction to the list of people after me and be no closer to escaping any of them and starting over. Maybe as someone who didn't have enemies.

Right.

"Look, there was definitely somebody lurking in the yard back there." I inclined my head over my shoulder. I still didn't feel a prickle in my skin, so whoever it was hadn't followed us.

Daniel's eyes moved past me then back to study my face. A siren growing closer helped him make up his mind. He dropped the poker to his side and headed to the sidewalk, but made no effort to stop me following.

Running the other way seemed like a better option, but the promised cash and passport niggled at me. The thought of dropping that bloody letter opener into a deep, gleaming blue ocean hit me harder. I'd do that before I lounged under a giant umbrella with a giant cocktail—also containing an umbrella—and forgot Faeries even existed.

I gave in and tailed him, catching up at the end of the street. "Where are we going?"

Daniel cast me a sidelong glare to say that 'we' had been too much. "Somewhere safe."

"Oh—okay." I sounded as stunned as I felt. I'd expected more of a fight. Common enemies made for strange bedfellows—or at least unanticipated familiar ones.

"That woman, Miranda, approached you in the hospital?" he prompted.

"We're not talking about the weird balloon fire?"

"Not unless you know more about it than you're saying."

"She showed up and told me I had to leave the hospital, yeah," I said. "Super vague and annoying. But she did say she'd been the one to keep the doctors from giving me iron to level it out to a normal person's."

"She probably saved your life." Daniel considered my answer. "Why?"

The genuine puzzlement in his question stung. "She and Abe were both pretty invested in me getting this spell."

"Who's Abe?"

"A cowboy I met at the safehouse. Empathic. Said he *sees* people's feelings."

"Only two of them?"

"Two's all I saw."

We took a left and headed down another block. The buildings thinned out and we passed more narrow, empty lots. Daniel stepped over a broken bottle and then veered to the right, making me jump to stay with him.

"Where are we?" I asked as we walked alongside a section of dark parking lots fenced in by chain-link and low, windowless buildings done in cheap aluminum siding.

He stopped. We stood in front of a warehouse with two boarded-over garage doors, and a smaller door to access the square hulk of the building.

Tucking the fireplace poker under one arm, Daniel removed a ring of keys from the front pocket of his jeans.

We entered through a loading dock. Another doorway at the far end led out into a larger room, where shadows moved under the overhead lights. I lifted my eyes to the ceiling as he closed the door behind us. My chest felt tight and goosebumps broke out over my arms despite the warm air inside. "Is this the new Consilium?"

"Consilium's gone." He set the iron poker aside, resting it upright against the wall beside the door we'd come through.

As I took another couple of steps inside the air seemed to grow heavier. An unfamiliar claustrophobia sucked my ribs against my spine. Under the weight of it, I didn't notice a pair of men who'd entered from a door off to the left until Daniel said something to them.

I only picked my name out of the quick stream of words—none of the others made sense. Was I having a stroke? *No, it's French. He's speaking French. Since when does he speak French?*

He'd been big into language before. Studied it, in fact, and translated Faerie scribbles. For somebody working through an inter-dimensional language, it couldn't have been hard to pick up an extra human one too.

I tried to wrench away when the older of the two men grabbed my arm. His tight grip kept me from turning gravity and fleeing to the high ceiling.

The younger man, a wiry Black guy, twisted my arm behind my back hard enough to make me lose my breath.

"Danny!" I hissed. "Goddamn it! Daniel!"

He didn't even look back over his shoulder as he headed into another room.

I tried to kick the younger man's knee, but he bent my wrist hard enough that I expected to hear a crack. I doubled over with a gasp, giving in to stop the pain.

The older white guy hefted me over one shoulder, knocking the wind out of me. He hauled me through a dark doorway off to the left and my vision blurred.

Focusing on the concrete floor, I tried to ignore the bouncing rhythm of his body under me and make myself heavy enough to drop him to the floor.

I couldn't. I couldn't focus my reeling thoughts. The intent seemed to slip from my mind like smoke.

Alert for another way out, my eyes caught on a bulge in the back pocket of his pants. My hand slithered down, fingers slipping around either side of his wallet. If nothing else, it would give me some extra weight to hit him with when he set me down.

The younger man opened a heavy door and they carried me into a little room, under a single overhead light. It looked like a bad movie's interrogation room, without the table or chairs.

The big guy tossed me down, landing me hard on my ass. Without another glance, they both headed out the door and shut it tightly. Not even time to throw a punch. A lock slid into place.

8

DANIEL DIDN'T STAY TO watch Jude get carted off to a cell. He shouldn't have brought her to the warehouse, but it had been the only safe spot he could think of. The iron in the walls gave him an advantage over her powers. He'd expected her to feel it before walking in, but maybe she'd been distracted with playing at her pathetic lost-and-confused routine.

Or maybe she'd walked in anyway, trying to prove something.

It didn't matter. She was here, like a bad omen.

Avoiding the voices in the cavernous main room for a few moments to think, he made for a smaller former-office to the left. It held a table, mismatching chairs, a mini-fridge and a microwave set on an unsteady packing crate. A handful of stacked crates opened on one end along one wall doubled as cubbies.

He found the one he'd staked out. His hands shook as he removed a change of clothing that probably needed a wash to uncover a pair of battered tennis shoes. The tremor sharpened the edge of dread that had played along his nerves since Jude's appearance.

Why couldn't she have just come through the window and attacked in a dizzying blur like a monster from a nightmare, given him an easy excuse to stab her with the poker? Instead of looking so fucking ordinary, putting that disarming, ironic twist into her voice as she spun a story where they were both in on the joke, where she wanted his *help*.

That *was* a joke. She wanted the incantation. But she hadn't just tried to take it.

"Thought you were bringing back pizza." Zeb's voice from behind made Daniel jerk upright. The other man leaned against the door frame, watching with something akin to concern.

"Shit." Daniel sighed at the reminder, snatching the shoes and putting a hand out for balance on the crates while he slid them on. He'd gone back to the apartment to pick up cash for that errand.

"You forgot in the midst of . . . meeting a chick and losing your shoes?" Zeb had clearly heard Jude's protests from the loading dock.

Daniel glanced past him to check for the others in the hall behind him. The rest of the team were professional enough to turn a blind eye to anything that didn't directly involve their paycheques. But Zeb had become a friend in the last six weeks—he'd insist on a real explanation, something Daniel wasn't used to providing.

"No excitement here?" he asked.

"Not 'til now." As expected, Zeb didn't appear satisfied with the vague answer, blocking the doorway. "Who is she? Some dangerous Faerie?"

The F-word made Daniel twitch. *Antagonist* had been the official term at the Consilium. Gracie liked to joke that the organization had adopted it because they couldn't take themselves seriously saying '*Faerie*', but it had worked its way into habitual vernacular.

"That was Jude," he said.

"*Tabarnak*." Zeb swore, taking a step back. He spoke fluent French but usually only dipped into it for the profanities. "How'd you find *her*? And, for the hell of it, why?"

"I didn't." Daniel gave in and shared the bare details of the last hour, leaving out only Mei's appearance.

Once he'd finished, Zeb shook his head in disbelief. "I can never tell if you're cool or cracked, man. *Yeah, the bitch who tried to murder me showed up and bombed my place, but it's cool. I'm fine.*"

The sarcastic response eased the tension in Daniel's muscles. *Congratulations, you're pulling off normal.*

Aloud, he said, "I don't think the bomb was her."

Admitting it made him uneasy. He didn't want to believe anything that had come out of Jude's mouth, but gasoline-filled water balloons paired with a Molotov cocktail didn't fit her. She was more spur-of-the-moment, and she'd probably rather use her own two hands.

"Two separate people trying to kill you? Now you're just bragging," Zeb said. "Is this how things always were in your old job?

"No. First time I've been chased out of a burning building."

"Congrats on learning new skills then."

Daniel laughed, but he didn't correct his friend. New skills they weren't. Rusty, half-remembered lessons, maybe. He'd had a childhood full of panic drills for insane shit like this, living with a paranoid mother who'd thought supernatural creatures were hunting her. Despite finding out everything she'd said was true after she died, and despite working for his father at the Consilium, he'd never had to put much of that old training into practice until recently.

"You think it was Aubrie, then? The—" Rather than finish, Zeb mimed throwing a bottle.

"More likely somebody in his employ." As if Spencer Aubrie would deign to get his hands dirty. "Let's finish up and everyone can get out of here."

"You thought up some way around the motion sensor while you rappelled down the side of your building?"

"Yeah, I brought her with me."

"*Puta madre*." Zeb's shock mirrored the sentiment Daniel had felt arguing the same point with Gracie an hour ago.

He couldn't help raising an eyebrow at the new Spanish oath, and Zeb scowled at him.

"Don't tell my *abuela*," he said. "She decided God only speaks Spanish, so if I swear in French or English, He won't hear it." He sighed, adding dryly, "Maybe you'll find out when your ex actually kills you this time around. You really think she's gonna help after you had the guys lock her up?"

"If she really wants the information she says she came for." Daniel brushed past him into the hallway to put an end to the conversation. The more Zeb questioned him, the more he'd question himself. Normally, he'd appreciate that skepticism in a friend, but he didn't have the luxury of a long consideration now.

"I wouldn't trust her," Zeb said, catching up to him.

With a flippancy he didn't feel, Daniel returned, "You can always quit."

"Just when shit's getting interesting?"

"Famous last words."

They reached the main, open room. Four men had a card game going, trading insults in French near the door: the two men who'd taken Jude to her cell and two of Daniel's newer recruits. Near the back, Fabiola stood over a table of blueprints tapping on her phone. She'd pared down to an undershirt and the polyester pants of her museum security uniform.

She frowned when she saw them, asking in accented English, "Zeb's taken the entire pizza?"

"Night's going to be earlier than we thought." Daniel stopped at the table. "That woman you mentioned coming into the museum yesterday—what did she look like?"

"She was tall, pale. Short red hair." Fabiola glanced to the ceiling as it might help her bring up further detail. "At first I thought she was just a museum donor. She treated the kids at the front desk like imbeciles." She shrugged. "It caught my attention when she started asking about artifacts in storage."

"Why's that matter?" Zeb asked.

"Jude's made some new friends," Daniel said. But Jude hadn't mentioned the cross, only the incantation. Either she wasn't working for the red-haired woman or she hadn't gotten all the information. Both scenarios were equally plausible. He'd need to talk to her again to figure out how many additional rivals he had, but that was the last thing he wanted to do.

9

I PICKED MYSELF UP, wincing against my bruised butt and sore arm. The goon's wallet hit the floor. Would he come back for it when he realized it was missing? I'd be ready if he did. The vise around my chest had eased but it still seemed hard to draw a full breath. I turned to the gleaming walls and the door. They weren't exactly mirrored, but they were metal.

I had to give Daniel credit: he'd gotten one over on me. Well, what now? If he wanted to kill me, he'd have run me through with that poker back at the apartment.

I walked on shaky legs to the door and put my hand against the cool surface. My skin prickled and goosebumps broke out again. I tried to alter my gravity, cling to the door, but nothing happened. *Just winded and fazed. Not 100% after the coma.*

Closing my eyes, I focused harder. This time I spun myself onto the wall, but the air tugged on me from all sides like it had gained mass, making me fight harder than ever to stay there.

With a grunt, I stumbled back to the ground, muscles quivering like jelly. I slammed my palm against the door. The force vibrated back up my arm, making me draw it back and shake out my fingers. *Iron.* It must have run through all the walls, given how I hadn't been able to catch my breath and shift gravity outside. This place had to be an old Consilium hold—I'd never set foot in one reinforced like this, but I'd heard stories.

Daniel'd said he was going somewhere safe—my fault for assuming that would apply to both of us.

At least I had more than Faerie powers at my disposal. I retreated to the big guy's wallet and went through it, pulling out a debit card. I slid the card sideways into the slot between the door and the wall, trying to work it in. I'd done this on occasion, never with an industrial door.

No dice. The card bent like it might snap and nothing happened with the deadbolt.

Frustrated, I spun and gave the door a swift kick. The motion made me tired and the door shook but didn't give. Not made entirely out of iron, just plated or reinforced. Just enough to keep me from climbing the walls.

I returned to the wallet and looked through it. Two twenties and some flimsy coffee joint punch cards—no help. I slipped the cash into my pocket anyway.

Returning to the door, I slid the debit card horizontally back into the frame, then bent it hard to one side until it snapped in half. Those halves snapped into even smaller pieces. They broke the way I wanted them to and I had long, thin strips of plastic. These I scraped against the wall. The sound of torn plastic riding over metal made me grit my teeth, but I kept it up. I whittled the strips down to give them narrower ends.

Armed with a flimsy, homemade lock-pick kit, I went to the keyhole. I stuck my tools into the lock, working them against each other. A bead of sweat trickled down the back of my neck, between my shoulder blades. I couldn't see see exactly what I was doing with the only light hanging in the centre of the room, but I kept working until I found the mechanism I wanted. I jiggled the pins, catching the tips of my fingers a few times against the hard edge of the keyhole.

My back ached from crouching for what must have been an hour. Impossible to tell time in this cell. I alternated between stressing my thighs in a crouch and letting my knees go numb on the hard floor. The plastic bent so far I expected it to snap in my fingers. Instead, the deadbolt slipped back with a satisfying click. *Jude: one, iron box: zilch.*

I shook my arms to loosen them, rubbing the sweat from my forehead. Grabbing the door handle and yanking it open, I found the hall empty. What—I didn't merit guards?

Reminding my pride that this was a good thing, I headed down the dim hall, still clutching the pieces of plastic in one palm. My legs itched to find the door and make a run for it, get the hell away from this iron prison.

I couldn't, though. I needed that spell. I wanted to burn it in front of Aubrie's face, and I wanted my passport and that damn letter opener. I could almost taste the salt of the first margarita I'd have once I was safe on some sunny, far away beach. Okay, it'd probably be a tequila shot.

That vision prompted me to follow the sounds of voices back to the place where Daniel and I had entered. Staying close to the door frame, I peeked out to take stock. The room just beyond the entrance held seven people. Daniel stood at a table, resting his palms on it, going over something that looked like a blueprint with a woman and another guy. My two goon buddies had a card game going with two other guys near the door where I peeked in.

The other guy near the blueprints—a young, Hispanic-looking guy with his hair buzzed short—tapped a pencil against the table as he stared down at it. "Car's gonna be crowded."

"Is that a real concern, Zeb?" Daniel's tone indicated he already knew it wasn't.

"Nah, man. You want to bring a plus-one, well, you're the boss."

"Tomorrow's good." The woman, an older Black woman as unfamiliar to me as the others, looked up from her phone. "Calendar says it will be busy. Two school groups."

"Kids are good?" the Hispanic guy, Zeb, asked.

"Kids are slow." This from one of the guys playing cards, a compact, middle-aged white guy who looked like he could bench press five of me with one arm. He had a ring of trim, white hair around his scalp and spoke in accented English like the Black woman. "Kids panic."

"That's dark, Olivier," Zeb replied.

The bald guy lifted his middle finger without looking away from his cards. "I know a good distraction when I hear one."

Zeb let the pencil roll out of his hand, then jerked forward to grab it before it hit the edge of the table. His gaze rose to the doorway as he straightened up, catching on me. His eyes widened and he cleared his throat, bringing everyone else's attention.

Too late to duck away. I took a deep breath and strode into the room. "Planning a bank heist?"

The muscular card-player knocked his chair back to come at me.

Unable to use my gravity to vault over him the way I wanted, I dropped to my hands instead, swinging a leg out to catch him in the ankles and knock him off balance as he loomed over me. He fell hard and I landed a sharp punch to his nose before getting to my feet, sucking in a breath to keep from showing how the sudden motion had winded me in the iron room.

The other three guys had risen too, but they waited, smarter.

"Your locks are shitty," I said, opening my palm and letting the pieces of plastic drop to the floor.

Daniel glanced at the two men who'd tossed me in the cell. One of them hissed in annoyance, recognizing the broken bits of his debit card.

The instinctive sting of fury wanted me to make them all hurt for parking me in a cell. I steeled myself and held my ground, fixing on Daniel to say: "I put you in the hospital, you put me in a box. Are we done?"

Once the words were out, my muscles relaxed, coming back under my control.

"Tell me about your hospital benefactor," he said.

"What?" Annoyance crept through me again at the demand. "You just locked me up. I don't feel like spilling my guts anymore."

His eyes moved over my shoulder and he gave a slight shake of his head.

I turned to see Baldie creeping up on me again, nose still bloody where I'd hit him. I tensed for another fight, but he backed off at Daniel's order. I was still surrounded and outnumbered, the iron in the walls pressing in to smother me.

"Miranda," I said, reminding him of her name, "was tall, skinny." I started ticking them off on my fingers. "Super pale. Red hair. In her fifties, maybe, if she were human. Cryptic as fuck. Wouldn't eat pancakes. You know her?"

Daniel glanced to the Black woman, who inclined her head in what was either agreement or uncertainty. He clearly understood which, but rather than indicate it, he studied the paper on table without seeming to see it.

"I'll give you what you want," he finally said, "but I need your . . . talents."

I kept myself from taking a step back, too startled to even make an inappropriate joke. "You want me to climb a wall?"

"To start."

"You might want to narrow it down. There's lots of walls in Montreal." I got within sight of the papers—definitely blueprints—and Daniel rolled them up, away from my prying eyes. I met his gaze when he turned back to face me, warning, "I'm not going back in that cell."

"Doesn't really look like you've got a choice."

Anger itched beneath my skin, ants in my bloodstream. I put my hands on the table and leaned on them to keep from letting a fist fly. Even unarmed, Daniel could probably take me on right now, since using my power would leave me gasping on the floor. The four other thugs waited behind me too, ready to pounce. Zeb and the woman across the table didn't look keen to get involved, but they'd probably jump into a fight if I started one.

My body made the decision almost without me—I couldn't go back into that iron box. I turned and ran. Ignoring the shouts and scuffle behind me as some portion of the room started to follow, I bee-lined for the exit. I could come up with some other way to get the spell from the safety of *not here*.

I burst through the door. The humid night air felt like heaven after the suffocating iron. I didn't pause outside, cutting across the parking lot to a street. I couldn't hear pursuers yet, but that didn't mean they weren't there.

I dashed across the road, deserted at this time of night, but found only a grassy park with a bike trail and the guardrail to a narrow body of water—a river or maybe a canal. City lights glittered across the water but no bridge was visible nearby in either direction.

Taking off down the paved path, I eventually reached a cross street and darted back across the road and down it. It took me back to a neighbourhood, dense duplexes and triplexes suddenly crowding the street like where the Faerie house had let me out instead of the shadowy warehouses.

I slowed to a jog to keep from attracting attention and kept going until I reached a more commercial artery and the welcoming neon advertising of a corner bar. Probably best to get off the street.

10

I SNAGGED A STOOL at the crowded bar and ordered a double whisky, which seemed to work in French as well as English. Two guys approached me between that and the shot of tequila I ordered next. The first inched away when I responded to his French pick-up line with a curse in English, but the other was bilingual enough to be persistent for another minute before packing it in. I probably should have let him buy me a drink. The twenties I'd pocketed from the goon's wallet weren't going to go as far as I'd like—preferably somewhere into blackout territory where I didn't have to consider my next move.

"Well, look who's awake." A voice broke through the din, the string of unprompted English words standing out in the ambient foreign conversation like an alarm.

A woman stood behind me: short with a shock of platinum blonde hair teased to fluffiness around her head. She wore a tight purple mini-skirt and fishnet stockings under a pair of lace-up boots. A black bra peeked out beneath her white ribbed tank and a collection of silver jewellery hung around her neck.

"Who the hell are you?" I asked.

"I'm Pru." She crushed in between me and my neighbours at the bar. Leaning close so I could hear her gratingly airy voice, she said, "Put us together and we're *Prude*. Funny, huh?"

"Are you hitting on me?"

She laughed, a silver stud gleaming in her tongue.

"Shit, no! I'm taken." She leaned in again, sniffing me in an exaggerated way. "Plus—I hate to be the one to tell you, girl—you *reek* of iron."

"Nice meeting you." I brushed her away as the bartender delivered my tequila.

"You ruined my night," Pru said. "I think you should make it up to me."

When I spun again she met my eyes, one side of her mouth twisting into a smile. "You've been playing in places you weren't supposed to be. But Spence'll be so happy to hear you're up and around again."

"You work for Aubrie." My chest tightened. So much for a safe, anonymous place. I downed my shot, sliding off my bar stool.

Pru didn't back off, even though I had a good couple inches on her. She grinned, clicking her tongue stud against her teeth. Her eyes flickered past me, catching sight of someone. She stood on tip-toe, lifting a hand to wave.

A lanky guy with spiked hair, dirty jeans and a leather jacket joined her, snaking an arm around her waist. Taller than her but still a shade shorter than me, and pale enough to almost glow in the dim bar.

"This is my boyfriend, Jasper," Pru said, cuddling against him. She batted her lashes at me to ask, "Where's yours?"

"My what? Oh." I got it: they were after Daniel. "So you're the assholes behind the water balloons? Which one of you was hiding in the backyard and chickened out when they saw the odds were a little different than you'd expected?"

Jasper darkened, eyes narrowing to slits. Bingo.

Pru scratched her head, laying her palm flat. She blew a cloud of something directly into my face.

My eyes stung. The room became a blur of colour, light and dark, melting together. It looked like a bucket of water had been dumped over the bar. I felt like I'd had about five more shots of tequila.

Somebody caught me as my legs gave out. Voices slid past my ears.

Warm air hit. I took a breath. I'd been led outside of the air-conditioned bar into the night. Things started coming into focus. I wrenched my arm out of Pru's cold fingers.

Jasper, on the other side, let me go to dodge my wild punch. He exploded into a shower of glitter.

I froze, brain not responding quickly enough to tell me whether that had actually happened. I shook my head to clear it. Didn't help. Stumbling backwards, I hit a brick wall and turned the world sideways. In what felt like slow motion, I flipped awkwardly onto my stomach, crawling on hands and knees up the wall out of their reach. My vision seemed to clear with every painful scrape of the rough brick against my palms.

My neck stung, just under my jaw. I stopped to touch it. My fingers came away from the spot with a smear of blood. The coppery scent brought me completely back to reality. Had one of them *bitten* me?

They stood below on the sidewalk, both their heads cocked to follow my progress up the building. Jasper glimmered, not a hallucination.

Pixies.

Full-blood pixies would have been even shorter. These two were definitely part-human like me. I'd been backup on the capture of a half-pixie assassin back in my Consilium days. They liked to draw blood first thing and ask questions later, because they could follow a blood trail better than a dog.

"Spence will want to see you," Pru called.

My breath caught in my throat. I wanted to see him too. He could tell me it had been some kind of misunderstanding in Toronto, that he hadn't meant to hurt me.

But he didn't have an evil twin who'd flung me off the balcony. I'd see Aubrie on my own terms to suss that out, preferably not outnumbered.

Moving faster, I continued up the wall to the top of the building. I hauled myself up onto the roof, relieved when my legs held me, then dashed across to the other side.

A burst of glitter flew past me, bringing me up short halfway across the room as it materialized into Jasper. A slower cloud became Pru beside him. She unfurled her fingers again to present a flat palm.

This time I saw the pixie dust coming. I managed a back flip, vaulting on my hands to spin my head away from the bulk of the dust. I stuck the landing at the edge of the roof, taking another step to jump. Shifting my gravity at an angle let me slide down the side of the building like a surfer on a hard, brick wave.

I faltered hitting the ground. The sky and nearby buildings veered to one side again. Turning upside down on pixie dust probably hadn't been the best move. Still, I managed to take off running in a position that felt upright.

My breath came in short gasps. Fuelled by only a handful of pancakes and some booze, I made it another block at speed before clipping a brick wall as I took the corner. I stumbled to my knees on the sidewalk, the jarring motion of the fall making the world tilt again.

Somewhere behind me, a car revved its engine. The sound grew louder, filling my ears, then slowed. The car skidded to the curb ahead of me and a figure jumped out.

I tried to make sense of my body, jumbled from the sudden stop, and get to my feet to fight, but the world spun around me with a speed that made my legs buckle. Warm hands slid underneath my armpits and the heels of my boots scuffed on the concrete as someone dragged me to the car and hauled me into the passenger seat like a ragdoll.

I tried to focus on the face but it wobbled, more an abstract smear than a person. Without my permission, my arms were lifted above my head. A sharp tearing sound echoed in my ears. I tried to yank my arms down, but they stayed stuck to the roof of the car.

Then we were moving, fast. Lights blurred through the passenger-door window. I clenched my eyes shut, trying to focus my orientation in the car. I still felt lightheaded when I opened them, but if I focused hard on one stationary thing at a time, my wavering vision held still.

The driver gave me a sidelong glance and the passing streetlights lit his face. One of the guys from the warehouse, Zeb. Close up, he looked about my age, with dark hair cropped close to his head, soft features and silver gauges in both ears.

I tugged on my wrists again, but they'd been securely anchored to the handle above the passenger door. The glove box hung open above my knees, its light shining on a roll of duct-tape.

"What hit you?" Zeb asked.

"Pixies." The answer slipped out in a half-slur before I could remember to be cryptic.

"No shit?" A note of curiosity tinged the skepticism in his voice.

"Love to tell you all about it over a whisky."

He snorted. "You're not really my type."

I yanked on my wrists again. They didn't budge. He'd used a lot of tape, an amount that would have been comical if it'd been somebody else's skin under the weight of it.

Amateur. "Were you Consilium?"

"Nope."

"How'd you wind up working for Daniel?"

He shrugged, then took another turn that felt like we went up on two wheels.

I couldn't tell if that was reality or the remains of the pixie dust. The cold shoulder also felt more personal than I'd expected. "Do you know who I am?"

"Yep."

And from the cool, sharp tone of his voice, he knew more than that. Who the hell was this guy that Daniel confided in him? No friend that I'd ever met.

Not that Danny had introduced me to his friends when we'd been hooking up. I hadn't been scheduling double-dates either. We'd kept our social spheres separate. He'd had co-workers. I'd had drinking buddies. And Aubrie.

I twisted a hand to try and pick at the corner of the duct tape. My fingernails were longer than usual from three months asleep. I managed to raise an edge but it was going to be a long process at this rate.

We slowed abruptly and turned into a dark parking lot that looked too much like the one I'd fled across leaving the warehouse. Zeb let the car idle as he studied two cars parked near a door up ahead. Then he steered into a spot some distance from the door, in the shadow of another building, before cutting the engine.

With a distracted irony, he told me, "Don't go anywhere."

11

"LATE FOR AN INTERROGATION." The bigger of the two guards folded his arms. He leaned against the heavy door to the cell as he stared at Daniel. "You think there's something we haven't wrung out of this bitch already? Or are you going to talk to her in that half-singing nonsense they switch to when they don't want to answer questions?"

"No." Daniel hadn't expected the guard, Marc, to remember that. He'd only mentioned learning the Antagonist language in passing when they'd met three weeks ago. "I can't speak it."

"But you understand it."

"Some." The written runes were much easier to decipher, but five-years study at the Consilium had brought him to the point where he could follow the other world's spoken language about half the time.

"And it has to be tonight." Marc sounded dubious. "Because an informant told you that Spencer Aubrie's coming here tomorrow to free her."

"Free her, kill her. I don't know. It doesn't matter." Daniel's gaze flickered to the second guard, hoping for an ally.

The other man just watched the exchange without comment.

"You plan to let this prisoner run out too?" Marc inclined his head toward the cell door.

News travelled fast to this end of the warehouse. These guards didn't regularly fraternize with Daniel's newer recruits, dedicated enough to their job that they hadn't even abandoned their post when word came months ago that the Consilium had fallen. Gracie had made sure they still got paid, at least, but even that hadn't endeared them to Daniel taking the warehouse over a few weeks ago. Their capitulation seemed to be some leftover deference to the memory of his father, but it was tenuous, so he hadn't pushed it.

Clearly letting Jude escape had been a step too far. Zeb had insisted on going after her and Daniel hadn't stopped him, but if he was being honest, he was glad she'd run. It would make things more difficult with the museum, but easier in every other respect.

The big guard spat an aside to his partner: "*Osti de traître. Le Consilium n'a jamais fait des accords avec les monstres.*"

Daniel tensed at the epithet. It wasn't the first time in the last few months that he'd been called a traitor. He didn't blunt his sarcasm to snap back: "One former contractor just broke out of here with a *credit card* and another's coming by tomorrow to kill us. Better to say the Consilium didn't make *good* deals with monsters."

The second guard, Gregory, chuckled. Ignoring his partner's resentful glare, he moved between them. "I don't think you'll get anything from her," he told Daniel with a shrug, "*mais si vous voulez y aller, ça nous derange pas.*"

"*Perte de temps*," Marc muttered, brandishing the key to the cell. He unlocked the door and shoved it open with a scowl.

Daniel stepped inside. When the door swung shut behind him, he fought to retain the bravado he'd shown the two guards. The lock seemed vindictively loud.

Harsh lights illuminated every inch of the tiny metal room, including a bed bolted to the far right side.

A figure sat cross-legged on the thin mattress. The overhead bulbs washed out her terracotta skin, giving her a sallow look that made the blue at the roots of her dark hair stand out. The colour appeared stronger in a disconcerting way when he looked at her closely, undulating just enough to give him a twinge of dizziness.

She caught him in a piercing violet-eyed stare.

"Hello," she said. "I know you. Cain's son—David?"

"Daniel," he managed to correct her, focusing on her face instead of the shifting colours in her hair.

"My apologies." She stretched her legs and got to her feet with the grace of a dancer, then extended a hand. "Ilse."

The original report of her capture had indicated she was a water sprite. The creatures fed on anxiety and fear, replacing it with a numbing bliss. Unfortunately for their human victims, that usually resulted in a numb, blissful drowning.

Even in the safety of the cell, with no water nearby, Daniel didn't shake her hand.

She dropped it to her side. "Perhaps that's inappropriate," she murmured. "The iron makes things a bit fuzzy."

He kept himself from flinching at the deceptively dry accusation. Setting foot in this warehouse, laying claim to whatever was still left of the Consilium, had always meant he'd eventually have to reckon with their sins. It had been much easier to pretend that they'd been all benign research and hadn't had secret prisons for their enemies.

"I don't want to keep you here," he said.

"How kind." The lack of irony in the sprite's voice made the words sharper somehow. Her eyes flickered past his shoulder as if there were a person behind him. "I would imagine, however, that you do want *something*?"

He fought the urge to glance back. Nothing had come into the room with him. "The entire formula you brought across with you. You had a list of ingredients but left off the amounts."

"Why would you want that?" Ilse's unnatural eyes gleamed in the overhead lights, too large if he looked at them too long. "I don't believe you have the ability to mix it yourself—you're human." She studied him again, as if verifying that fact. "And to use it, you would have had to have broken the incantation." She lifted her voice to make it a query.

"You answer my question, you get out of here," Daniel said. "That's the only way this works."

"I see." She paused. "I propose instead that I'll answer your question, then you answer mine. Then you can let me go, and I'll owe you for that."

"I don't want anything from you except those numbers."

"You should be aware that the Mab will hunt you down purely to purge the world of your name."

"The Mab's dead."

"A Mab's dead." Ilse pressed her lips into a straight line. "I suggest you show proper deference to the new one. Perhaps you could tell me what you plan to do with the incantation. Then I can—"

Before she could finish, the room's door rattled like something heavy had been hurled at it. A second impact echoed off the walls, making the door shake under the force of a sickening crunch.

Ilse remained stationary, eyes narrowing at the door in suspicion rather than relief, as if she'd already guessed who'd be coming through it. At the sound of keys in the lock, she spoke suddenly in a high-pitched tone, almost a song.

The translation of the foreign word came to Daniel automatically. *Ink.*

The staccato of sounds formed a melodic lilt as she continued with a simple list of words. She spoke slowly, as if to someone not fluent in her mother tongue, aiming just over his shoulder again. "*One bottle. Half. Three—*" the next syllable wasn't as easy to transpose, something like rain—maybe drops? "*Eight leaves. One whole.*"

He couldn't discern the last thing she said, but her tone softened for it. When she finished, her vivid eyes met his.

"Damn it," she said in English, looking dismayed as she realized he'd understood her. With a sigh, she added, "No matter. We may both be dead, soon enough."

12

AUBRIE STEELED HIMSELF AGAINST the initial shock of the iron as he stepped into the warehouse. It hit like plunging into freezing water, sucking the air from his lungs. He breathed in, focused on quelling the nausea that twisted his insides. The Consilium had kept more than one building like this and it wasn't his first time in one. He'd had practice around iron. The feeling would fade.

The toxic construction didn't seem to slow down the eight others he'd brought with him, though they all shared his weakness to it. He had warned them, tried to help them anticipate what it would feel like so they could barrel through. Despite the weight of the tainted air around them, they'd made short work of forcing the loading dock door open, then fanned out into the echoing space to secure the warehouse.

Now, though, the ones he could see were breathing hard, sweating, winded.

Coming earlier than he'd planned due to the Mab's attack at the airport, he hadn't been able to assemble his full force. He hadn't even bothered to call Mei. She'd probably have demurred in favour of her business dinner anyway.

The cavernous building went quiet after an initial spate of shouting. It hadn't been left well-defended. There weren't many people left who could defend it.

"This door's guarded." One of his team got Aubrie's attention from further inside, beckoning to a hallway.

Was guarded, Aubrie amended, reaching it with several of his people trailing. The two men who'd been protecting the door lay in a motionless pile to one side. The bleeding tears in their skin matched the still-exposed claws of a man in his employ whose name he didn't remember.

The half-griffin man had clearly followed Aubrie's advice to practice wielding his powers while near—or ideally holding—a piece of iron, to learn its limitations and start building an affinity with it. His transformed paw shook but he flexed his talons, strain etching across his face as he held the partial shift of his flesh against the building.

Should learn that one's name. He's promising.

"Take a minute," Aubrie told him. "Relax." He might need those claws to go to work for him again, once they got the door open.

The griffin allowed the claws to vanish, his hand reforming into five fingers. He hissed, clutching his hand as the weight of the iron bore down on him, but kept his spine straight.

After a search too slow for Aubrie's liking, another woman dug the keys from one of the pockets of the bodies by the door. He wanted to tear them from her hands, but held himself in check and stepped aside to give her access to the door's lock. Better someone else enter first, just in case.

She tried two keys before finding the correct one. The deadbolt shot back and she pushed the heavy door open. Four others followed her in, spreading out at the entrance to ensure no one got past them.

Relief Aubrie hadn't expected flooded him upon seeing Daniel with an unfamiliar woman. He'd expected the Mab's messenger to be someone he knew, but a stranger without any accompanying baggage of past history made things much easier.

Daniel's stance with the Faerie indicated an interrupted conversation, or some flimsy facsimile of an interrogation. Pru and Jasper had clearly failed in their mission to rout the human, but no matter. This might even be the better outcome. *Two birds, one cage.*

He met Aubrie's eyes but kept his expression unreadable. The Consilium had always trained their people well—and not just field agents who regularly ran headfirst into danger. Everyone from janitors to bookkeepers had been drilled to die for the cause. Most of them already had.

The Faerie woman took a step forward as Aubrie approached, extending a hand. Blue danced in her black hair as it caught the light. Her time in the iron prison had probably decayed her glamour.

"You must be John Aubrie," she said.

The name set Aubrie's teeth on edge. He glared at her, at the sly hint of mocking underneath the guileless question. He didn't know her, but she knew him. Knew he didn't use that name. Probably knew why. The Mab must have told her to call him that, to twist the knife and throw him off. She wasn't planning to be cooperative. He'd expected no less, but one always hoped . . .

"Is this not how humans greet each other any longer?" The woman looked from him to Daniel, then down at her own hand before returning it to her side.

"He wouldn't touch you either?" Aubrie glanced to the younger man. "Learned a lesson in the last few months, then?"

"Fuck you." Daniel's hands tightened into fists at his sides. Not as well-trained as he tried to project.

"Let's be civil."

"*Civil?* After you *massacred* hundreds of—"

Aubrie spun and punched him in the stomach, cutting off the accusation. The weight of the iron in the room made the force of his blow closer to human. If he'd been anywhere else, using his full strength, the jab would have killed the other man.

Seeing Daniel gasping on the floor, a pang of pity went through Aubrie, and not for the first time. He'd thought more than once over the years that it would have been kinder for Alan Cain to have drowned his progeny like unwanted puppies rather than trying to mould them into Consilium soldiers. But zealots needed followers.

He looked back to the blue-haired woman. She hadn't moved, staring at the open doorway as if she hadn't even heard the disturbance. A small 'v' quirked between her eyebrows.

"You're giving away royal secrets to humans now?" he asked.

That got her attention back on him but didn't faze her the way he'd hoped. "Nothing was given."

"It was taken, then. Or traded," he said. "Whatever semantics you want to use to save face. The Consilium got the incantation from you one way or another." He inclined his head toward Daniel. "Comparing notes?"

"Not with a human. Nor with you." She said the words with no vehemence.

"I won't waste time negotiating."

The warning rewarded him with a gentle smile. "Waste your time as you like. You don't have much left."

"Because of your new Mab?" Aubrie shook his head. "She hasn't got control of the realm. She can't raise an army. She barely speaks the language anymore."

"I wouldn't count on that." The woman grabbed his wrist.

Warmth flushed through his skin where she touched him. It bled up his arm, through his muscles, making them ache to loosen and relax. Her fathomless eyes gleamed as she wrapped her other hand around the back of his neck to pull him into an embrace.

Calm flooded Aubrie's body like a warm wave. His shoulders slumped without permission, melting into the creature pressed against him. The warehouse around him faded, sounds of shouting, footsteps and a commotion somewhere near the door growing distant.

The scent of iron cut through the magic like a knife and let him fight his way back to himself. He could feel the hunger on her, desperate to pull energy from him.

Being half-human, he wasn't immune to Faerie magic. He twined his fingers into her hair, intending to yank her head back and extricate himself. Brittle as ice, it stung when he touched it.

She burst into a splash of water.

Aubrie jerked back, covering his face with an arm against the spray. The force of it sent him stumbling back, tripping and ending up on the floor. He wasn't wet, though—all the water had gathered back together and flown from him as if tossed from a bucket at the next closest person: the woman coming to assist him.

Metallic clanking echoed outside the room. A high-pitched creak preceded the sudden hiss of fire sprinklers bursting to life from the ceiling in the hallway.

The sentient water splashed from one person to the next until it reached the doorway, then disappeared into the rush of the spitting sprinklers.

Aubrie got to his feet in time to see Daniel reach the door when the misty form of the Faerie did. He hadn't seen the younger man run, but he must have bolted as soon as the woman attacked.

Daniel spun to swing a fist at the half-griffin man, who ducked, then lunged forward, claws outstretched. The talons caught him in the back of the lower leg, throwing him against the doorjamb. He managed to stumble through the doorway, leaving a trail of blood behind as he fled.

The half-griffin and another woman other took off after him.

The blue-haired Faerie had probably already found her way down a drain, on her way back to her queen.

Aubrie reached down to help his nearby compatriot up. Fury and shame burned in his chest. They'd spent too much time in this poisonous building. He'd overestimated his people's ability, and his own, to withstand the iron. Practice did not make perfect. He'd let the Faerie distract him for too long, let her spring an attack. He'd known better than that. It stung his pride, but he tried to push the feeling aside and focus on more pertinent concerns.

The blood in the doorway told him Daniel wouldn't get far while injured, not with the two others on his tail and a few more people outside to aid them.

The iron frayed his nerves, a low hum at the edge of his perception. He looked to his last remaining accomplice, hovering awkwardly by the door as she awaited instructions he was more than happy to give. "Let's burn this goddamn place to the ground."

13

DANIEL STAGGERED INTO THE loading dock. Multiple sets of footsteps echoed in the hall behind him. Every step he took sent a bolt of pain up through his leg, but he darted for the dark outline of the iron fireplace poker still resting against the wall beside the door where he'd left it.

He put his weight on his good leg to spin and swing the weapon up as his nearest pursuer reached him. The metal rod slammed into the side of the Antagonist's throat, knocking him backwards with a grunt.

Four others reached the room and stopped short when they saw the weapon in his hand. One woman bared her teeth in a hiss, pressing in a step closer.

Daniel shoved himself out the door, slamming it behind him. He almost slipped the iron poker through the handle to jam it shut, but he couldn't bring himself to give up the weapon. He scrambled out of the dim circle of light that fanned out over the parking lot outside and took two turns between buildings.

He limped to a stop as he reached a dead-end: a high chain-link fence covered in a network of heavy vines that separated the row of warehouses from the residential neighbourhood to the southeast. He'd gotten lost in the dark, missed the break in the fence that should have led him back to a populated area. His leg throbbed hard enough to indicate that climbing the chain-links would be difficult. The rows of razor wire glinting under the leaves at the top upped that to impossible.

Shoes clicked on the pavement at the mouth of the alley. "Ollie ollie oxen free!" came a female voice. "Nowhere to run."

He ducked behind a broken wooden pallet propped against the wall of the building beside him, holding his breath as she approached. By the light leaking into the alley, she slunk past: a slender woman, no more than five feet tall. He had at least eight inches and fifty pounds on her, but his injury would be a handicap . . .

The woman vanished.

. . . *And there's that.* Daniel held as still as he could.

Sharp fingernails dug into the back of his neck. The air around him shimmered and he jerked sideways, thrusting the iron poker toward the distortion. It smashed into her jaw as she re-materialized fully.

He lurched to his feet, almost losing his balance when he landed on his injured leg. He threw himself forward and rounded the corner.

Headlights blinded him. A car swung up alongside with a squeal of brakes.

"Daniel!"

At Zeb's familiar voice, he shoved himself off the wall and made for the car. He had only enough energy to open the back door and tumble onto the backseat.

Zeb turned in the driver's seat, managing to yank the door shut. He laid rubber with a squeal.

"You hurt?" His eyes flickered back in the rearview mirror.

"Yes." Daniel forced his fingers to release the iron weapon and dropped it on the floor of the backseat. He examined the tears in the leg of his jeans and the bloody gashes underneath, unable to see much in the dark. His leg throbbed.

"Bad?"

"ER."

"Got it." Zeb took another turn that almost had Daniel on the floor of the backseat.

"*Alive!*" he snapped.

"*Osti de câlice de tabarnak.*" Zeb didn't slow the car. He let a breath hiss between his teeth with the string of profanities.

Daniel almost let himself relax into the pain, but a new voice made him freeze.

"What happened?" Jude slouched in the passenger seat, craning her neck over the seat toward him as much as she could with both wrists duct-taped to the handle above the door.

"You *found* her?" Daniel couldn't hide his amazement, and it made Zeb cast him an insulted look in the rearview mirror.

"He got lucky," Jude grumbled, giving a half-hearted tug on her bonds.

"Prisoner and no prison," Zeb said. "*Putain de chanceux.*" He directed the next question over his shoulder, "That was Aubrie?"

"Yes." The memory of looking the bastard in the eye and then doing no more than run made Daniel sick with shame. He should have fought. He should have done . . . something. He'd had the advantage. Or he should have had it—he hadn't expected Aubrie and his people to do so well against the iron in the building.

"You saw Aubrie?" Jude's question came out quiet and strained.

Zeb ignored her, his voice grim. "Everybody's dead?"

"Greg and Marc are." Daniel had seen the bodies of the guards he'd seen as he fled the iron cell.

"Jean and Olivier too. Probably Martin and Simon."

"You went inside?"

"I got back with Little Miss Sunshine here, and there were two new cars outside the loading dock," Zeb said. "I parked around the block and went in through the side door to investigate. Saw Jean and Olivier and all the blood there in the break room and I got the hell out. I'd have kept going over Pont Champlain to the South Shore and maybe the American border, but you came shooting out of that alley."

"You thought they wouldn't notice *this* at the border?" Jude demanded, tugging her arms again.

"Fuck." Daniel slumped back against the seat, blinking at streetlights that still seemed to be rushing by too fast. *We should have been ready. I let Aubrie walk in and murder everyone again.* He hadn't been there the first time, three months ago at the Consilium, and he should have been. He'd thought if he had a second chance, he could . . .

What? Get a lucky hit in and run for your life?

Zeb's voice lifted in alarm. "What about Fabiola?"

"She left before they got there." Daniel hardly remembered that far back in the evening. "Maybe ten minutes."

"Okay. Okay, good." Zeb hesitated, asking with sigh, "Is there a chance she sent them?"

"No." He couldn't believe Fabiola had any ties to Aubrie. He'd only come into contact with her because she worked at the museum and she'd been willing to provide security information for a price. Aubrie didn't even know about the museum.

Although, given that all of the blueprints and plans had been left at the warehouse, he probably knew now.

"Should I call Grace?" Zeb asked. "She could meet us at the hospital."

"No." Daniel didn't want to explain his stupidity to his sister. He thought better of the initial answer: forewarned was forearmed. Not that Gracie would ever be far from a weapon.

A siren wailed behind the car.

"*Tabarnak*," Zeb hissed.

"Hey!" Jude sat up straight, turning toward the back window and trying to angle her pinned wrists into the headlights coming up on them.

Daniel glanced back at the police cruiser. A chase was the last thing they needed. He worked to concoct a legitimate explanation for the blood, for his injuries and their speeding to the hospital. Maybe a dog attack. No good explanation for the duct-taped captive in the front seat, though.

Zeb took a sharp, sudden turn that dumped him onto the floor. The flashing lights behind them dimmed momentarily.

Daniel propped himself on one elbow.

"Are you sure you can outrun them in this?" The car had to be at least twenty years old, and the floor of the backseat smelled like it.

Zeb snorted. "Offended you have to ask. We'll be invisible in five blocks. They saw a silver sedan doing ten over the limit with a white guy in the backseat. They've got better things to do."

"*Ten?*" The incredulous word came from both the back and front passenger seats in unison.

Zeb stifled a laugh but didn't correct his conservative assessment of their speed or his prediction. After a moment, he inclined his head back to tell Daniel, "You're gonna want to stay down—there's no airbags back there."

"That's another joke?" Daniel shifted to ease the pressure on his throbbing leg.

"Don't worry, man, we're not going to hit anything." Zeb's tone changed from dismissive to thoughtful as he took another two hard turns in a row, putting the sirens further behind them. "For real about the airbags, though."

14

THE BUZZ OF AN automatic car lock jolted me awake. I blinked against harsh sunlight and focused on a passenger seat and glove box below me. The one Zeb had closed before locking me in the car at a far corner of the hospital parking lot back when it had still been dark out.

With my arms duct-taped to the handle above the door, pins and needles had set in before we'd even reached the ER last night. Or this morning? The only way to ease the feeling, once I'd been left alone in the car, had been to shift gravity and stretch out on the ceiling above the passenger seat. The blood had flowed back into my hands, but the fuzzy upholstery up here was not as comfortable as it looked.

"*Merde, c'est cool.*" A voice said from behind me.

I cast a glare over my shoulder at Zeb, his head poked through the open driver's door to regard me with an impressed look.

"It's pretty basic for her, actually." Daniel stood at the open passenger door beside me.

Whipping around to face him, I shot back, "I don't remember you calling it *basic* in bed."

He ignored that. "Want to do something more interesting?"

"If it involves being separated from this car."

"No sudden moves." Behind me, Zeb brandished the iron fireplace poker from last night. He rested it on the steering wheel like a warning as Daniel produced a

77

pocket knife and cut through the duct tape around my wrists.

I pulled my arms to my body as soon as they were free, rubbing the tape residue on my skin. Fury flared like a match struck in my chest, spreading into my limbs. The guys had the advantage of space and time—it'd take me more of both to jump out of the car than it would them to flee. Plus that damned iron poker. I wouldn't be able to do a lot of damage. My muscles still ached to try.

Curling my legs into my body, I twisted my hips and stepped back down into the passenger seat. I took a deep breath to extinguish the anger gnawing at me, then leaned back in the seat and regarded Daniel. "I still need a spell from you."

The threat in my tone didn't faze him. "And I still need you to climb a wall."

"Well, it's been a shitty night and I need a fucking coffee," Zeb said.

Turned out there *was* something I liked about him. I raised my hand, wiggling my fingers to ease the tingling sensation. "Okay, second."

Daniel and Zeb exchanged a look over the roof of the car, then Daniel looked back to me and inclined his head to indicate we weren't taking this car.

Leaving the silver sedan unlocked, they led me through the parking lot toward the hospital entrance. I didn't relish the idea of walking into another hospital so soon, but the only other option was running.

Daniel at least wouldn't be able to chase me—he favoured his left leg. Not a limp exactly, but I couldn't imagine him running on it easily after seeing the dark bloodstains that had glistened under the street lights when he'd collapsed in the car last night.

He had new jeans now, sans blood, and carried a plastic grocery bag with contents I couldn't discern. Definitely a file folder of some kind, and something else bulky. He hadn't had that pocket knife last night either. Maybe Zeb had taken the bus to pick stuff up while I snoozed in his car last night. The idea of that lead-footed asshole stuck on a slow-moving bus made me smile to myself.

Rather than heading into the hospital, Zeb led us to a dark blue car parked near the entrance. He produced the keys and slid into the driver's seat. Daniel took shotgun.

I hesitated at the back door, trying to focus on my beach and my umbrella drink. I'd get maybe a week out of Lilah if I ran now—assuming I could even get back to Toronto—then I'd be sleeping under a bridge. Plus those Faeries would come after me. Miranda had proven she could. So I might as well hear Daniel out. Maybe I could get the spell without any fuss or bloodshed. After all, as the saying goes: there's a first time for everything.

Suppressing a growl of annoyance, I climbed into the backseat. I had to hurry to buckle my seatbelt as Zeb brought the engine to life.

Twenty minutes of silent city driving and an enviable parallel parking job later, Zeb brought us to a neighbourhood diner he seemed to know. The guys chose a table behind the half-wall jungle of fake plants.

The waiter saw us through them and came over carrying the coffee pot. He spoke in French but I recognized the word *café* and nodded, pointing to my mug. He filled it to the brim.

He filled Zeb's too, but Daniel shook his head. I'd have thought he'd want the caffeine after last night. In the sunlight filtering through the window blinds, he looked worn out. I wanted to ask about his injury—and Aubrie—but I already knew I wouldn't get a satisfactory answer and I didn't want to put myself further in his debt.

Once the waiter had gone, I swallowed a mouthful of *café terrible*, then set the cup aside to rest my elbows on the table. "So, are we pulling a bank job or what?"

"What," Daniel returned.

"If you want my help, you'll actually need to let me in on it."

"It's a museum."

"New side gig? Hocking priceless treasures online?" When I got an annoyed sigh in response, I said, "You're not really selling the plan here."

"I don't have to *sell it*," he said. "This isn't a partnership."

As if I needed the reminder. "Fine," I said, lifting my coffee cup again "When?"

"As soon as you finish that coffee."

I gaped at him, setting the cup on the table hard enough to slosh hot liquid over my fingers. "This morning? Right now? Are you nuts?"

"Does it matter?"

"It does, actually. I've been duct-taped to the ceiling of a car all night. I'm going to need more than coffee to fuel criminal activity." I flipped open the menu the waiter had left, scanning the breakfast specials.

"I could go for a *poutine déjeuner*," Zeb admitted.

Daniel just rested his elbows on the table and rubbed his temples with a sigh, but he didn't argue.

After we'd all put in a breakfast order, he produced a manila folder from the plastic bag he'd carried in from the car. Wouldn't be Consilium without the paperwork.

"O'Meara Celtic Heritage Museum," he said, passing it to me.

"Never heard of it." I flipped the folder open. "This little nobody museum got the money to snatch your artifact?"

"The last owner's estate donated it."

"This thing?" I found a photo of a necklace. It sat on a white background, tiny wooden beads running the length and meeting at a heavy-looking, greyish cross. Probably stone. The pixelated picture made it hard to see the carving around the edges and across the centre. A ruler ran down the left and across the bottom, indicating the cross was about an inch and a half by an inch. "Doesn't look that special. What's it do?"

"Shoots lasers."

"Faerie laser pointer? You're not even trying."

Daniel pulled a paper from underneath the photo and placed it in front of me: a sketch of the layout of a room.

It looked like it had been drawn from a blueprint. He pointed to a pencilled circle. "The cross is in second-floor storage," he said. "Storage has motion-tripped sensors that get switched on with the rest of the system when the building is evacuated. Here." He traced a straight line with one finger across the room, starting inside the doorway. "Every metre across, about knee-height, until the shelving units that hold the artifacts."

"Good security." I studied the blueprint, trying to commit the room to memory.

"Insurance requires a lot of it," he agreed, "but the room's ceiling is out of range."

"What about cameras?"

"Only on the first floor. Nothing operational on the second floor yet."

"Easy mark." I fixed on something else he'd said. "Why's the building going to be evacuated?"

"We're going to pull the fire alarm."

"Ah, the old junior high manoeuvre." I traced a finger along the blueprint. "Just the three of us?"

"Four," Daniel said. "Fabiola's already in position."

"In position, huh?" I repeated. "I guess that should give me confidence, you guys talking like you know what you're doing."

"What's supposed to give us confidence about you?" Zeb returned.

The waiter interrupted with our breakfasts. I flipped the folder shut and swept it into my lap. It helped make way for the steaming plate of eggs, fried potatoes and toast set in front of me.

"What happens after we pull the fire alarm?" I asked as soon as the waiter was gone, keeping my voice low even though we were hidden behind the fake plants, far from the other customers.

"You and I need to get up to the second floor, get the cross, then let security kick us out," Daniel said, shaking some pepper onto his scrambled eggs. "We've got about seven minutes between the time the alarm goes off and when the fire truck arrives."

"I can do seven minutes."

"You'll have to come down on top of the storage shelves and saw into them. The cross should be on the top shelf. Third from the left."

"Saw into them with what?"

Zeb pulled a white leather purse from the plastic bag between him and Daniel and passed it to me.

I opened it to find a hefty, battery-powered handsaw inside. "I don't do purses."

"You do today," Daniel said.

"What if someone looks inside?"

"It should only be Fabiola."

"That's the second time you've said *should*."

"Retrieve the cross and pop it in here." He showed me a slab of polished rock swirled orange and red, hanging from a chain, about the size of a Zippo. He slid his thumbnail along the bottom of the pendant and it came off, revealing a narrow hollow. "The cross will fit. Cut it off the cord. It'll be invisible to the security we'll have to pass through on the way out."

"Why are we going through security on the way out?"

"There's no better way out. Fabiola's going to catch us at the bathrooms and escort us out. Just pretend you couldn't be bothered to rush."

"I don't need pointers on being a bitch."

He didn't rise to that. "Make sure the cross is in that necklace," he said. "Fabiola'll have to search us with the other employees there. Pockets, shoes, everything."

"I guess it's a good trick, getting caught." I couldn't help smiling, imagining the reaction as I asked, "And where's *Zeb* during all this work we're doing?"

Zeb paused with a forkful of French fries, peppers and egg to cast me a dark look. "Waiting to get your dumb asses out of there before anybody sees whatever mess *you* leave in the storage room."

Okay—getaway driver. That checked out.

Daniel pulled a pill bottle from the bag and opened it. The label indicated some over-the-counter painkiller. He took two pills with a swig of water.

"Your leg's messed up," I said.

"It's fine."

"The hell it is."

"It doesn't preclude you doing your job."

"Because this isn't a partnership," I finished. "But we're going into this place together. If you want the stupid cross, you're going to need to watch my back, and be in a fit state to do that."

"You've got nothing to worry about."

I stifled a laugh. Nothing to worry about, my ass. Just Faeries dangling an incriminating weapon over my head in one hand and a promised passport in the other. Though Daniel was half-right—his potential to compromise me at the museum was probably the least of my worries.

15

WE GOT TO THE O'Meara Celtic Heritage Museum just before ten-thirty. A two-story stone building with a pointy roof, it nestled in among shops and restaurants on the street without fanfare.

Daniel and I clambered out, letting Zeb drive off to our rendezvous point. Daniel moved more easily now. Those pills must have done their job.

A short line of people waited inside the museum doors to pay the entry fee. Overhead lights gleamed off the slick cement floor, making the place extra bright. At the counter, two men in matching t-shirts took money and a security guard checked bags.

The purse felt heavy and awkward hanging off my shoulder. It seemed weird to see anybody else in a little museum like this, especially on a weekday. At least, I thought it was a weekday. Days of the week remained kind of fuzzy since the end of my extended nap.

To my right, what looked like a school group swarmed in the little glassed-in gift shop, terrorizing the clerk. The guys at the warehouse had been talking about kids last night. Whoever'd remarked on it was right: nobody would pay attention to Danny and me with that chaos going on.

That told me it was a school day. I reminded Daniel as we neared the front desk: "I still haven't got any cash."

"You can pay me back when you lift the next wallet." He spoke to the guy at the counter in French and shelled out twenty bucks to get the two of us in.

Fabiola waited in the uniform and cap of the security company. She said something to me in French that sounded like "vote sack." My blank look made her frown and repeat, in English, "Your purse, please?"

I held it open so she could shine her little flashlight in over the saw. She nodded without a flicker of recognition, and I zipped it back up.

We entered into a room of paintings and glass cases of jewellery. I skimmed a couple of English captions as we walked past. All the stuff was old and Irish or Scottish. A bunch had been found in bogs. *Should have left it there.*

Daniel led me to the hallway with the sign for the bathrooms and water fountain, pausing outside the door to the men's room. He stood underneath and behind a security camera, avoiding being seen.

I'd stopped right in front of the camera, so I approached the drinking fountain between the bathrooms.

"What are you doing?"

"I'm not good at this part." I turned my head from the water without really drinking anything. "Is anybody watching these cameras?"

"Someone's supposed to be." He pulled a utility knife from his pocket and unfolded a tiny pair of scissors. With those, he clipped the wire at the bottom of the security camera monitoring the hall.

"You don't think anyone will come to check that?" I asked.

"Not while they're trying to empty the building." Camera disabled, he crossed the hall and pulled the fire alarm on the wall.

I jumped at the sudden, pulsing whine.

The two of us hid in the empty men's room, door ajar, until we heard footsteps stop coming down the stairs beyond the hallway.

Daniel pushed the door open and we made for the stairwell. The fire alarm rang as we mounted the stairs.

He used a knuckle to tap a code into the keypad at the top of the stairs.

"No alarms here?" I asked, before setting a foot in the short hallway beyond the door. One other doorway stood open at the end, leading into a single, giant room.

"No." He glanced to the ceiling, as if double-checking for cameras.

A rush of relief flooded through me as I went first into the hallway and nothing bad happened. I stopped at the entrance to the storage room. The employees had left the lights on in their haste to leave, but I wasn't about to bank on them forgetting the security system.

I studied the doorway and the ceiling inside, quickly determining the best way up and across to the cabinet.

Daniel nudged me and handed me the pocket knife he'd used downstairs.

Good thought. I'd need something to cut the string on the cross. I tucked it into the purse with the saw, then zipped that up and slung the strap across my chest. I stood on tiptoe to take a hold of the top of the doorjamb, then spun my gravity and let myself slide in a slow, curling somersault to twist onto my hands and knees.

It didn't take me long to creep over the ceiling tiles, firmer than the ones at the hospital. Newer, maybe. The purse banged uncomfortably against my bruised hip and the bleat of the fire alarm drilled into my head.

In my haste I scraped my elbow coming down on top of the cabinet. Good thing there weren't noise sensors, because with only half a metre between the shelf and the ceiling, I hit my head twice as I crawled across.

The whir of the saw retrieved from my purse joined the whine of the alarm as I cut a triangle in the top of the cabinet large enough to fit my arm through. It fell through the top, making me thrust an arm in to retrieve it. Just my luck if that had smashed the stupid cross I needed.

After retrieving the bit of wood, I searched blindly for the cross. My fingers brushed several things and each time I brought the item up, studied it in the light, and set it aside.

On the fifth try, I grabbed the wooden beads of the necklace. Bingo. I pulled it up and laid it on the top of the shelf, then reached back into the purse and hooked the pocket knife. I cut the cross from its string and slipped the artifact into the hollow stone on my neck. Then I slid the closed knife into my pocket and used the bottom of my t-shirt to wipe my fingerprints off the saw. I dropped that through the hole into the cabinet. New artifact, not found in a bog.

"Got it," I said, raising my voice enough to let it carry across the room.

"Three minutes," Daniel said. As soon as the words were out, he grunted like he'd been hit.

I smacked my head on the ceiling for a third time as I spun to see what had happened.

The doorway had disappeared. I couldn't see Daniel anymore, or even the outline of the wooden doorjamb where he'd been standing. Just a blank, white wall.

Glamour. Goddamn it.

I narrowed my eyes and tried to peer through the new wall. The magic started to come apart like mist when I focused on what I remembered being there before. Two shadows moved behind the rapidly fading white fog.

I jumped off the shelves, hitting the floor in the same instant I remembered the motion sensors.

A second alarm joined the whine of the fire bell. Luckily, there was no heavy door sliding shut to trap me in like in a movie—just the two deafening sirens.

I sprinted through the foggy, glamoured doorway into the hall, colliding with someone I didn't recognize. My skin tingled as I grabbed his collar.

He disappeared, leaving me blinking at my empty hands.

To my right, Daniel picked himself up from whatever scuffle they'd been having before I'd barged in.

Something smashed into my face, knocking me to the floor. A hand slid into the front pocket of my jeans and I snapped my fingers around an invisible wrist.

The Faerie flashed back into view, straddling me as he dug through my pockets.

Daniel hauled him off me, letting me scramble backwards. I used the wall to get to my feet, ready to toss myself into the fight, but I stopped when Daniel wrestled a plastic bag from his pocket.

He tore it open, flinging the contents at our adversary as the other man darted in with a punch. The tiny pieces flying from the bag gleamed silver under the lights.

The Faerie shrieked and stumbled backwards, hissing in pain as his hands moved to cover his face.

I joined Daniel in a dash for the stairwell door at the end of the hall. It closed hard behind us but we didn't have long before the guy would be on us again.

"What did you throw in his eyes?" I demanded.

"Iron filings."

"Where the fuck did you get—?" Distant voices from beyond the door below us drew my attention. "Can't walk out the front door now, right?" Without waiting for an answer, I wrapped the purse around my fist and used it to smash the delicate glass out of a small window in the stairwell.

Daniel hesitated, considering the proximity of the voices below us, then frowned at my exit route. "Always the window with you."

The opening was just big enough for us to slip through: first me, then him, onto a narrow ledge high above the sidewalk. At least we'd come out on the side of the building, not in view of the crowd in front of the museum.

I shifted gravity to lay with my back against the building, but Daniel pressed himself against the bricks, one hand still tight to the side of the window.

"One story," I said. "You probably won't die." More like one and a half—the museum had high ceilings. I leaned out to look past him to the street, then turned my head toward the back of the building. "Around the corner?"

"Right, let's inch down the ledge." Despite the tight sarcasm, he seemed resigned enough. He kept his head tilted back against the bricks, refusing to look down.

I slid sideways along the narrow concrete shelf, letting my gravity press me to the building. Since I was safe, I put an arm out sideways, across Daniel's chest. I didn't know if I could catch him if he actually lost his balance, but I could try.

"What are you doing?" he asked, pulling back.

"Adding 'guardrail' to my resumé."

We reached the back corner of the building, and edged around to a spot above a tiny private parking lot. No convenient dumpster full of discarded foam or soft trash bags presented itself to catch us: only cars and asphalt.

"Hold still," I said.

"No problem." Daniel'd already pressed his back as tightly to the building as he could manage.

I swung one leg out and around to lie on top of him. My throat tightened, unprepared for the warmth of his body against mine, the familiar scent of his soap mixed with the tang of sweat.

He tried to jerk away but had nowhere to go. Meeting my eyes, centimetres apart, his voice came out strangled as he prompted, "And now?"

"We jump. Ready?" Without waiting for an answer, I pulled backwards, tugging him with me. I tried to work between his gravity and mine to keep us close to the bricks, sliding down toward the ground rather than falling.

We still landed in a rough heap on the asphalt.

I pulled myself up using the bumper of a nearby car. "Okay, needs work."

Daniel steadied himself against the wall. He reached under his t-shirt to his shoulder, hand coming away with some blood on it from scraping against the bricks.

Without commenting on that, he nodded toward the edge of the parking lot.

"Wait," I said, noticing blood creeping through the jeans on the back of his leg too.

"It's fine. Let's go."

Since it didn't appear to be bothering him enough to stop, I gave up and followed. "Who was Invis-o-Guy? One of Aubrie's?"

"Probably." Daniel checked his phone as we neared the sidewalk on the next block. We slowed as we moved into the open. From the sound of it, a fire truck had arrived at the museum entrance, and maybe the cops, too.

The necklace felt heavy and conspicuous around my neck, so I reached up and unclasped it. I nearly shoved it into my pocket, but that had been the first place the invisible man upstairs had looked. I bent down to tuck it into my sock, where it dug into my ankle just under the lip of my boot. Then I hurried to follow Daniel around another corner as he led us toward what must have been the rendezvous point with Zeb.

"You do stuff like this all the time now?" I asked, getting only a sidelong glance that either meant he did or he wanted me to think so. I'd half-expected him to panic going off-script, but he'd taken the plan's adjustment with surprising calm. The jump out the window, well, that was another story. Nice to know some things stayed the same.

Around the corner, we came to a deserted street. An eerie stillness calmed the air, making it heavy. My muscles tightened in anticipation.

"I think this place is glamoured," I said. "Do you have more iron?"

Before he could answer, music poured out of the air around us. One voice somehow sang two parts: a high, airy tone and a lower bass. I'd never heard anything so beautiful or awful. It snaked through the air like a physical cord, spiralling around me. My blood ran ice cold and my body felt heavy and distant, like it wasn't under my control anymore.

Daniel's expression had gone blank, head turned in the direction of the music. He swayed on his feet, a second from collapse.

A blonde woman stepped out of a shadowed doorway. Four shapes melted out of the building beside her. The split voice twined together again to form a word, ringing in my head like a bell: "*Sleep.*"

Then I was on the concrete on my back, head lolling off the curb. Had I been hit or had my legs just given out? I fought the command and struggled to focus beyond the voice the way I had peered through the glamour at the museum. My muscles didn't respond. My vision dipped and blurred. The twin voices spun inside my head, tossing a heavy, fuzzy web over my thoughts. Nothing existed but the song.

16

"It sounds like I'm going to need another week here to finish with the sale."

"Isn't that what we're paying lawyers and real-estate agents out the nose for?" Gracie lifted her arm to keep the cellphone between her shoulder and her ear as she sorted a handful of papers.

"Yes," her husband Ted agreed, a smile in his voice, "but there's understandably a lot of . . . weird layers of ownership on these Consilium places. I just want to make sure we're clear from a liability standpoint and everything's a done deal."

"Mmm, say liability again—I love it when you talk lawyer."

"I think I could pass the British bar at this point," Ted muttered. "Probably make a lot of money doing real-estate law in London. I could specialize in firebombed secret headquarter tear-downs. We'd make a mint."

"But you'd have to wear a funny wig." Gracie sat on the floor, surrounded by stacks of papers. The room she'd used to call Ted's office had become the Consilium archives. Boxes of files, books and assorted papers lined one wall, with more of the same unboxed on every open surface. Some had been singed in the fires, but most were intact: a few of the satellite offices hadn't been so badly charred. Everything digital had been wiped by a supernatural EMP during the attacks, so she, Daniel and Ted had spent the last two months collecting what hard copies they could. No other survivors had seemed inclined to do so.

Given no other pressing tasks to save the world this morning, she'd taken it upon herself to keep organizing the mess.

"What's going on there?" Ted asked. "Things still in a holding pattern?"

"Not . . . exactly." Gracie glanced to her son Riley, drawing stick figures on scrap paper near the doorway. She didn't want to be too detailed with the two-year-old in earshot. "There were some setbacks. But Danny should have the cross by now."

"Something bumped the timetable up?" Ted's voice said he knew he wouldn't like the answer.

"Aubrie attacked the warehouse last night."

"So, 'setbacks' in the evasive sense."

"I didn't want you to worry. It's under control." Gracie winced at her words, which could have been construed as callous.

Without remarking on it, Ted asked, "Daniel went to the museum? Him and Olivier and Zeb?"

"Olivier's dead. They took Jude." Gracie waited through the silence, then added, "They needed a way around the motion sensors."

"And you supported that?"

"I suggested it."

"Knowing it's pretty much the last nail in the coffin for getting any more help?"

"No one else was going to help us anyway." The handful of remaining Consilium survivors had been dodging Gracie's calls and slamming doors in Ted's face for the last month. "They're all too scared to fight a war without a chain of command."

"Too certain your brother conspired with that woman to murder their boss."

"Don't repeat that bullshit." Gracie couldn't stand to hear the rumour, even though she knew her husband

STEPHANIE CAYE

didn't believe it. Daniel had always been kinder than her, more willing to trust despite the lessons to the contrary that their parents had laid out. His relationship with Jude had made him a useful scapegoat to the remnants of the Consilium who couldn't possibly take responsibility for their own misguided trust in Spencer Aubrie.

"It doesn't look good, working with her," Ted pointed out.

"Doesn't matter how it looks. Those cowards are all in hiding." Gracie didn't care that her epithet included some of her husband's old friends. "They weren't sticking their necks out for us."

"It's done now." Ted sighed and didn't argue further. "What's Rye up to?"

"He just woke up. We're drawing."

"Let me talk to him?"

Gracie passed her son the phone. "It's Daddy."

She steadied it in his hands as Riley clamped his chubby fingers around it and put it to his ear.

With her son focused on the phone, Gracie continued sorting the papers in front of her. She'd been alphabetizing the files and separating out whole ones from pieces. Doing that, she'd come across the bare bones of Spencer Aubrie's personnel file. *John* Spencer Aubrie, to be precise. According to interviews conducted when the Consilium hired him, *John* had been bestowed by his Antagonist mother. Aubrie's middle and surname had been added along with foster parents when his mother disappeared, presumably back to the Faerie realm.

Gracie had hoped, opening the file, that she might stumble onto some weakness that could be exploited. Instead, she'd ended up stunned that the Consilium would even have taken this man on and deeply ashamed of the crush she'd harboured on him as a teenager.

He'd spent a lot of time at their house during her high school years under the guise of being a friend of Alan's. She doubted now that he and Alan had ever

94

been friends—her father had sorted people into two categories: soldier and enemy. He'd embodied the adage about keeping enemies closer.

The file said Aubrie had committed his first homicide at sixteen: his foster mother, the last in a string of temporary homes. Officially, her death had been ruled an accident since no one could determine how a person—even an athletic football linebacker like Spencer Aubrie—could have hurled the woman down the stairs with enough force to shatter more than half the bones in her body. The police didn't have a lot of experience with Antagonist powers.

Riley thrust the phone back at her. "Beep," he said, imitating her call waiting.

Gracie accepted it. "Hey, I've got another call," she told Ted.

"Take it. Love you." He hung up.

She switched to the new call. "Hello? Zeb?"

"Hey, Grace." He sounded reluctant, as if he were afraid to talk to her.

"Tell me you're not in jail."

"I'm not, no. I'm out here on the sidewalk. And it's been, uh, it's been half an hour since I should've seen Daniel or whatshername—Jude."

Zeb's pause gave Gracie's heart time to drop into her stomach. "Did you go back to the museum?" she asked. "Did *they* get arrested?"

Those were the wrong questions, stupid ones. *Daniel's not there and I did this. I pushed him back to that woman.*

"I talked to Fabiola," Zeb said. "She didn't see them come out, but the motion alarms went off."

"Then—"

"Listen." Zeb blazed forward without acknowledging her interruption, "On my way to meet them, I knew I was heading down the right street, but then the scenery, uh, changed?" He picked his way over the words like he thought he wasn't choosing the right ones. "Just long enough to make me take another turn, and then I was back heading the wrong direction. That's some kind of magic shit, right?"

Glamour. Shaken, Gracie couldn't get the word out.

"What should I do?" Zeb asked.

"Keep looking!"

"Looking . . . where?"

"I don't—!" Gracie lowered her voice when her son's eyes widened in alarm. She turned away from him. "I don't even know. Didn't you have some contingency plan?"

She should have gotten all the details, should have been involved, but she'd let Daniel push her out of it. Why had she done that? Because it was easier to pretend to be normal for once, let her brother shoulder the supernatural stuff.

Zeb sighed. "*Crisse.* It was her, wasn't it? Jude. Taking her along was a bad idea."

"I'll call you back." Gracie tapped the phone off. She couldn't stand the reminder. *My bad idea.*

Her eyes flickered back to her son. She couldn't take him with her to search. Not that she had any idea where to start looking. Not with Ted—the only one on speaking terms with anyone who might know how to help—on the other side of an ocean. It wasn't like she could just call the cops. *Hello, officer? My brother's been taken by Faeries. Yeah, either the royal Court or a rogue cell of half-human hybrids.*

The bitter thought stirred a reminder. Gracie scrolled through the contact list on her phone until she came to a number without a name, one her brother had given her. She put the call through and waited, heart pounding.

"Hello?" A familiar voice came on, suspicious.

"Mei, it's Grace. Daniel's missing."

"Grace, I'm at work," Mei said, voice low. "And I don't care."

"You do if you want that incantation."

"What am I supposed to do about it?"

"Find him."

"How?"

"Call Aubrie. See if he's behind it." Gracie hated herself as she added, "Daniel was with Jude this morning. That bitch probably turned him over to your boss for a pat on the head."

"Last I heard, *that bitch* was working for the Court," Mei returned. "Her pats on the head are coming from a whole new set of hands now."

"I need to know who has him."

"Because you're going to do what?"

The harsh response made Gracie set her jaw.

"I have some ideas," she said. *None of them good.* Her thoughts went to the inconspicuous lock box in her bedroom closet. It held the only thing that might get her brother back, but giving that up would probably bring about the end the world in return.

Worth it, said her mother's erratically bestowed value system. Consequences be damned, family was the only thing that mattered. *You always look out for each other.*

That from the woman who'd fled both her own parents and then her husband in search of some fever-dream of safety from the supernatural world.

Alan's ethos had been simpler: anyone was expendable if the price were too high. Pragmatism came easily. But Gracie had cut her father out of her life for a reason.

"I will *try* to find out if Aubrie has him," Mei finally said. "But if it's the Court, Grace, there's nothing I can do." She finished with venomous sarcasm, "Though I've heard they'll usually accept first-born children in return for favours."

She ended the call without giving Gracie a chance to snap a response.

17

DANIEL WOKE TO SOMETHING sharp pricking the sole of his foot. He tried to move but couldn't, bound upright against what felt like a wooden beam. Coarse rope cut into his wrists, pinning them behind him. A quick assessment told him he still wore jeans and a t-shirt, but no socks or shoes. He shifted to move his legs—one folded uncomfortably beneath him and the other stretched in front of him—but stopped when someone's fingers curled around his heel.

As his eyes adjusted to the dim light, he made out a woman with long, blonde hair sitting in front of him. She ran the tip of a hunting knife lightly down the length of his bare foot.

"I thought I might have to break skin to wake you," she said, reaching up to take the cigarette from the corner of her mouth.

Aubrie's. Daniel's body went cold with fear. The memory of the Antagonist in the museum came back to him, and, in a haze, the singing on the street.

"You really did a number on Ilse," the woman added.

Not Aubrie's. The Court. That recognition brought no relief. "I didn't—"

"You could have let her go three months ago."

"I didn't know she was there."

"Until?" She slid her hand along his left leg, scooting forward to lift it into her lap. His jeans had been slit up the back to the knee, exposing the dark stitches from last night's injury and the blood already leaking out from his escape from the museum. "Your team had her in an iron cell for five months, dying slow. I'd say that gives me four months, thirty days and twenty-six hours with you. But I doubt I'll need that long."

The woman turned his leg and began cutting each stitch with her knife, reopening the largest gash in his calf. "You've got that spell Ilse brought with her?"

"I don't have anything." Blood trickled over his skin as a hot ache crept up through his leg. Shadows behind her seemed to shift and spin. His body felt tight, muscles tense. All he wanted to do was bend his knee and pull away from her.

"No? Huh." With a shrug, she jammed the knife into the wound in the centre of his calf.

Daniel bit back a wail as pain like lightning surged through his leg. He tried to tug it away, causing the knife sink deeper into the muscle.

"Where's the incantation?" The woman rested a hand on the weapon. "You have it written down somewhere?"

"No." He barely got the word out, unable to breathe, as he forced himself to hold still to keep from jostling the blade.

"Memorized it?" She lifted her hand to take a drag from the cigarette. "That was stupid. Recite it for me."

"I don't—" Daniel choked on another howl when she put pressure on the knife and twisted, tearing new trails through his flesh.

"You do." She pulled the blade out with surprising care.

He sagged against the wooden beam, blinking through tears as he managed to suck in air. His leg throbbed, but the wound felt distant without the knife's insistent, burning pressure.

The blonde stubbed her cigarette out on the concrete floor. She ran the tip of the knife lightly down his knee, making his body go taut again. "One more time."

"I can't tell you." Maybe she would free his hands to write it.

"Humans are shit with our language." She shoved his leg off her lap hard enough to make him gasp.

Straightening up, she dug a pack of cigarettes and a lighter from her back pocket. "And I hate hearing any of you butcher it," she continued, "but you can tell me rune by rune. You're a translator. You know the alphabet. I read your file."

She flipped the lighter closed after lighting a new cigarette. "Yeah, we've got files on you assholes too."

Daniel struggled to remember the names of the runes to give her false ones. His mind reeled, still fixed on the pain.

"Need some help?" The woman cleared her throat.

Music seeped into his thoughts. It started more quietly than it had on the street: first a high, delicate female voice, then a deeper male voice. The two twined together, wrapping around his mind like fingers. The notes echoed with a strange comfort, and the tension left his body.

The song crept around his head, leaving the dulcet whisper of a question: "*Tell me the incantation.*"

"I don't have it." His own voice startled him, coming out without permission.

The music danced through his head, whispering, "*Who does?*"

Gracie. The name stuck in his throat. He couldn't say it aloud, fighting the siren's song harder at the thought of his sister. She'd taken the written incantation for safe-keeping. He couldn't give her up.

The music conjured up images and memories of Gracie as if trying to flood his memory and force her name to spill out. The last time he'd seen her, both she and Riley singing some annoying song from a cartoon . . .

A song. He fixed on that memory. That goddamn tune had been stuck in his head for days afterwards.

Wracking his brain for the catchy melody distracted him from the music around him. He replayed the simple, insistent pattern his nephew had been singing on a loop, filling his mind and blocking out the siren's voice.

"Fucking earworm." The words came sharply out of the music, shattering the sonic walls that had pressed in around him. "You want to be clever, we can go back to cutting."

Daniel choked on the sudden pain in his chest, eyes snapping open to see the knife lodged low in his left side, between his ribs. Blood bloomed across his shirt. He could only draw short, difficult breaths with liquid surging up his throat. It hurt almost too much to try.

The blonde crouched low over him, her hand still on the knife's handle. She leaned in close to whisper in his ear, "Just tell me and I'll sing you to sleep. Pain goes away. You won't feel a thing."

Lingering for another second with her cheek brushing his, she pulled back when she didn't get a response. She brought the lit cigarette within centimetres of his face. "Otherwise I'll put *this* out in your goddamn eye—" She grinned, showing more glittering, shark-like teeth than should have fit into her mouth—"then we'll go on from there."

"Soren!" Another figure appeared from one side, shoving the blonde woman away.

With the newcomer back-lit, Daniel couldn't see his face. He made out the silhouette of what appeared to be a Stetson as the shadow knelt over him. Still unable to draw a full breath, he cringed as the man moved his leg. The room spun.

"What the hell did you do?" the man demanded.

"Exactly what he'd do to either of us if he had the chance!" The woman's voice came from somewhere to the right.

"Out, Soren," the man snapped.

"I'm not finished."

"What'd you think you'd get out of him after puncturing a lung? You'd better pray to whatever's holy in that mercenary head of yours that I can repair this."

"You of all people should be with me," the woman said. "What the Consilium did to your mother to see how she could heal herself—"

"Don't need a reminder," the man snapped. "I lived it. You just read about it, so go ahead and dial that righteous anger the hell back."

"You could do with a little more righteous anger yourself, boss. But I guess you come by human *sympathy* more honestly."

The man surged to his feet, making the siren hop two quick steps away.

"I had the Mab's permission." She threw the words out like a shield.

"Go run and tell her then."

Daniel shuddered, hacking more blood into his throat when someone touched the throbbing wound on his ribs. Dark spots danced in his vision.

The man's voice seemed to come down a tunnel. "Probably best if you go ahead and pass out, son. This is going to hurt again."

18

I WOKE LYING ON my back, staring at a white ceiling. No machines beeped in the room this time. Everything seemed sharp, like I'd just closed my eyes on the street and opened them again here. The voices in my head, the singing, felt like a distant dream.

No. I *had* been on the street. Standing there with Daniel. And now I lay on a generic, flowered polyester duvet in a bedroom with a painting of a horse on the wall, like a cramped version of a Best Western.

Western. Abe. Things popped back into my head, unscrambling my memory. I had to be in the Faerie safehouse, floating somewhere in the space between worlds. The window to my right showed sunset on a suburban street.

I checked my pockets, startled to feel the bulge of the slim, narrow pocket knife Daniel had given me pressing into the bruise on my hip. Nobody had frisked me before dumping me here?

When I stood up, something bit into my ankle. I fished the stone necklace out of my sock, stuffing it back in my pocket so I could walk normally again.

The door to the room swung open when I turned the knob. I'd expected it to be locked. Slinking down the hallway on the way to the stairs, I glanced into the open doors. The whole place seemed empty.

A sudden instinct to bolt brought me down the stairs to the front door in record time. Time to get out while the getting was good.

The sounds of another door shutting and water running from the kitchen stopped me short. Guilt twisted my stomach. Daniel had to be somewhere in this damn house too. I couldn't just leave him.

Why not? He would leave you in a heartbeat.

And he'd have good reason. I *owed* him, over and beyond our deal about the stone cross and the Faerie spell. Besides, the Faeries had manipulated me, coerced me into fucking him over only to toss me aside the same way Aubrie had.

Fury burned in my stomach as I crept back to the kitchen doorway, peering around the side. Abe stood at the sink washing his hands. He looked tired, shoulders low, cowboy hat pushed back on his head. He rested his elbows on the edge of the counter as if he needed it to keep himself upright. Beyond him, the window to the backyard showed twilight. I'd been here all day.

That was long enough. I dug Daniel's utility knife out of my pocket. The short blade seemed better than nothing.

Moving quietly into the kitchen, I grabbed Abe's arm, bringing the tiny blade to his throat. My fingers tightened around it when I saw the distinctly pink water swirling the drain. Blood. A lot of it.

Abe turned his head just enough to see me. "You really think that'll take me out, darlin'?"

"I think it's worth a try." I tightened my fist to keep from pressing the edge into his skin. "What the hell happened? You *ambushed* us?"

"Soren saw an opportunity and she took it," he said. "I didn't know she meant to do it."

"You *created* the opportunity," I snapped. "You tricked me into walking Danny right to you. You sent me to him because you could track me, right? Sniff out my blood but not his? Then sicced a—what the fuck was that—a *siren* on us?"

"That wasn't my intention." Abe's hands tightened on the edge of the counter. "I give you my word it wasn't."

"Is that the Faerie *word*, or the human one?"

"It's mine," he said, voice firm.

Being part-human like me, whatever word Abe gave was only as good as he wanted it to be—he didn't have to worry about a broken promise tainting his magic. I hated that I believed him anyway. That stupid hat made him look like the good guy in an old movie.

Keeping my fist clenched around the knife, I pulled it back and stepped aside, letting him turn to face me. He didn't seem like a threat, resting heavily against the sink. He hadn't been faking that fatigue.

I still kept a healthy distance between us, just in case. "Where's Daniel? You have him somewhere?"

Abe inclined his head sideways toward a door on the opposite side of the fridge. Not the back door, something else. A basement?

I stepped toward it, then stopped myself. "There's spells on that?"

"Yes."

"Undo them and take me down there."

"That's a bad idea. Jude, just . . . trust me."

"Oh, I don't trust anybody." I brandished the knife again. "Least of all people who trick me into playing offence in a war they say is over. You missed some blood under your fingernails."

He sighed, examining his hands.

"It was all bullshit, huh?" I asked. "Telling me Daniel had something Aubrie wanted. Turns out it was something *you* wanted."

"That wasn't a lie," Abe said. "I haven't lied to you once. He has an incantation that Aubrie's already killed for. He's safer here."

"So that *wasn't* Daniel's blood you were just washing off your hands?"

Abe nodded to the doorway that led back to the front hall, sounding reluctant as he said, "I can show you."

"And while my back is turned, somebody else can swoop in and take Danny."

"No one will touch him. No one else is here." He looked toward the ceiling to indicate the silence in the house. "Everyone's got a job to do, darlin'."

"And yours was torture?" I gestured to his hands again.

The cowboy's shoulders stiffened. His expression darkened. "No," he said. "Don't much cotton to torture."

Ignoring the weapon in my hand, he brushed past me and strode out of the kitchen.

I turned to the basement door, but I had no idea how to undo the spells. *Never should have lowered the knife.* Squeezing it in my fist for reassurance, I followed Abe.

He headed into the living room, stopping in front of the mirror that hung over the boarded-up fireplace. Taking off his hat and tossing it on the nearest table, he turned to see me hovering in the doorway. He took his amiable, calm tone back up as if that flash of anger in the kitchen had never happened. "One of our people, Ilse, brought the incantation over here five months ago," he said. "Consilium captured her right when she came across and they took it."

"Took it?" I repeated. "Like, she had just written it down and put it in her pocket?"

"Committing spells to memory is dangerous. They're powerful, mess with your head. Plus they're hard to get rid of when you don't want them anymore."

"Well, writing them down is a good way to get them lifted."

Abe nodded as if to grant that. "After the attacks in Toronto," he said, "we figured Ilse was dead. Turns out, the Consilium had her at a facility in Montreal."

"You said the Court hit all the satellite offices."

"Place in Montreal wasn't an office. We didn't know where it was until yesterday."

"When you *followed* me?" I snapped. Had they watched while I walked into that iron-walled warehouse and just left me there?

THE FLAWS OF GRAVITY

He continued without addressing that. "Couple days ago, one of our people bound a sylph to your ex so we could try to find our messenger."

"A what?"

"Sylph." Abe gauged my expression. "An air sprite. Dumb as a housefly, but they operate well enough under command. They're easy to glamour, easy to bind to a human. They observe, experience, then you can pluck out their recent memory and play it back through a mirror."

I stared at the mirror, working through that insane explanation. "You bugged Daniel with a . . . sprite? But you couldn't track him with it. You had to send me?"

"Sylphs don't emit much of a magical signature. It's why they're so useful. Makes them easy to lose, though." Abe reached toward the mirror and pressed his fingers against the glass, saying a string of high-pitched words that I didn't recognize as English.

Nothing happened. He frowned and tried a second time.

The mirror started to ripple. I took a step back, expecting something to come out of it. Instead, the reflected scene changed from us to another familiar place: the inside of the iron room at the warehouse. A bed in the corner showed me this room wasn't exactly like the one I'd been in. This was long-term prison.

I had to come closer to see better, but I kept my distance from Abe.

The sylph's view shown in the mirror came from over Daniel's shoulder, maybe half a metre behind him. A woman stood in front of him. She looked more or less human, apart from the shades of blue dancing through her hair and the violet gleam of her eyes.

"Last night." Abe had brought us into the sylph video mid-conversation.

From what I could tell, Daniel had come to ask the Faerie, Ilse, for parts of a recipe. They never answered each other's questions directly, but Abe had been telling the truth: from the way Daniel spoke, he definitely had whatever this incantation was.

I opened my mouth to ask Abe to fast-forward, but Ilse's eyes shifted past Daniel and looked right out of the mirror at me.

A chill ran down my spine. I fought to keep from taking a step back.

In the glass, they reacted to noises I couldn't hear—the audio on the sylph wasn't great—then Ilse looked past Daniel again. She produced a string of sounds similar to ones Abe had used making the mirror work. In contrast to Abe's halting delivery, the words Ilse used flowed easily and made my skin itch like I'd pulled on a sweater full of static electricity.

Lost, I opened my mouth to ask Abe to back it up. Ilse had recited something past Daniel, right out of the mirror at me.

Not at *me*. At the sylph.

"She knew it was there." I didn't look to Abe for confirmation. Ilse had sensed the sprite or seen through the glamour. Something about her expression struck me, though. She seemed . . . sad. Longing, even.

"What did she say?" I asked.

"The amounts for the ink."

"That's it? To who? You?"

"Miranda."

In the mirror, a door slammed open, drawing my attention. Another tremor ran through me at Aubrie's reedy voice. I looked to the edge of the glass, not wanting to see him. My tense body ached to run and I couldn't focus on the rest of the conversation.

Something happened, some kind of fight. The sylph's view veered toward the ceiling, then spun to one side, making it dizzying to watch.

Abe put his fingers against the glass, pausing the show. It shimmered and changed to throw our reflections back.

"Haven't had time to get further yet," he said, as if inviting me to fill in the blanks.

No way was I telling him about the museum. I was supposed to be looking for Daniel, not watching Faerie spy footage. "What was that meant to prove?"

"That Aubrie's after that incantation."

I blinked away the memory of the blood I'd seen on the cowboy's hands in the kitchen. "He's obviously not the only one."

"We don't need it, darlin'. Just need it contained."

"Like locked up in a basement, bleeding out."

Abe frowned. "That spell was written specifically to hurt somebody half-human."

"Somebody like Aubrie?"

"And somebody like you."

"Where was all this concern for my well-being when you sent me off to pump Daniel for information?"

"That was before I liked you." The cowboy's quick smile faded as he added, "and before he had all the pieces to use the thing."

If Daniel'd wanted to kill me, he'd had plenty of opportunities last night. And even if he could target me with this spell, he didn't have all the pieces like Abe thought. The stone cross in my pocket had to be part of it.

"You think you're the bad guy," Abe said. "You betrayed him. That doesn't mean he's right from here on out."

The words stung but I flashed the little knife again. "Stop telling me what I think and take me to the basement."

My blade may have been ridiculous, but Abe understood the steel behind it. Without argument, he led the way back to the kitchen. Pulling the basement door open, he slashed his hand downwards and muttered something to undo the spells.

The two of us descended into a damp, gloomy basement that stunk of cigarette smoke. The place was clean and empty except for shelves running along the walls and a dim form off to the left: Daniel, propped upright against one of the wooden support posts with his hands tied behind it. He didn't stir when we entered, chin on chest, one leg folded under him and the other out straight, resting in a pool of blood. More of it had seeped through his t-shirt from a wound in his ribs.

Bile rose in my throat again, making it hard to catch my breath. "What were you saying about bad guys?"

Abe snorted. "Enjoying that high moral ground now?"

I stalked past the cowboy to crouch beside Daniel. Leaning in, I parted the torn t-shirt to take a look at his ribs, where I expected the worst to be. Instead of a fresh wound, a puckered scar ran across his skin. I found the same on the back of his leg. The raised lines looked like they'd healed weeks ago. I remembered him favouring the same leg at the museum, and the blood on his jeans after our escape. He'd been injured then.

Something magical had gone down. I sat back on my heels, looking to Abe.

He hadn't moved from the stairs. "I healed him."

"You what? I thought you were an empath."

"Mixed family. Came to see you in the hospital, in fact, but you wouldn't remember."

"You healed me too?"

"Really think you bounced out of that coma good as new all on your own?"

"I'll bet now you wish you hadn't."

Abe gave a short laugh, shaking his head as if to disagree. He kept a hand on the wooden banister for support.

"Healing Danny's why you're almost dead on your feet?" I asked.

"Humans are harder to fix," he said. "Their bodies fight the magic that ours soak up like a sponge. Though you were no picnic either."

"One of the nicer things somebody's said about me." I moved my attention back to Daniel. "Why waste the energy to heal him if he's so dangerous?"

"The *spell* is dangerous," Abe said. "He's an idiot for taking it, but that's not a capital crime in my book." He

THE FLAWS OF GRAVITY

sighed, glancing up the stairs. "Look, you've seen he's alive. Let me try to solve this. Soren, the others, they reacted badly. Things are . . . confused right now. Just give me a little time."

"No." The word didn't come as easily as I wanted. It seemed like Abe was being straight with me, but he wasn't in control here. I couldn't trust him.

I reached out and tapped Daniel's cheek.

"Danny? Wake up." Leaning around the post, I used the pocket knife to saw through the rope around his wrists. I asked Abe over my shoulder, "Is he still bugged?"

"Had to unbind the sylph to run its memories."

Daniel's eyes opened just as I broke through the first piece of rope. He blinked, turning toward my voice. As soon as he recognized me, he winced away.

The last piece of rope broke in my fingers. I guided one of his arms back around the post. "We're getting out of here. Can you stand?"

He didn't answer, grimacing as he bent his leg and got to his feet, using the wooden beam for support.

I looked to Abe. "You're going to let us walk out?"

The cowboy gave me a weary look. "I'm not going to fight you."

"Good call." I snatched Daniel's shoes from the floor nearby and passed them to him. After waiting a moment while he fumbled to put them on, I led the way to the stairs, slipping past Abe, who watched us go.

I pushed the door open to the kitchen and came face-to-face with a blonde woman in the process of heading down the stairs.

"The fuck is this?" she snapped, bouncing back on her heel. Her dark eyes took on a predatory gleam as they moved past me to Daniel frozen behind me.

Even though my vision had been hazy from the song on the street, I still recognized her as the one who'd knocked us out. Abe had called her Soren. Soren the siren. Cute.

I returned the favour and swung a fist before she could snare me again.

While the siren stumbled backwards and collided with the kitchen table, Daniel darted past me to the back door. He yanked it open, letting the blank white space bathe us all in light.

"Shit!" I pulled him back, slamming the door. Tugging the knob again in the same motion, I snapped, "Montreal!"

The void had filled with buildings and a street. Despite the twilight I'd seen out the kitchen window earlier, night had fallen fully wherever the house had dropped us.

I pulled the door shut as we rushed out, in case it might keep the Faeries from following us too fast. We ducked into the mouth of an alley around the next corner and then down a shadowed walkway between two tiny garages.

I relaxed when I didn't hear any footsteps in pursuit.

"You okay?" I asked.

"I don't know." Daniel sank into a crouch, pushing through the bloodstained fabric of his t-shirt in search of his wound. He didn't look surprised to feel the scar.

"Abe healed you," I prompted.

"I remember." He shuddered, slumping back against the wall.

"I wasn't in on this! I didn't do it, and I didn't know about it." Lowering myself down beside him, I ran both hands back through my hair to smooth it back from my face.

He kept his eyes on the ground to ask, "How did we get out?"

"I held Abe hostage with your tiny knife," I said. At the mention of the pocket knife, I withdrew it and offered it to him. "Here."

He accepted it, studying it like he couldn't quite remember what it was.

"I've still got the cross," I said, voice too bright as I patted the lump in my pocket. "And if those Faerie assholes were smarter, they'd have searched me. I guess they didn't get far enough into the sylph video to see the museum."

"The—"

"Yeah, they had a sylph on you. It's some kind of air sprite that—"

"I know what it is." Daniel turned his head as if he might catch sight of the creature. "Is it still active?"

"They took it off to see what happened to their messenger."

He sank back against the wall, lowering his head. He didn't say anything further and after a minute passed, twinned anxieties about our exposed position and his mental state made me reach out and touch his face like I might need to wake him again.

When my fingers brushed his cheek, he jerked back, smacking into the wall behind him. With a hiss of pain, he put a hand to the back of his head.

"Sorry!" I stammered. "I'm sorry, but . . . who are they? The crazies with the house. I assume you know."

"Are you fucking with me?" He met my eyes, voice ragged but blunt.

"No, I really don't know who they are." I re-thought the question. "Or did you mean in general? Because, no—still no." Regretting both my barrage of information and that jumbled, awkward response, I waited in silence while he considered it.

"Your new friend Miranda is a distant cousin of the last Mab," he said, finally sounding more like himself. "We assumed—the Consilium assumed she was dead, but it looks like she's been hiding here."

"A distant cousin." I thought of Miranda, about everything that had gone down while I'd been napping in the hospital. "But not anymore, because the Mab and all the other cousins over in the Faerie world are dead. So you mean she's the Mab now."

"You really didn't know?" He studied my face.

"She wasn't wearing a tiara or anything." My heart tapped against my ribs to remind me that the Faerie queen had an army. "We can't stay out here."

I stood and extended a hand to urge him to do the same, expecting a fight. "If you want to argue about the 'we', I've still got this cross thing and if you want it back—"

The words died on my lips when he gripped my hand. He didn't meet my eyes as he pulled himself to his feet, and he yanked his fingers away from mine as soon as he had his balance.

"Do you have somewhere to go?" I asked.

"I have another apartment. One that hasn't been blown up yet." The words should have been droll, but he just sounded exhausted. He turned to take in the alley around us. "Where are we?"

"Montreal, but I didn't specify an address." I shrugged at his raised eyebrows. "It's magic. The house is on a separate plane. Blah blah blah. Let's find a cab."

19

DANIEL TRAILED JUDE THROUGH a dark neighbourhood, dogged by the sharp, raw certainty that something could attack any second. Following her was stupid, but she was there, in front of him, and thinking harder than that for another option just ended in static.

They walked three blocks before they found a street large enough to have cabs. Jude scanned traffic for a taxi topper as Daniel checked his pockets and found his wallet, but no phone. The Antagonists in the house had probably taken it.

Jude's jumping up and down and waving both arms in a display at odds with her usual behaviour caused a cab to veer across a lane of traffic and pull to the curb.

Daniel scrambled into the backseat, forgetting about the blood on his clothing until the driver turned around.

"Hé, attendez," she said. "Ça va?"

"Ça va bien." The answer came automatically, but he struggled for a more coherent explanation. "C'est juste—"

"Zombie pub crawl." Jude jumped in.

The driver's attention snapped to her. "In June?"

Jude pulled the door shut behind them, settling into the seat. "Yeah, it's like . . . zombie summer . . . something." Apparently unable to find a plausible detail for her lie, she concluded: "Whatever. Any excuse to bar-hop, right?"

"Huh. Cool." The driver seemed to buy it, facing forward again to steer the car from the curb.

Daniel pulled himself together enough to give her his address, then Jude took over and kept up the inane conversation for a few minutes, inventing some kind of story for the blood on his clothes. He couldn't follow. He stared at the pattern of the fabric on the seat in front of him and counted the squares in it to keep his mind from wandering back to the shadowy basement.

When they finally reached his second apartment, he paid the fare and dug the spare key out of his wallet to get them inside, then left Jude in the living room. He went first to the bedroom and retrieved a cellphone from the desk drawer. Holding down the button on the side, he waited agonizing seconds to find it still had adequate charge.

He couldn't stay in the bedroom. Two giant windows bored into him like fixed eyes. Instead he went to the interior bathroom, locking the door. Turning the shower knobs, he let the water run to cover the sound of the phone call.

Gracie picked up after one ring. "Where the hell have you been?"

"Court." The accidental pun almost seemed funny. Daniel sank down against the bathroom door, fighting to loosen muscles still primed for flight.

"What happened?" his sister demanded, voice harsh through the phone.

"Nothing." The afternoon had already begun to feel like a distant nightmare, slipping away as soon as he woke up. He couldn't get stuck on it, couldn't lose sight of his intent.

"You're lying! I can *hear* it." Gracie snapped him out of his thoughts. "Danny, come over here. I need to see you. I need to see that you're okay."

"I'm fine." He couldn't help running his fingers along the scars on his leg.

"Fuck *fine*! Someone grabbed you, right? After the museum? Was it Jude herself, or did she just lead them to you? God, when Zeb called and said you'd disappeared, I knew she was behind it."

"I'm not sure she was."

Jude hadn't expected the ambush in the museum. She'd tried to steer him away from the glamoured street. She might have collapsed to the sidewalk when the siren attacked. He couldn't be sure any of that was right, after the infernal singing that had left his memory hazy.

"She got me out." If he said it aloud, maybe it would make sense.

It didn't.

"She's got the Agate Cross in your necklace," he told his sister. "She didn't give it to them, and there's no way the Court would let me keep the cross if they'd known we had it. I need to decrypt the incantation now."

"Wait, she's still *with* you?" Gracie's voice rose an octave. "Get rid of her!"

"Send me a picture of the incantation and then burn the paper."

"You really think right now is the best time to do this?"

"Yes." Getting his mind back on what needed to be done would let everything else seep away.

"Then come over here and get it."

"I can't."

"Why not?"

Because I'm not sure I can leave this bathroom again. He hated the thought. It sounded like something his mother would have said. She hadn't been crazy like they used to think—she'd had legitimate reason for her paranoia, for her terror, but she hadn't always been functional. He couldn't succumb like that. He had to put aside what had happened, forget that it could happen again, and stick to the plan.

"Send me the photo, then burn the paper," he repeated.

"Fuck." Gracie said nothing else for a full ten seconds. Then she sighed. "Okay."

"Can you call Zeb? Just tell him I'm fine."

"Because you're always fucking fine. Anything else I can do for you?"

The sharp sarcasm made him feel better. "Be normal."

"None of this is normal."

"It's getting there."

She sighed. "Are you hurt?"

"Not anymore."

"What does that mean?"

"It means I'm—" Daniel stopped himself before saying the word that would set her off, "—not hurt."

"I hate this," Gracie said. "Come over here as soon as you can." She disconnected the call.

A minute later, the phone buzzed in his hand. He tapped the message to find a photo of the paper with the incantation. He forced each stroke of the foreign runes into his brain to block out the other recent memories.

The second buzz delivered a photo of paper burning in a metal mixing bowl on Gracie's counter, accompanying a text that said: *Done. Now come over.*

Delete the pic, he texted back.

Not an idiot. It's gone.

Daniel set his phone on the tile, relief fusing through him. With the spell out of his sister's hands, there would be no danger of pointing the Court toward her if they came for him again. She was safe.

In the clean, familiar bathroom, the day seemed unreal. If he hadn't had the wounds to prove his involvement, it might have been a cautionary tale he'd heard about someone else—something from his mother's disjointed warnings, or from the stories of his Consilium colleagues who went regularly out into the field.

He didn't have wounds, though—he had scars.

The vivid memory of having them healed shocked him upright, struggling to pull in a breath. The healing had burned, ten times more painful than the original claws through his leg last night, or even the agony in his chest when his lung filled up with blood. Worse than that had been the proximity to something massive and unnatural, something that could swallow him and barely notice.

The cold tile felt like the concrete floor of the basement. He lurched forward and fell to his knees in front of the toilet just in time to throw up. The nausea passed a minute later, but the fear held on. Fear followed by shame, as if he'd just admitted it aloud to his father and been jeered for cowardice.

He collapsed onto his back again. He had something both Aubrie and the Mab wanted—something that vicious siren had tried to take by force hours ago. The realization should have frozen him, sent him into the spiral of numbing panic he'd been anticipating for years. Instead, he stared at the bathroom's stark white ceiling with a calm certainty. If he ran, if he surrendered, then either the Mab won or Aubrie did. Neither outcome was acceptable.

So he had work to do. He had the incantation and he had the cross—well, Jude had the cross. Or she said she did. He hadn't verified. *Careless.* Maybe she'd tricked him into bringing her here for . . .

For what?

He didn't have the energy to examine every traitorous scenario. Nothing made sense right now. She'd still be out there beyond the door, probably pacing the apartment and looking for a drink.

A drink wasn't a bad idea. The warmth of alcohol dulling the razor edges of his nerves, blotting out his lingering memory of the day, sounded goddamn amazing.

But he'd still have to deal with her, and sobriety might be his only advantage at this point. Probably too much to hope that she'd gotten bored by herself, taken off and left the cross behind.

20

I took the self-guided tour of Daniel's second apartment, keeping an eye out for liquor bottles. This place was bigger than the one last night, on the fifth floor of a tall building with a nice view of the downtown skyline lit up against the dark. The microwave clock said it was nearly midnight. The apartment wasn't at all like how I remembered his place in Toronto. This one felt a little closer to how I'd expect somebody with money to live—newly built, blocky and modern with a leather sofa in the living room. Daniel's late mother had been loaded, if I remembered correctly, which had facilitated her dragging her kids all over the country. Alan definitely hadn't lacked means, either.

Anxiety buzzed in my veins. Abe had let me walk out with Daniel, but he didn't speak for Miranda, and it was the new Mab of the Faerie realm who had the letter opener poised over my neck and the army to back it up.

Somebody knocked on the front door.

I froze. The knock had been quiet and tentative, not the heavy fist-pounding that usually preceded a gruff voice shouting: *Police! Open up!*

What would they shout here in Montreal? I didn't know enough French to venture a guess.

Nothing followed the knock. We'd only been here fifteen minutes. Awfully coincidental to have a visitor stop by at midnight. I crept to the door and peered through the peephole.

A woman stood outside—the one who'd been at Daniel's apartment last night. I hesitated, watching her turn to glance down the hall. Daniel might have called her. I didn't know who he was running with now.

One easy way to find out. I pulled the door open just enough to face her. "Hi."

She took a step back, surprised.

"Wrong place," she said.

"You're looking for Daniel? He's in the shower."

She cocked her head as if listening for the distant rush of water that would back up my story. Her surprise faded into a chilly smile. "That was quick."

The scorn in her voice raised my hackles. "And you are . . . ?"

"No message necessary." Her eyes flashed gold when she shifted her gaze back to me. She turned without another word, heading back down the hallway.

I leaned out the door to watch her disappear around the corner, then ducked back inside, locking it. The shower had stopped, so I perched on the armrest of the sofa and waited for Daniel to emerge.

When he finally did, in clean clothes and moving a lot easier than he had before, I told him, "You had a visitor."

"What?" He stopped, looking somewhere between puzzled and exhausted. "Who?"

"The woman who beat me to your place last night."

"Mei? Mei came here?" He tensed as if regretting giving me her name. "Why the hell did you answer the door?"

"Because she knocked instead of kicking it down."

My lazy attempt at humour triggered an exasperated look.

"Don't answer the door," he said.

"She didn't seem like the jealous type." I leaned forward and something poked me in the thigh. I pulled the sharp stone necklace from my pocket, digging my fingernails into the grooves at the bottom to dump out the stone cross. It looked like I remembered—etched with little vines and decorative patterns around the edges. It had two strange symbols carved on the front, deeper than the other designs.

"What is this thing anyway?" I asked.

"You do have it." Daniel sounded relieved, reaching for it.

I closed my palm and held it over my shoulder. "I told you I did." Shouldn't have been surprised he hadn't believed me, but then why let me tag along? "What is it?"

He withdrew his hand. "The two runes are the key to breaking a code."

"A coded incantation?" I guessed. At his dismayed look, I added, "So, it's a good thing Miranda's brigade didn't get all the way through the sylph-vid and realize I had this baby, huh?"

I held the cross between the tips of my fingers to study it again. "What's the incantation do? Abe implied you could hurt me with it."

"He's right," Daniel said. "It would neutralize your Antagonist blood and strip you of your powers."

"It *what*?" I almost dropped the stone, but my muscles constricted into a fist around it. I glared at him. He'd been blunt on purpose, wielding the honest answer like a baseball bat. "So you just . . . you whisper some words in my ear and I'm not climbing walls anymore?"

"Calling it an *incantation* is misleading," he said. "Speaking the words aloud isn't powerful enough. It would have to be painted onto your skin."

"That's why you needed the recipe for some special ink."

His turn to be surprised. "How do you know about that?"

"I saw what happened last night on the sylph. Or, in the sylph's memory . . . ? Whatever." The specifics of that weirdness didn't come close to the question weighing on me. "Are you planning to use the spell on Aubrie? Is that why he wants it?"

Daniel avoided my eyes. "He didn't tell you?"

"He left that out, along with teaching me how to fly," I reminded him, wrapping my fingers around the cold, stone cross. "Look, unless you think you can *take* this thing from me, you should probably explain a little. How exactly do that incantation and this weird little stone figure into Aubrie's goal of jumping through a portal and finding Faerie magic?"

"The only way he can access what he wants is to merge the worlds."

"Merge?" A chill ran down my spine.

"Exactly what it sounds like. Our world and the ... other one, they lie on separate spheres in the same space," Daniel said. "The barrier between them can be torn apart, but the rush of magic flooding this world would mess with magnetic fields, global weather, tectonic plates—"

"Four horsemen, seven plagues and a partridge in a pear tree." I ticked them off on my fingers. "Bullshit. Aubrie wanted to break into the Faerie world. He thought they owed us some magic. The Consilium were obviously going to be assholes about it—Alan wouldn't have wanted *any* power falling into grubby half-Faerie hands, even ones on his side—so we had to go around them, but Aubrie wouldn't have—"

I couldn't finish the sentence. I didn't know anymore what Aubrie would or wouldn't have done.

Daniel's expression made me wish I'd kept that outburst to myself. Not like he'd forget our past, but I didn't have to keep throwing out reminders.

"Okay," I said, backtracking, "suppose I go with this. If that incantation takes Faerie power out of somebody part-human, what for? To turn guns into daisies and make the sky rain candy?"

Daniel hesitated like he might not answer, then said, "The excess magic produces a key that reveals the original text of an Antagonist grymoire containing the spell to merge the spheres, among others."

"Why does it have to be worked out on somebody part-human?"

"From what I've read, human blood is more . . . stable." He didn't seem certain of the word.

"Less likely to absorb magic." Like Abe had told me about Faerie healing.

"The spell needs that stability," Daniel said. "It uses the magical energy of the . . . the other half—"

"Faerie blood."

"—and shorts it out."

"Use up all the magic to make the key and leave whoever gets painted up fully human." A bitter taste filled my mouth imagining that some words painted onto my skin could erase my powers. How could ink just soak through and take part of me away? Goosebumps broke out. Not my magical early-warning system, just the discomfort at realizing I would be so disposable to the Faerie world.

Big surprise. You knew that. The voice in my head sounded like Aubrie's. *Faeries lie.*

So did humans. I thought of Abe's supposed concern about my well-being with Daniel having all the pieces to use the incantation. He was right that Daniel did owe me some payback.

"So, why do *you* need the incantation?" I asked.

"The grymoire has to be unlocked in order to destroy it."

Not exactly the denial I'd been hoping for. I took a different tack. "Are you planning to paint Aubrie up with it? That won't be easy, but I think you and me and Zeb and Fabiola—"

"Not Zeb and Fabiola. They're civilians. And not . . . you and me." Daniel extended a hand for the cross.

I didn't have a good reason not to drop it into his waiting palm. He'd answered my questions. Not his fault I hadn't liked the answers. And what was I going to do with it anyway? I couldn't read Faerie runes.

Once he had it, he disappeared down the hall. A door clicked shut.

He hadn't even told me to go or thrown some new mode of raw iron at me. He'd just left me here alone in his apartment for a second time. Breaking that incantation must have been pretty important.

Duh. My stomach churned again at the thought of the spell burning up my powers like kindling.

And at something else. I'd been running on a breakfast plate and coffee all day. Granted, I'd spent almost the whole day passed out in the Court's magic house, but my appetite had caught up.

I headed to the kitchen I'd found in my initial survey of the apartment and flipped the lights on. Despite the size of the place, the cupboards were almost empty. I pushed aside a canister of ground coffee to find a box of instant mac and cheese and a box of crackers. Not in the mood to cook, I grabbed the crackers. The fridge held a small carton of milk and jar of mustard, a frozen pizza in the freezer.

Opening the cupboard above the oven, I scored a half-empty bottle of Scotch. As I turned around, the box of crackers under one arm, prying up the cork top from the bottle, I slammed my hip on the handle of the oven door. It creaked open.

"Ow!" I took a swig of the Scotch, eyes catching on something beyond the half-open door. With one hand still around the bottle, I eased the oven door down to peer inside. A mess of papers rested on the top rack. I placed a finger on the first thing and slid it out just enough to peek.

It had my full name printed on it. I set the Scotch aside, pulling the papers out and moving them to the kitchen counter where I could see better. The top sheet looked official. A report. A very boring, clinical evaluation of my Faerie powers, with my full name and some numbers printed along the top. Consilium paperwork. Maybe part of my personnel file. When I'd started there, they'd done a lot of tests and interviews to see what I could do, how I used my ability.

The next several sheets underneath weren't about me—what looked like a years-old credit report for someone I didn't know, and part of a spec on a security system that was probably from the O'Meara. I shuffled through the jumble, hoping to find more from my own file.

Yes, another paper with my name printed on top. This one was a transcript of an interview I'd had with . . . someone. Maybe a shrink? I didn't really remember who all I'd talked to during my entrance exams because it had all seemed so formal and ridiculous.

The text on the page started partway through the interview. I was talking about my mom. The first line had me saying, "No, *all I got from her was her ability to drink anybody under the table. Probably not magic, huh?*"

I started skimming, not wanting to revisit my old thoughts on my mom. Sifting through the papers with one hand, looking for the next page of the transcript, I reached for the Scotch bottle. It slipped through my fingers, landing sideways on the stack of papers.

"Because of course that happens," I told the bottle, snatching it up. I took a drink before setting it aside again, then shook the Scotch off the papers. It looked like it had only soaked through a few layers. I laid those out on the far counter to dry off.

I found a photograph, printed on regular paper like a photocopy. It had my name and that same set of numbers printed at the top. A cold feeling spread through me as I lifted the paper away from the rest of the pile.

My mother stared up at me in black and white. She was young in the photo, before the lines on her face had deepened and her hair had thinned. This pretty girl looked younger than me now, her dark hair in a ponytail, long legs running up into a pleated cheerleader skirt. Maybe it had been taken post-football game. Several other cheerleaders clustered around her. She had her

THE FLAWS OF GRAVITY

arm linked with a young man, whispering something to him with her doe eyes fixed on his face. His gaze aimed between her and the camera, as if caught in the act of turning his head.

Was it my father? Not beyond thinking. I had never seen him. My mother had erased him from her life even before I'd been born.

Something struck me like a gong. I'd seen this face recently. I wanted to set the picture aside, keep moving through the rest, but I couldn't put the paper down.

Laying the picture on the counter, I placed my hand on it to block out my mother, then twisted my wrist to cover the man's body. Adding the other hand, I extended my fingers to make a frame around his face, eliminating his hair, neck, shoulders. I narrowed the square until I gazed at his grainy black and white features.

When it hit me, I let go of the picture to grope for the bottle of Scotch.

The sound of the door being splintered in almost made me spit out the mouthful of liquor. Swallowing and gagging as the Scotch burned down my throat, I spun, still clutching the bottle, and darted out to meet whoever'd broken in.

Jasper and Pru entered in full punk club getup.

"Can't you assholes just glitter under the door?" I huffed, indicating the mess they'd made kicking it in. Pixies were stronger than I'd thought, or maybe they'd blown it open with some ridiculous toy like last time. "No stupid water balloons tonight?"

Pru grinned. "That was fun, huh? Too bad you ruined it."

"It's a bad habit I have." I brandished the Scotch bottle by the neck, turning it upside down and inadvertently pouring the rest down my arm. I swung the bottle at Jasper when he took two steps toward me.

He bounced back, brushing liquid from his leather jacket. His eyes flickered behind me, as if he'd guessed that I stood between him and what he wanted. "Where's your boyfriend?"

I let him get within inches again before I executed a back handspring, one-handed, still clutching the bottle. It took a nudge of my gravity to make it. My boots connected with his chin as I came over.

Upright, I spun and dashed further into the apartment before Jasper got back up. The heels of Pru's shoes clicked on the floor behind me. I made for the closed door at the end of the hall, shoving the door open and hitting Daniel with it on the other side. He must have been going for the lock.

"Pixies!" I twisted it, pressing my back against the door. It shuddered under the weight of what I assumed was Jasper's shoulder. "Tell me you have more iron pokers in here."

"I don't." Daniel retreated to a desk and searched the drawers. Not finding whatever he was looking for, he grabbed a lamp.

I'd expected him to wield it like a weapon, but instead he slammed the base down on the stone cross sitting on the desk. He hit it three times, pulverizing it.

"Damn it!" I gaped at him. "I hope you got what you needed from that thing! Not like it was easy to get."

"Don't worry about it." He yanked the lamp cord from the wall, apparently intent on using it as a weapon now that the cross was dust.

"I'm worried about these glittery fuckers. This door's not going to hold." At least it had ceased shaking against my back for a moment. "What's that one?" I nodded to the door behind his desk.

"Closet." Daniel stopped, turning toward it like he'd remembered something.

"We'll go out the window again."

"No." He sounded like he'd rather fight both pixies empty-handed than descend the side of a building with me again. To be fair, we were higher up than at the museum.

"Come on, Jude! It's like a double-date." Pru's voice came from outside the door.

I rested my head against the wood, watching Daniel haul an upright vacuum out of the closet. "Are you kidding me? They're not *dogs*, they're"—It dawned on me what he meant to use it for—"oh."

"Open the door and take a swing at her head." Daniel nodded to the empty Scotch bottle still in my hand. He plugged the vacuum in at the outlet beside the door, then untangled the hose attachment.

"My pleasure." I waited another moment to make sure he had a finger on the vacuum's 'on' switch. Both of us ready, I flipped the lock, yanking the door open in the same motion I swung the bottle at Pru.

She slashed down with a knife the moment the door opened, then burst into a cascade of glitter to avoid the bottle.

Daniel brought the vacuum to life, its loud whir droning in the hallway as he jabbed at the floating dust with the hose attachment. Pixies could only stay in glitter-form for a few minutes before it would kill them. At the very least, this would injure her long enough for us to escape.

I dove forward into the hallway to head off Jasper, who'd started back to the door when I opened it.

He realized what Daniel was doing and shoved me aside hard, into the wall.

Daniel kicked the vacuum into Jasper's path, but instead of moving around it to attack, Jasper grabbed it as it toppled and hit the hardwood floor on his knees.

Preoccupied with freeing his girlfriend, he didn't lunge for Daniel as he darted past and joined me at the ruined front door. An anguished howl ripped from Jasper's throat like a battle cry, following us into the hallway.

On the ground floor, I nearly nailed a guy with the glass door as we dashed out onto the wet sidewalk. He shouted after us, but we didn't stop.

Adrenaline coursed through me. I drew deep breaths of the damp night air to try to fill my lungs. Should have eaten a couple of those crackers.

We slowed to a walk once we'd put enough distance between us and the building, trying to look less conspicuous. Warm rain hung like a mist in the air.

Memory of what I'd seen in those papers sizzled through me. I spun to face Daniel, stopping him short. "Miranda! It's *her* face in that picture with my mother!"

"What picture?" He looked lost, torn out of his preoccupation with escape from the pixies.

"The one in your oven. Am I related to her? Was that my father?"

"Jude—"

"Tell me right fucking now."

Rain fell harder. Daniel turned toward the nearest building, lit windows belonging to a restaurant.

"Inside," he said, pushing past me.

21

I FOLLOWED HIM TOWARD a booth at the back, avoiding the other diners near the windows. The place was busy. The clientele digging into poutine and burgers—mussed women in short, sequined dresses and men in colourful, patterned shirts with pit stains—seemed out of place for the homely building and time of night. We'd found the city's after-party.

On closer inspection, the patched green vinyl and faded hardwood around the booths made the place look less like a retro-themed hangover diner for club kids and more like one that had actually opened sometime early in the twentieth century and then hunkered down for the duration of time.

A waitress set down laminated menus on the Formica table and looked from me to Daniel. "*Bonjour* hi."

It sounded like a choice, so I went with: "Hi?"

That won me English.

"Something to drink?" she asked.

"Whisky." I leaned forward with one elbow on the table, shoving back the wet ropes of hair around my face. The few mouthfuls of Scotch hadn't done anything for me except make me feel like I'd swallowed a campfire.

Daniel said something to her in French. I had no idea what—he spoke almost as quickly as everybody I'd encountered so far in this city, though he definitely had an accent they didn't. Still, better than I could do with my basic half-remembered primary school vocabulary.

I watched the waitress saunter away from behind my fingers, then lifted my head as Daniel pulled a wad of napkins from the dispenser. He pressed them to the back of his hand to mop up a bunch of blood that I hadn't noticed until then. He'd hidden it under the table when our server came by.

"Pru got you with the knife?"

"Yes." He grabbed more napkins to clean the blood between his fingers and wipe it away from the gash on the back of his hand.

"Are you okay?"

"It's not deep." He flexed his hand, then glanced around us to see if anyone else had noticed.

I blurted, unable to help it, "I didn't know you spoke French."

He hesitated, puzzled by the jump. When it became apparent that I expected an answer, he said, "My maternal grandmother was Québécoise. She insisted we learn. My mother used it as . . . kind of a secret code when we were living out west. It comes back fast."

We hadn't covered grandparents or childhoods in our casual hookups—I didn't know why his mother had moved them all over the country, why she would have needed a coded communication.

"Secret from who?" I asked.

He gave a slight shake of his head to dismiss that, then asked instead, "What's the picture you were shouting about outside?"

Whatever family stories he was avoiding must have been uncomfortable to actually take one of my questions head-on. I ignored his patronizing tone. "The one in your oven. The one of my mother in a cheerleader outfit."

"I think it's from her yearbook," he said. "It was in your file."

I leaned forward to rest both elbows on the table, my shoulders bunching forward. "But you don't know anything about it?"

"It wasn't dated or labelled."

I stopped myself before bringing up the resemblance the guy had to Miranda again. Daniel already had enough reasons not to trust me—I didn't need to hand him another weird tie between me and the new Mab.

Instead, I asked, "Why do you have pieces of my Consilium file in your oven?"

"Why were you going through the apartment?" he countered.

"I wasn't. I accidentally found that stuff while I was raiding your booze."

"I don't keep that in the oven."

"It was an innocent mistake. A *lot* more innocent than you having information on me hidden around your place." I put a hand down on the table and repeated, "W*hy* do you have parts of my file?"

He matched my tone. "I have *parts* of a lot of Consilium files."

Abe had told me that. Daniel had all the leftover information that hadn't been destroyed when the Consilium had fallen. It still seemed shady that my stuff was so front and centre, but it hit me that there was a good reason for that. One I didn't want to approach right now.

The waitress returned, granting me a pause in the conversation. She set down two glasses of water, then posed with her pen and pad.

I didn't need to understand the French to know what she asked. I skimmed the menu, starving and desperate to think about something else even for a moment. "Two hot dogs, with everything. And a Coke."

"*Vous, monsieur?*" She continued jotting my order as she turned to Daniel.

"A cheeseburger. No onions."

"Fries?"

The follow-up question seemed to throw him. "Sure. Yes."

As she bustled off, I turned in my seat to put my back against the wall, stretching my legs out along the rest of the bench. Resting an arm on the table, I glanced to Daniel. He watched the front windows without seeming to see them, avoiding my gaze. How the hell was he just sitting there across from me, waiting for food? Was he trying to keep me close so he could use the incantation on me? It didn't seem like his style, but I was thinking of the man I'd known three months ago, the one who'd maybe thought I was a decent person.

My wet hair dripped onto my shoulders, chilling me in the AC the restaurant had going full blast. My body felt too tight again. I wanted to be up and moving. But the food coming was worth waiting for, especially if I'd need to run soon.

"You solved the thing?" I asked. When Daniel raised his eyebrows, I realized that I'd brought him into my thoughts mid-conversation. Rather than say the word aloud, I drew a cross on my collarbone to indicate what I meant. "You smashed it, so I figure you decoded the incantation. That was fast."

He hesitated like he might not confirm my guess, then said, "It was just a simple substitution cipher. Replace one rune with the other."

"I didn't know Faeries did 'simple.'"

"I've actually never come across an equivalent word in their language."

"Figures."

The waitress arrived with our food. I dug right into my hot dogs. It seemed like it had been forever since I'd eaten. I finished both in two minutes flat, then I washed it all down with the Coke and the full glass of water.

On the verge of ordering two more, I tensed when Daniel sat up straighter, eyes fixed on something over my shoulder. He grabbed the steak knife that had come with his burger. I turned in my seat as the glass door to the restaurant slammed open.

The people sitting close to the door jumped as Jasper stormed in, eyes blazing. He came straight for us.

I slid out of the booth in time to meet him as he reached the table. He knocked me back across the table with both hands around my throat.

Daniel tried to stab him in the back but Jasper burst into glitter and the knife came down hard into the Formica just beside my shoulder.

Catching sight of the gash on the back of Daniel's hand again told me exactly how the pixie had found us.

As the murmur of voices in the restaurant grew into shouts, Jasper reappeared in the booth behind us. He reached over the back to grab Daniel and shove him out onto the floor.

I jumped to the ceiling and down onto the pixie's back. I got his collar in one hand and one brittle spike of his hair in the other. As soon as I gripped him, he exploded into dust. I fell hard on the top of the booth seat, pain shooting through my ribs.

The front window shattered. Something large, dark and not-human-shaped raced through it. All of the other diners who hadn't already taken cover at Jasper's entrance started running.

The creature moved fast. It went straight for Jasper and Daniel, bowling them both over and separating them in the process. Once it held still enough, I gaped at the dragon, its red and yellow scales glittering in the fluorescent lights overhead.

As long as a crocodile but taller, it stood on four legs with huge claws. A long tail whipped powerfully back and forth, and a line of raised, furry scales ran down its spine to the tip. It had large, golden eyes and a long snout like a dog's, with rows of sharp teeth inside that it bared at Daniel as he started to get to his feet. Moving like something between a stalking cat and a snake, the dragon reared up on its hind legs.

I leapt off the table, letting gravity move around me to extend my jump and bring me down onto the slick scales of the creature's back. The scales felt pliable, not hard like armour. I slammed a fist into flesh, right beside the dragon's spine.

It screeched, throwing its head back and knocking me onto the floor. I rolled to avoid the skittering claws of a back foot, starting to run while still climbing to my feet. A roar of flame seared my back as I threw myself into the nearest booth. I struggled upright in time to see Jasper take another run at Daniel.

The dragon wheeled around toward me, snapping its tail to the side and catching the pixie across the chest. The force flung him backwards into the window, where he hit hard with a thud and collapsed.

Startled by the good luck that had narrowed our odds, I almost got singed by another belch of fire. I dropped to the floor, looking for cover. The safest place seemed to be behind the counter that housed the cash register, but the dragon stood between me and that. I shifted gravity to fall up to the ceiling, crouching and running over its head.

The creature tilted its face up to watch me. A spray of fire made me drop too early. I bounced off the edge of the counter, falling in a heap behind it with a grunt.

Our waitress crouched there, her hands over her head. She peered out at me, opening her mouth. Nothing came out.

"Have you got a knife?" I asked. "Something big? Anything sharp?"

"Là—there!" She pointed to a drawer.

I inched across the open space between the register counter and the half-wall that separated the dining room from the kitchen, fumbling for the knob she indicated.

A huff behind me made me yank my hand back and hit the floor. A spurt of flame shot over me. On the tile, I snatched a crumpled towel and wrapped it around the handle of a heavy, cast iron skillet that had fallen off a hook on the wall during the creature's grand entrance through the window. The iron still triggered an itch in my hands that started to work its way up my arms, but at least it didn't burn.

Claws skittered on the linoleum just beyond the counter, letting me gauge its location. Leaping to my feet, I swung the skillet, slamming into the edge of the counter and catching the dragon across the face with the heavy iron pan.

With a high-pitched scream, it recoiled. As it wheeled away from me, its tail snapped over the counter and stung across my cheeks.

I hit the opposite wall with enough force to send pain rocketing through my back. I dropped the skillet, spinning to yank the nearest drawer open and coming up with a sharp cake knife.

When I whirled back around, the dragon had shrunk back into human form. All of its flaps of skin and flags of tail pulled back in, wrapping around a human body until it reassembled into a woman in navy slacks and a yellow button-down shirt.

The woman who'd come to Daniel's apartment earlier tonight, and last night. Mei.

Her hair fell loose in a curtain over her face, half-hiding it. A giant, red welt across one side was still visible. Had the iron forced her change?

"You stupid bitch!" she snarled.

Catching a glimpse of a forked tongue, like a snake's, I raised the knife and flipped it around to clench a fist on the handle and point the tip at her.

Approaching sirens interrupted Round Two. She glanced over her shoulder at the ruined storefront, then took a hasty look around the restaurant and fled.

I slid over the counter, wiping the blood from my face with the back of one hand, still clutching the knife in the other. Jasper lay unconscious by the window. Tempting, but no time. The sirens sounded close.

I crouched to check under all the tables and see where Daniel had ended up. He got my attention from the mouth of the back hallway. A group of kitchen workers and restaurant patrons who must have been clustered behind him there had started fleeing through the fire exit at the end of the hall. He inclined his head toward it to indicate that we should follow.

"It's okay to come out," I called to the few people still sheltering under the tables. "Cops are on the way."

I set the cake knife down on the counter, adding over my shoulder, "Tip your waitress. She's had a hard night."

22

"I MEAN, SURE, IT crossed my mind that dragons were real." Jude practically skipped down the sidewalk. "But holy shit, dragons are *real*!"

Her adrenaline seemed to be running strong because of the fight, but Daniel's had cut out already, leaving him sore and exhausted from grappling with the pixie. He couldn't share her enthusiasm, too mired in questions about Mei's sudden appearance and her motives.

He pulled his phone from his pocket to find the closest bus stop, saying, "She'll try again. Or Aubrie will send someone else."

"She's with Aubrie?" Jude stopped short, rubbing a palm against her jeans, then fell back into step with him. "Aubrie's got a *dragon*?"

"You jumped on her back. Who'd you think she was?"

"Hey, I saw a dragon bust through a window and I reacted."

Daniel laughed despite himself, but he couldn't bring himself to thank her.

After a moment, Jude added, "I guess she didn't make such a big entrance at your place last night."

Her airy, innocent tone erased any levity he'd felt. She'd mentioned that earlier, seeing Mei at his apartment before she swung in, but it hadn't registered at the time.

Now it had enough weight to put him back on guard. "How long were you lurking outside yesterday?"

"Long enough to see you give her something." She paused, looking thoughtful. "And as much as it hurts my ego, if Aubrie sent her, she should have tried to grab *you* back there at the diner, not fucked around spitting fire at me to give you time to run. Was she *protecting* you?"

"That's ridiculous." He looked back down at his phone, mind racing for a better story, but nothing came. What did it matter how much Jude knew anyway? If she planned to take the news of Mei's betrayal back to Aubrie, well, last night's assault on the warehouse said Mei may have already beaten her to it.

Jude wiped the back of her hand across her cheeks, rubbing away the blood from cuts probably made by the dragon's tail. Showing him the red stains, she said, "If your dragon BFF didn't kill Jasper, he's going to track us again."

Daniel nodded to the bus stop on the corner. "Not if we break up the trail."

When they reached it, he turned to search traffic on the street for the headlights of what he hoped would be a very conveniently timed bus. No luck.

Jude sat down on the bench, stretching her legs out. They spent a minute in silence before she asked, "You ever think you should just high-tail it to Rio?"

No sarcasm in the question. Daniel glanced to her to gauge more from her expression but found her studying the curb. "What's in Rio?"

"More like what's not. No Aubrie, no dragons, no sphere-merging nonsense. No Faeries." She used her fingers to count off the examples, a frequent habit of hers, then amended, "Okay, there might be Faeries, but they wouldn't know you and you could just politely ignore each other."

The idea of Jude ever *politely ignoring* anyone stirred another unwelcome laugh in Daniel's chest. He swallowed it. "Sounds perfect."

"Yeah." She flashed a half-smile, as if she'd expected the flip response. "Then why are you still here running Consilium Part Two?" Before he could object, she continued, "Planning heists, translating secret magical incantations, running all the time—like, in the fleeing sense—that's not normal. Plus, you called Zeb and Fabiola *civilians.*

"You could have disappeared, you know, ignored this incantation thing, forgotten about Aubrie and his stupid plan—"

"His *stupid plan* to kill hundreds of thousands of people?" Daniel interrupted.

She sat back. "How do you even know he can do it?"

"He already killed hundreds at the Consilium. People I knew, people I worked with."

"So, it's revenge, then." She appeared to be waiting for confirmation. When she didn't get it, she concluded, "Revenge I could get behind. But it doesn't track." She clasped her hands between her knees, focused on her entwined fingers. "Why Aubrie and not me? You had my file in your oven. You were obviously looking for some way to pay me back."

The pure ego in her accusation left him speechless. As if he'd had nothing better to do the last three months than scour her file for some weakness and plot revenge? He should have left her distracting Mei at the restaurant.

Jude stood up. "I stabbed your father—" she punctuated each word, "—and then I came back to your place and *slept* beside you for a *week* before I fucked you over too."

"I haven't actually forgotten," Daniel snapped.

March. Waking in the middle of the night to find her at the desk typing with two fingers at his laptop. Sitting up and putting on his glasses automatically, even though he could see her there well enough, and wondering for an instant if he were dreaming. Jude's expression as she noticed he was awake: her momentary surprise and desperation replaced with panic, then something closer to anger.

"*I'm guessing you're not going to give me the password to this.*"

It had taken him too long to realize what was actually happening, and by then she'd already attacked. He'd gotten in one good hit before she knocked him down. A knee on his chest had cracked two ribs when she manipulated her gravity to make herself heavier and hold him against the floor, then she'd hit him in the face. He didn't remember the broken lens from his glasses going through his eyelid, or whatever blow had caused the hearing loss in his right ear.

"It wasn't self-defence. Obviously not with you, and not with Alan either." Jude hovered beside the bench. "I didn't mean to kill him. But it wasn't . . . I can't say it was an accident. It just wasn't a plan."

She launched into it before he could stop her. "He called me into his office when I was leaving work, and he knew . . . everything. He knew what Aubrie was doing—or at least what I thought Aubrie was doing. He knew I was involved. The things he called me. I wasn't human to him." Her voice turned bitter. "I was a *tool*. He'd always meant to use me and toss me, just like Aubrie said."

Alan had said as much, more than once, trying to warn Daniel off. *She's a weapon—nothing more. You'll regret letting that Antagonist mutt into your bed and you'll get no sympathy from me when she—*

"I told myself I'd just get the codes while you were asleep and disappear and you'd never know," Jude said. "But then you woke up, and . . . "

"And you decided the best response was to smash a fist into my face until I blacked out," Daniel finished. "Thanks for the explanation."

"Aubrie said you were only getting close to me for the Consilium. Keeping an eye on me," Jude said, voice straining. "And given every fucking thing he said about Alan turned out to be true, how could he be wrong about you?"

The flimsy excuse cut deeper than Daniel had expected. "Right," he said. "My fault for having a manipulative bigot for a father."

She shook her head. "I'm sorry, I'm just trying to—"

Tensing, she cut off then drew a breath.

Firmer the second time, she repeated, "I'm sorry."

She slumped onto the bench like her legs had given out. "I know it doesn't fix anything," she told the sidewalk, "but I wish I could do it all over again."

Daniel couldn't make his muscles work to run. He should have done it the moment she'd launched into her explanation, kept her from dragging him back into her twisted version of their past.

The memories blurred to mix with more recent ones: Jude hauling him out of that basement, jumping up and down and waving her arms like a lunatic to summon a taxi to get them away, barricading the two of them in his office against the pixie attack.

She could have left him in any of those situations. Moreover, she'd had the cross half that time—she could have held that over his head, demanded the incantation she'd come for. Yet she hadn't even asked for it.

That didn't mean she was genuine, that she wouldn't lash out and turn on him again if it suited her. It didn't mean he should address her inexplicable apology. It didn't make them allies.

A jarring ring from his back pocket jolted him back to the empty bus stop. It took him a minute to remember exactly what the sound was, but once it registered, he pulled the phone out and answered without looking at the screen.

23

MEI CROUCHED BEHIND HER sedan, parked at the curb across the street from the restaurant. The sirens sounded too close to make fleeing an option. A police cruiser rounded the corner as she eased the passenger door of her car open, reaching in without standing to grab her purse from the centre console.

She slunk down the street, staying behind the parked cars. Police officers rushed into the restaurant as a second squad car pulled up. No one had noticed her at half a block away.

Safely around the corner, she continued another block before mapping her location on her phone and bringing up a ride-hail app. She'd have to come back for her car in the morning.

The side of her face stung. She hadn't meant to get involved in that mess at all, just trying to approach Daniel and see if he'd gotten the rest of the recipe for the ink. Encountering Jude at his apartment had been an unpleasant surprise, then seeing the pixies arrive after her hasty exit had made things worse.

How had Daniel and Jude gotten away from them? Pru and Jasper were unpredictable and childish, but they weren't to be underestimated. They usually had the temerity to come out on top.

Still, the escape had suited Mei. She should have been quicker following them into the diner before Jasper arrived, but her leeriness of speaking to Daniel in public—where someone might see, where it could get back to Aubrie—had kept her away. Especially with Jude there. It was bad enough that she'd answered the door at the apartment.

Mei's car arrived. Her driver was polite and quiet, letting her relax and giving her the ride home to plan out her story.

At least she had plausible deniability. Smacking Jasper with her tail to get him away from Daniel could be explained as an accident. And it would be, when Jasper inevitably reported her participation back to Aubrie. Assuming he was still alive. She'd knocked him hard into that window.

Her phone started to ring in her purse as she came through her front door. When she saw the screen, she took a breath and prepared herself for the call. "Spencer."

"What are you doing?" He didn't sound angry, only curious.

"You spoke to Jasper. Did he get arrested?"

"He managed to avoid it."

Jasper had probably flashed into glittery dust in front of the police. Pixies were never inconspicuous. *Says the woman who went through a plate glass window as a dragon. But that won't happen again.*

"There wasn't time to take him with me," she said.

"I was surprised to hear you were there at all," Aubrie said. "It was my understanding that you were too *busy* to involve yourself."

"Well, I didn't like the way we left things yesterday." Mei allowed a note of apology into her voice.

"I didn't either." He sounded relieved. She hadn't aroused suspicion.

"What happened to Pru?"

"She's no longer with us." Aubrie didn't sound troubled.

Mei wasn't sorry to hear it either. "No wonder Jasper went mental. He'd have killed them. But I'm sure you'll be able to watch the whole thing online from some idiot's phone." She didn't want to rehash the fight, putting her fingers to her cheek where she still had a painful welt.

"I already have," Aubrie agreed, startling her. "Poor quality video, though. Most of the comments called it out as a hoax with bad CGI. I don't think it'll go viral."

Mei's anger flared despite his warm, ironic tone. A *hoax with bad CGI. My fucking life.* She waited to see if he would say anything more, like whether the camera had captured her face. She hadn't intended to shift back into human form there in the diner, but she thought she'd at least been careful about it.

When he said nothing else, she went into her kitchen and found a bag of peas from the freezer to hold against her cheek. "Do you want me to try again?" she asked, with no intention of doing so. "I'm not sure I can find them a second time."

"No. Pru, before her untimely passing, put me in touch with a mage. She'll have more luck scouring the city."

"How did Pru meet a mage?" As far as Mei knew, most mages didn't leave the Faerie realm, and they didn't associate with grubby half-pixies. Then again, there were bad apples in every bunch. A Faerie with mage abilities—magical powers learned and cultivated above and beyond the typical sort they'd been born with—would certainly be a faster and more efficient option for capturing Daniel and Jude.

"She was resourceful." Aubrie finally sounded a little wistful to have lost the pixie.

Mei rolled her eyes. Useful even dead, damn Pru.

"I'm in Niagara," Aubrie said.

"So soon?" She hadn't realized he meant to head down there this quickly. The Court must have rattled him yesterday.

"You should come here. The others are making their way down but it's very quiet right now. We could have some privacy before things start moving again."

"I'll check my calendar."

"You're not suited for an office job, Mei."

"I enjoy it." She tried to block the memory of the rush that went through her when she morphed into a dragon. She didn't even worry about the witnesses and their cellphone videos. No one could recognize her. They were all terrified of her power. When she became a dragon, everyone else was simply a spider: tiny, insignificant.

But that memory belied the intense pain it took to make the change, the daily struggle to be normal.

"You used to enjoy this," Aubrie said.

"Did I?" Mei's thoughts had already travelled back to her human life. Maybe breathing fire and brute strength meant power in the Faerie world, but she couldn't live in that world. Didn't want to, in fact. "I'll call you tomorrow," she said.

"Early," he urged. "Goodnight."

"Goodnight." Mei hung up. Hand trembling, she set the phone on the counter and left the bag of frozen peas beside it. Her cheek felt numb. She went into her bathroom to check the damage to her face. The pan hadn't touched her for long. She assumed the redness came more from the impact than the iron itself. It itched but the colour had already begun to fade.

She caught her own golden eyes in the mirror. Her mother had taught her the simple glamour early, around the age she'd started walking, to make most humans overlook her strangeness. To keep them from singling her out. Mei had cast it every day of her life. Now it took no conscious energy to maintain, the first step to putting on her makeup in the morning.

As she reached for the faucet, her wrist brushed a plastic bag. Normally immaculate, her bathroom counter held a clutter of bags and bottles of ingredients that had taken her five trips to specialty herb stores and two to shady Faerie dealers to gather. She didn't enjoy dealing with the brokers, preferring to pretend that other world didn't exist.

Soon it wouldn't. Not for her.

Her mother had married a human, stifled her nature and shaped it into a human body until she thought nothing remained. It hadn't worked. Smoke drifted out of her nostrils when she was upset, flames started on her fingertips in moments of passion. She'd swallowed a bottle of pills in the bathtub and slit her wrists for good measure, to make sure that the dragon wasn't strong enough to pull her back from death.

Well, death wasn't the only path out of Faerie.

Mei returned to the kitchen and punched Daniel's number into her phone, waiting through five rings before he answered.

"What I told you yesterday was true to the best of my knowledge," she said, skipping pleasantries she wouldn't get. "Aubrie didn't tell me he'd moved his attack up, so I couldn't tell you. Bad luck, certainly, but *not* a double-cross."

"Bad *luck*?" Daniel sounded incredulous. "That's really what you're going with?"

He didn't hang up. She took that as a sign to continue. "Did you manage to get the recipe?"

"Yes." He sighed.

"I'm impressed. I've got all the ingredients. Tell me and I'll mix it."

"I'll text them to you."

"Perfect. Then there's just the matter of a private meeting spot to perform the spell. I was thinking St. Catharines." The city would be close enough to Niagara to assuage Aubrie without putting her directly in his path until she was ready.

"Where is that?"

"South of Toronto, around the lake."

Silence, then: "Did you throw a dart at a map?"

"Aubrie's near there now, in Niagara."

"Then why the hell would I go to St. Catharines?"

"Because he's alone. Could be a good time to play offence." Mei waited, and when she got no immediate argument, she lied, "He's expecting me. Just me. You meet me down there, work the spell, I'll take you to him. Besides, you can't stay in Montreal. He's called in a mage to find you. You're not going to be able to run much further here." She touched her aching cheek. "Bring your bodyguard with you if it makes you feel better."

24

GLUED TO THE BUS stop bench, I tried not to eavesdrop on Daniel's conversation or draw attention to myself. How hard would it be to just bolt? Conspicuous, yeah, but he probably wouldn't follow me.

Even though the thought cheered me, my muscles refused to follow through.

Daniel didn't speak after putting the phone to his ear, listening as someone else did.

"Bad *luck*?" he finally said. "That's what you're going with?" He moved toward the curb, as if aware of my presence but only doing the bare minimum to cut me out.

I focused on the empty street, watching for the bus as I refused to let my mind wander back to the last five minutes. It was impossible not to hear Daniel's end of the phone conversation: short, clipped sentences. Why the hell was he talking about St. Catharines? What weird Faerie shit could be going on there?

Finally, he hung up, staring down at his phone like it might crack and start spilling secrets.

"Planning a trip to the Greater Niagara Region?" The casual sarcasm in my voice startled me, but I went with it.

He turned as if to snap at me, but he didn't have to. The bus approached, pulling to the curb with an unpleasant screech of tires, and he moved to the door instead.

I checked my pockets and found some change from last night's thwarted bender—the pixies had kept me from spending everything I'd stolen, not that a couple of dollars would have gone much further in the bar. It was probably enough for a bus fare, though.

After Daniel had tapped his fare card on the reader and moved toward the back of the bus, I fed coins into the slot until the fare light turned green a second time. I took a seat up front, near the driver.

My splurge left me with a single quarter and I turned it over in my fingers for a long time as the bus bumped down the street, taking a turn every now and then. Heads, I'd go back and talk to Daniel. Tails, I'd stay here, face forward and ride until . . .

No viable second choice presented itself. Twenty-five cents would get me nowhere in a strange city at two in the morning, especially with pissed-off Faeries out there after me.

I stuffed the quarter into my pocket and headed to the back of the bus, shifting my gravity to keep from tumbling to one side as the floor bounced beneath me. I dropped into a seat across from Daniel.

He'd hunched forward to tap on his phone, and even when his fingers stopped moving on the screen, he didn't lift his eyes to me.

Since he hadn't actually told me to fuck off yet, I pressed my luck. "What's in St. Catharines?"

"Aubrie's in Niagara Falls."

The quick response stunned me. Mostly the fact that I'd gotten one after our conversation at the bus stop. Maybe he'd done the mental coin flip too and come up devoid of options the same way I had. "Why?"

Daniel kept his eyes on his dark phone screen. "He needs to perform the spell there. But he doesn't have everything he needs yet so I'm not sure why he's there now."

"And why are you going after him?"

"Mei said he's alone."

"Ah ha—Mei! I knew it! I *knew* she was protecting you!" My voice got too loud. The driver glanced back to us in

STEPHANIE CAYE

her mirror. I moved across the aisle into the seat beside Daniel, my lower back throbbing at the memory of the dragon. "You could have just told me she was helping you."

He sat back. "I wasn't sure she still was."

"But you are now?"

"No."

"So going down there might be walking into a trap."

"Yes." His resigned tone stopped my next logical question. He wasn't going to run the other way, disappear into the crowd, like any sane person would.

Well, neither was I. "Can I come with you?"

"Why?"

Such a good question. "Well, I'm obviously not getting paid by the Faerie Court to steal a spell from you anymore," I said, "so my second wish is to throw Aubrie out a window. And I can't do that if I'm stuck in Montreal."

"What makes it *obvious* you're not working for the Court?" Daniel shot back.

"I held a cowboy at knife-point and punched a siren in the face to get you and that stupid stone away from them, remember?" I squared my shoulders against the plastic seat. "I don't want the fucking spell."

After taking a moment to consider that, Daniel asked, "What were they really going to give you in return?"

"The money I told you about." Ugh, might as well be honest at this point. "Double what I told you—twenty thousand. And a passport." I still couldn't be honest enough to mention the letter opener, though.

He looked skeptical. "You don't have a passport?"

"Why would I?"

"Where were you going to go with it?"

"I *am* going to go to a beautiful, *expensive* private beach with killer margaritas and no Faerie magic." I sighed. "But since I'm unclear on what the margarita situation will be if Aubrie smashes the worlds together, I figure better safe that sorry."

Daniel rubbed his forehead with one hand, still not meeting my eyes, but I thought I caught a smile.

"Fine," he said.

"Okay." I sank lower in my seat. Relief fused through me. Even if he didn't actually want me along, he'd agreed. It was on him now.

I nodded to the phone in his hand. "Where are we headed? Borrowing a car from Zeb?"

"That would have been easier." He sounded as if the thought hadn't occurred to him.

"Easier than . . . ?"

"My sister."

"I thought your sister lived in England."

He looked surprised, like he didn't believe I'd remembered. "Not anymore."

"She moved to Montreal too, huh?" I asked. "What are the odds?" I knew the answer to my next question before I asked it, but I needed it confirmed: "She was Consilium?"

"Yes." He tugged the cord against the window to request a stop. The bus slowed.

"Family business."

"Family malady."

"Says the guy who *still* won't tell me why he hasn't run the hell away from all of this." I hadn't expected to get an answer to that and wasn't disappointed. After we'd stepped off the bus and headed down the street, I asked, "What'd your sister do for the Consilium?"

"She was in Antiquities. Archaeology. London was just a home base. She's been in India and Russia the last few years."

"Now she's your partner in whatever Consilium Part Two is."

Daniel considered that. "Don't say that to her face."

After another two blocks, we came to a row of narrow townhouses, most dark inside. He led me three buildings down and then mounted the steps two at a time up to the front door, where he tapped into his phone again.

I jumped when the door buzzed, but followed him inside. He led me straight to the first plain wooden door. It had gold numbers nailed to it: 2945-B.

He rapped on the wood with one knuckle. It opened a moment later to reveal a woman silhouetted by a dim lamp.

She threw her arms around Daniel, pulling him into a tight embrace. Catching sight of me over his shoulder, she stepped back. "What the hell's going on?"

"Sorry it's so late." He didn't answer her question. Nice, it wasn't just me he evaded.

"Early," she corrected. "Insomnia's making a comeback. And I hoped you'd be by at some point. Sooner would have been my preference. And *alone*."

Moving aside to let him in, she hesitated, eyeing me. After a second, she reluctantly gestured me inside too. Shorter than me, she had long, dark hair pulled back in a braid that fell over her shoulder.

"This is Jude," Daniel said, as an afterthought, once we were inside the apartment.

"I figured." Voice flat, the other woman told me, "I'm Grace."

I tightened my jaw to keep it from dropping as the name registered. No wonder it had sounded so familiar when Zeb mentioned it this morning.

Grace hugged a long, threadbare sweater around herself, still looking like she wished she hadn't let me in. She turned to her brother for an explanation.

"I need cash, if you've got it," he said, "and your car."

She frowned. "Where are you taking the car?"

"Ontario."

"Why?"

"Everywhere I go the last two days, somebody comes crashing in after me an hour later." Daniel glanced to her window, adding, "If that. I need to keep moving."

"You look dead on your feet. You're not driving my car."

"I can drive," I said. "I'm super awake. Couldn't sleep if I tried."

Grace glared at me, not appreciating the attempt at problem-solving. She turned back to her brother. "Just stay here. Get some sleep."

"I can't," he said. "Not here."

"Why?" Grace's eyes flickered to me, but I could only shrug. If Daniel didn't want to tell her what he'd told me about Aubrie's location, I wasn't going to be the one to bring it up.

As it turned out, she didn't need me to. "Aubrie's down there," she guessed. To Daniel's surprised expression, she added, "I read the same information you did. Sphere-merging requires a bunch of natural energy and where better than Niagara?"

She turned on me. "You talked him into this?"

"No," I said. "All his idea. I don't know anything about sphere-merging."

Unconvinced, Grace looked back to her brother. His expression seemed to tell her more than it told me, because she sighed. "I'll get you the cash."

She headed up the stairs across the room, disappearing to the condo's second floor.

A metallic gleam in the corner behind the television caught my eye. I went toward it and lifted a heavy, long-handled battleaxe from the corner. The sharp blade shone in the overhead lights. I balanced the axe in my hand, marvelling at the weight. Turning to Daniel, I clarified, "Archaeology?"

"That shouldn't be there." Grace came back down the stairs and straight for me. She extended her hand to take the axe, the sleeves of her sweater pushed up to reveal smooth lines of muscle in her arms. She could use this weapon, no question.

"What happened?" Daniel asked, nodding to the axe.

"I couldn't sleep so I was doing a few exercises when you texted." Grace carried the weapon to the front door. She fished a necklace from underneath her sweater: a chain strung with a little key and another charm. The key unlocked the closet, and she placed the battleaxe inside.

I craned my neck to try to see what else she had in there, but she closed it before I could. She asked her brother, "Should I be expecting someone?"

"The Court had a sylph on me. They could know where you are."

"Great." Re-locking the closet door, Grace gave Daniel a dubious look. "What have I got they'd want now?"

"Just . . . " Daniel thought better of whatever it was he'd been about to say. My money was on 'be careful', but he probably figured Grace didn't need that advice. The axe told *me* she didn't.

She handed him a wad of cash. "I hope this is enough."

"It's great. Thanks."

Gracie hugged her arms to her chest. "Where's the cross?"

"I smashed it."

"Why?" Her eyebrows shot up.

"To keep Aubrie's pixies from getting it."

"Then you've—?" She stopped, casting me a furtive look.

"He decrypted it or whatever." I jumped in to let her know she didn't have to speak in code. "We've been through that already."

Grace gave her brother an exasperated look. I got the idea she would have said more but didn't want to with me there. "I can wait outside," I said, gesturing to the door.

"Can you?" She glared at me. "That'd be awesome."

"No problem." I swallowed the initial fury that reared up, walking to the door and letting myself out into the hallway. Outside, I leaned against the wall and dug my fingernails into my palms. She had every right to hate me. Daniel shouldn't have brought me here.

As minutes ticked by, I expected cops to show up and drag me away. The building stayed quiet. The silence gnawed at me. The front door was too thick to hear anything through. I fought my itchy muscles, refusing to give in and run.

I tensed when the door finally opened and Daniel stepped out. He closed it behind him, saying nothing, but I fixed on the car keys in his hand.

"Did you knock her out and steal the keys or what?" I made the joke without thinking, wishing the words back in the same breath. Of all the stupid things to say . . .

"That's not everybody's go-to solution." His sarcasm startled me. Maybe my ridiculous apology had actually made a difference. Or maybe the lack of sleep was just making him punchy.

Either way, I matched his tone. "And that's not a 'no.'"

25

"Daniel's going to Niagara with Jude." Gracie kept her free ear cocked toward the baby monitor in case Riley should wake as she spoke into the phone. "I want you to follow them."

"Wait—what?" That snapped Zeb more awake. "Follow Daniel? To . . . where?"

"No, follow Jude. Especially if she and Daniel part."

"Grace, I'm not really trained for—"

"I haven't got anyone else!" Gracie said. "Just go and I'll call you as soon as I know where they are."

"Maybe it's just the fact that it's two thirty in the morning, but I don't understand," Zeb admitted. "You told me earlier that Jude got Daniel away from the Court."

"That's what he said."

"Don't you have people who do this for a living?"

"Not anymore. I'll pay you overtime."

"It's not the money—though I will take you up on that. It's just . . . I don't like the idea of tailing Daniel."

Gracie couldn't be surprised at his loyalty, seeing as how she'd only met him a few times, whereas he'd been working shoulder-to-shoulder with her brother for a couple of months now.

"He needs backup," she said.

"Doesn't sound like backup. Sounds like surveillance. You think he's, like, compromised?"

She stifled an inappropriate laugh. "Under a spell? No."

Not that she hadn't tried to check. Lack of familiarity with the signs meant she couldn't say for sure, but as far as she knew, Jude didn't have that kind of power. Her brother had only seemed tired, on edge, and anxious to be out of the city—not in any kind of trance.

Gracie's fingers tightened around the phone. "I've already got you booked on a nine a.m. flight to Toronto." She ignored the incredulous laugh she got in response. "There'll be a rental car waiting for you—be careful with it, will you?" She hated to add a barb as she asked a favour, but she knew how he drove. "I'll call you when I get their exact location."

"It better be a good rental. None of that sub-compact shit."

She gave him the flight information, then hung up and listened again for noises from upstairs. Maybe Riley really was learning to sleep through the night.

Grabbing the baby monitor, she headed upstairs to her bedroom, leaving her cell on the bedside table with the monitor beside her pillow as she lay down. Her mind kept coming back to the way her brother had sounded on the phone earlier that night—afraid, in pain, and trying desperately to hide it.

She shouldn't have let him leave. He'd tried to explain it to her in what he thought were rational terms—Mei insisted on meeting in St. Catharines, and they needed Mei's cooperation to destroy the grymoire. As for Jude, well, she was a weapon, useful.

Now who sounds like Alan? Gracie hadn't told him that, because she hadn't really bought the mercenary excuse. Her brother was flagging, exhausted, making bad decisions. He didn't need to be under a spell to make a mistake. Had it occurred to him that Jude might be leading him into a trap? That the smartest thing to do with the information he had was to run in the opposite direction?

She put a hand to her face, pinching the bridge of her nose. Of course that had occurred to Daniel. Of course he'd considered all his options. She wasn't giving her brother any credit. She was supposed to have his back. He'd always had hers.

But he'd been different since the attack in Toronto. He was becoming someone she didn't understand. She should have fought harder to keep him there, but she'd been thrown off her game by him walking that woman into her home. *I never should have pointed him back to her.*

A noise from downstairs made her sit up. Certain for a moment that it had been the sound of the front door swinging open, she told herself she'd imagined it. Hearing nothing more, she had to get up anyway and go the hallway. She moved to the next bedroom and checked on Riley, sleeping soundly in his crib. At the doorway to the nursery, she tensed at another sound—a creak on the stairs.

Doing a hasty mental inventory of the upstairs rooms, nothing presented itself as a usable weapon except the baby monitor in her hand. She kept all the real weapons in the front closet downstairs.

The dark nursery gave her the advantage of shadow against the light from downstairs. She darted forward, swinging the baby monitor up with as much force as she could into the face of the person just gaining the top of the stairs.

The form fell backwards, thudding down several steps.

Gracie leapt over it in a dash down to the front hallway, tearing the chain from her throat and jamming the key into the closet lock to get it open.

Before she could reach inside, an invisible force struck her, slamming her backwards and pinning her to the wall. Gracie managed to turn her head and see what appeared to be an old woman with one hand thrust out, picking herself up from the stairs.

The woman came closer. Tiny, with a shock of white hair pulled into what had previously been a tight bun, probably before the tumble down the stairs, she sized Gracie up with sharp, dark eyes. "Where's your brother?"

A question Gracie should have expected.

"Gone!" she snapped.

"Where?"

"Don't know." She fought to extend her hand toward the closet, but she couldn't move a muscle. "Who's asking?" She'd have put money on Aubrie, since the Court seemed to run in a pack.

The old woman kept a hand out, pressing her so tightly against the wall that it became hard to draw a breath. She twisted her fingers and Gracie collapsed to the floor in a heap, stunned by the sudden motion.

Something hit her shoulder. Her own cellphone, summoned somehow from the bedroom upstairs.

"Call him. Bring him here."

"Fuck no." Gracie let out a weak laugh at the command.

Another twitch of the woman's hand knocked it out of her, slamming her head backwards into the wall hard enough to make her see spots.

A sudden noise cut through her: Riley crying from upstairs.

The other woman lifted her chin. "You won't bring your brother back to save you? Maybe *he* will."

As the Antagonist turned toward the stairs, Gracie tried her muscles. She could move again. Closing a hand around her phone, she chucked it at the woman's head.

When her opponent threw up a hand to block it, Gracie shoved herself into the closet, grasping for the first weapon she could find. Her fingers closed around the long-handled axe she'd just returned there. She hauled herself up, brandishing the blade.

The Antagonist took a step away from the stairs, startled.

Relief fused through Gracie. She liked the axe because it was scary as hell and made people think twice. She swung it but missed and sank the blade into the carpet when the woman disappeared. Yanking it free, she put her back to the wall, searching the room for any glimmer or sign of the woman reemerging.

Unable to wait any longer with Riley still wailing in his room, she shoved herself from the wall and dashed to the stairs. She smashed into an invisible barrier at the bottom, knocking her away. Her first instinct was to try again to break through it, so she fought against that to spin around, swinging the axe down.

The blade found flesh, sinking into the outside of the Antagonist's thigh as she came up behind. The other woman screamed, throwing up a hand and sending Gracie backwards with a burst of energy, onto her back in the middle of the living room.

Gracie clutched the axe to her chest as she hit, narrowly avoiding bringing the blade into her own cheek. She struggled upright.

The woman lay in a heap on the floor, blood running from her leg. For an instant, her glamour gave way and rather than the tiny, white-haired woman, she became a bright, terrifying form too thin and ethereal to be human. The glimpse of the naked Antagonist made Gracie's blood run cold.

The creature shoved itself back along the floor, trying but unable to stand on its legs.

Gracie blinked and the thing was human-shaped again, hissing at her in fury and pain. Jamming the axe handle into the floor to pull herself to her feet, the weapon became too hot to touch. She flung it down, swearing, and pushed herself up. She didn't dare move around the woman on the floor between her and the closet, going instead for the kitchen. She grabbed a knife from the block on the counter and swung around, expecting the Antagonist to be there.

The old woman remained on the floor near the front door, one hand to her bloodstained thigh. Red leaked out onto the carpet around her as she hissed words in a language Gracie didn't know.

Gracie knelt beside her, jabbing the blade toward her throat but not pushing it through. "Who sent you?"

The woman replied in the same language—Antagonist, probably, though Gracie had never heard the delicate, sing-song words aloud.

"Who sent you?" she repeated, making sure the knife blade cut slightly into the woman's throat. "The Mab?"

The Antagonist couldn't keep a flicker of disdain from crossing her features at the suggestion, even with the knife pressed to her throat.

"Aubrie, then," Gracie concluded.

Of course he'd try to use her to get to Daniel. He'd known them since they were teenagers. It should have occurred to her sooner. That was probably why Daniel had left so fast. *Always one step ahead and not bothering to tell me about the view.*

The old woman flexed her fingers against the rug. Cold pressure wrapped around Gracie's throat, cutting off her air and making her gasp. The same pressure bore down on her hand, tightening and pressuring her muscles to drop the knife.

Before her fingers could fully betray her, Gracie jerked an arm forward and jammed the blade through the Antagonist's chest.

The weight crushing her throat and hand dissipated and she sucked in a breath. She whipped her head to one side to keep from watching the thing's face contort as it died, forcing herself to remember the inhuman creature under the old woman's face.

Her son's cries from upstairs reached her again, and she sat back, drawing a deep breath to suppress the urge to vomit. The woman's glamour held, even in death. Gracie focused on the carpet beside the corpse's head rather than the human face.

She got to her feet, swaying to one side before finding her balance. Leaving the knife where it was, she dashed up the stairs to the nursery to pull her crying son out of his crib. "Shhh, it's okay, Rye."

He quieted, one hand clutching the collar of her sweater, as she held him against her chest.

Gracie collapsed with him in the nearby rocking chair. Her eyes caught on the blood on her hand, resting against her son's back. Her stomach recoiled again but she almost laughed at the first thought that came to mind: she couldn't tell Daniel what had happened. He'd come back.

The Antagonist had been stronger than she'd anticipated, tossing her around like a puppet. Telekinetic, maybe, but paired with the barrier that had stopped her from reaching the stairs, and the way the axe had grown hot in her hands, that didn't fit. Spells, too many different tricks to be an ordinary Faerie. She hadn't considered that Aubrie would have people like this, assuming his recruits would all be half-Faerie hybrids. Nothing to scoff at, but not this powerful. If not for that lucky swing with the axe . . .

Tremors ran through her body but she refused to consider the other way that fight could have played out, focusing her thoughts like a laser to keep the terror from breaking through.

She needed to get rid of the body in the living room. Zeb probably wouldn't be amenable to coming to help her with that before flying to Toronto, and she hadn't made any friends yet in Montreal who might help her dispose of a corpse. She'd have to call Ted in London and see if he knew anybody here to take care of it.

26

EVEN AT THREE IN the morning, the Fallsview Casino buzzed with noise and life. Tinny melodies designed to draw players to empty slot machines warred with the pop music piped in over the speakers and sharp laughter mingled among the voices of table dealers calling cards.

Aubrie downed the single shot of whisky he'd allowed himself to assuage his nerves against the jarring stimulation. He'd have preferred to be in bed in his quiet hotel, but he had it on good authority that his quarry was a night-owl, and there would be no better place than Canada's largest casino—open twenty-four hours—to find a Faerie who fed on luck.

He left his secluded booth at the back of the bar for a table closer to the action, scanning the section of the casino floor he could see. Trying to open himself up to any tingle of magic nearby, his thoughts wandered unbidden back to the phone conversation with Mei. He wanted to be pleased by her desire to help him, despite all her earlier insistence to the contrary, but guilt lingered.

She'd been conflicted for months now—more mistrustful, quicker to anger. She wasn't ready for their plans to come to fruition, to give up her silly, suffocating human life: capital raising and corporate dinners.

Soon, though, it wouldn't matter, this friction between them, their petty spats. He'd show her how much better the world could be for them. She could have everything.

When nothing magical piqued him from his current location in the bar, he had to get up and walk the casino floor. It took several passes before the tell-tale electricity danced across the hairs on his arms, letting him know a Faerie was close-by.

Turning a corner, Aubrie found him.

The *houle* sat on a stool beside a man playing something on a horizontal screen. Three other people sat at similar screens, arranged in a circle around a taller, vertical screen that showed the outcome. Digital Roulette.

With a narrow nose and dark, sunken eyes, the Faerie had an owlish look to him that matched the term the Consilium had chosen to define his kind. He watched the taller screen with anticipation, squeezing his companion's knee.

The human with him had patchy skin and greasy hair, eyes scrunched like he'd been at the roulette screen for hours—maybe days. Sweat stained the underarms of his rumpled button-down shirt. He watched the digital ball on the screen and then his shoulders slumped as the inevitable occurred.

His gangly companion leaned over without taking a hand from his leg, whispering something into his ear that was likely meant to goad him into another game.

The man retrieved a wallet from his back pocket.

It turned Aubrie's stomach. He steeled himself to keep from yanking the inhuman creature away from its victim. Watching a Faerie feed on a human had never become palatable, even if the Consilium had insisted that this one-on-one interaction was inevitable and impossible to chase down in every instance. They'd always preferred the big picture.

He walked up beside the *houle* and waited a full minute in silence before the Faerie noticed him.

"You want to play, there's a spot open there," the creature said, jerking his chin toward the empty slot in their game without taking his eyes off the screen where one of the other players had set the computer-generated roulette ball going.

"No, thank you."

The other man cast Aubrie a sharp look, eyes narrowing. Then he shifted on his stool, moving nearer to his mark and not taking his hand off the man's thigh.

"I've only got twenty bucks left," the man murmured, blinking hard as he licked his dry lips. "Fuck, I was supposed to pay Stacey back . . . "

"Next one's your spin, baby," the *houle* told him. His voice lacked conviction as he kept one eye on Aubrie.

"Maybe pass this round." Aubrie put a hand on the Faerie's shoulder and squeezed with a modicum of his own supernatural power.

The owl-faced man glared up at him, lifting his hand from his victim to swat Aubrie away.

At the break in contact, the roulette player jerked upright, startled, like he hadn't realized there was anyone around them. He stared at the *houle* and Aubrie with wide, uncertain eyes, then glanced to the other players with him as if he didn't remember where he was.

"Let's talk," Aubrie told the Faerie.

"I don't consort with abominations like you," the man growled under his breath, flashing his teeth.

Aubrie tightened his fingers into the creature's shoulder, making the *houle* hiss in pain. He pulled it back before the Faerie could latch onto him and siphon out whatever luck he might have on the way. He'd made his point, and he'd need whatever fortune was coming to him.

The gambler got to his feet, eyeing them with a face drawn like he might scream. Instead, he shook his head, shoved his wallet into his back pocket, and scurried away with his head ducked down.

With another disdainful glower, the Faerie slid off his own stool. He towered over Aubrie by three inches.

Aubrie gave him an impassive look and offered, "Buy you a drink?"

"To make up for the meal you cost me? It better be the good shit," the *houle* huffed, then led the way back to the bar.

The Faerie ordered a double of the most expensive tequila the casino had, downed it at the bar, then ordered another.

Aubrie joined him in the second and they moved to the secluded booth at the back of the bar.

"What do you want?" the *houle* asked.

"Your kind finds hidden items."

"When we're satiated."

"I'm not going to send you off to drain some other sad gambler."

"Look who's gloating because his *limited* powers come without strings," the *houle* crowed, throwing back the double in his glass.

Aubrie choked on a laugh. No strings? What about being unable to set foot in his own mother's world—unable to go after her when she'd abandoned him? Or being refused his birthright—the deeper magic all other beings born Fae were granted?

"What are you looking for?" the other creature asked, leaning back in his seat with hooded eyes. "And what's the finder's fee?"

"I'm seeking a grymoire, and I'll—"

"Oh shit." The *houle* perked up, studying Aubrie with new eyes. "You're the half-breed that wants to merge the spheres. The new Mab's after you."

Aubrie tensed at the slur but focused on the pertinent section. "You're a devotee of the new queen?"

"That human-reared imposter? Nah." The man waved a hand dismissively, then slapped it down on the Formica table. "But she's got the keys to the treasury and she's got a bounty on you. Big one."

Aubrie's hand darted under the table to free the tool he'd taped there during his first trip to the bar that night. He used his power to slam the iron corkscrew down hard through the back of the *houle*'s hand and deep into the table. It burned against the skin of his own palm but he was quick to release it.

The creature across from him hissed and sputtered as breath left his lungs in surprise. He tried to yank his hand back but thought better of it when the iron started to tear his flesh. Blood pooled under his palm. Glaring at the top of the corkscrew, he flexed his fingers with difficulty and spat, "I can't just *find* things. I need a starting point. I need someone that's touched it, or something that's—*fuck*, can you pull this out?"

Aubrie clenched his fist, trying to ignore the sting in his palm that lingered even after releasing the iron. "That's not what I was told."

"Then you were misinformed, asshole." The *houle* sucked in a sharp breath and doubled forward, hacking as if he might vomit on the table and then gritting his teeth. He added, as if Aubrie didn't already know, "Nobody's seen that book in twenty years."

It had been Pru who'd told him that *houles* could locate any hidden object. She hadn't mentioned any caveats, but she wouldn't have. The pixie liked to please. So much so that she didn't always get the full story.

That meant the early detour to Niagara to find this idiot had been a waste. Not that Aubrie had had any reason to stay in Montreal with the Court already alert to his presence there, but he might have gone to Mei and . . .

"Maybe I can find something else for you," the *houle* interrupted, pressing his hand flat against the blood on the table as if trying to minimize contact with the iron.

"There's nothing else I need," Aubrie said. The mage dispatched in Montreal would bring him the incantation. He didn't have any further leads on the grymoire. The most likely possibility was that Miranda already had it.

If so, though . . . perhaps he could take it from her.

"Could you find the Mab?" he asked.

The *houle* gave him a dark look. "What do I get in return?"

"Your life."

The other creature snorted. "And?"

Despite himself, Aubrie found he liked something about the Faerie. "Find her for me and I'll leave you to your—" he gestured to the casino floor behind them, "—feast. You'll never seen me again, nor will I report you to any relevant authority. Including your Mab."

"The old Consilium compromise." The *houle* flashed his teeth in something between a grin and a grimace.

Aubrie stiffened but took a breath through his nose to loosen his muscles. He'd faced down his own hypocrisy before. "That's a 'yes'?"

"Can't do it with iron stuck in me." The *houle* nodded to the corkscrew in his hand.

"You'll have to give me your word you won't retaliate."

"Buy me a bottle of that pricey tequila from the bar, pull the iron out, you have my word I'll tell you where the Mab is and I won't harm you now or in the future."

"You'd sell your queen out for a bottle of liquor?"

"I told you, she's not my queen."

At least they had *that* in common. Aubrie grabbed the stack of bar napkins he'd left on the table earlier and used them to yank the iron corkscrew from the other creature's hand. He left it resting on the table in the nest of soft paper that hadn't completely blocked it from twinging the burn on his palm again.

The *houle* yelped at the motion, pulling his hand back to his chest and cradling it. He lifted his chin to see if anyone had noticed, but no one heard them over the noise of the casino. Leaving a bloodstain on the front of his shirt, the Faerie started to get up.

"Wait," Aubrie said. "You're meant to find the Mab."

"Can't find her without somebody who knows her intimately," the *houle* said dismissively, then nodded toward the bar. "I told you, I need something to build off. Now, my booze?"

He thought he could swindle Aubrie on a technicality. *Faeries lie.*

"I've known her for years," Aubrie said. "We've never been *intimate*, if that was meant as a euphemism, but let's say I have physically touched her and in addition I have a very clear picture of her as a colleague and former friend."

The other creature paused. Hadn't expected that. With a frustrated growl, he dropped back into the booth and offered his uninjured hand to Aubrie.

"Think about her, then," he muttered.

Aubrie pictured the Miranda he'd known years ago, before their interests had diverged. Before she'd sent him to spy on the Consilium and become furious that he'd liked the purported goals of the human organization, that he'd stayed on. He saw in his mind's eye her proud, stiff stature, her flashing electric green eyes, the dismissive sneer she'd turned on him at every opportunity.

The *houle* made a confused noise in the back of his throat, jerking back and breaking contact. Meeting Aubrie's eyes, he hesitated and then said, "She's here but she's not. It's a . . . it's like a place—a house." He thought again, eyes on the ceiling as if that might provide answers. "A house between the worlds."

"And can you find it?"

"It's not hidden. Well, it is, but it's . . . it's not my kind of 'hidden', if that make sense?"

"No. Elaborate."

"Yeah." The *houle* frowned over Aubrie's shoulder, considering his options. Finally he said, "I might know a guy who can help. But he'd negotiate his own contract and I'm gonna need an extra fee for the introduction."

27

I offered to drive Grace's black hatchback, so Daniel tossed me the keys and directed me out of the city with directions on his phone.

He fell asleep once we were on the highway headed west out of Quebec and stayed that way for a few hours through Ontario. It probably had more to do with exhaustion than any faith in me, but things had been different between us since that awful conversation at the bus stop.

Finally copping to everything aloud had left me feeling. . . well, not better. But something different, something less bad.

I couldn't explain why I wasn't high-tailing it for Rio and out of this mess, except that I didn't want to lose the fight. I *couldn't* lose the fight. I couldn't let Aubrie win.

Even if part of me still ached to hear him say how the balcony, the coma had all been a mistake. I'd just misunderstood his intentions, his meaning.

Maybe the Consilium had known I'd killed Alan. Maybe they'd been closing in on me and that was why Aubrie had told me to steer clear of his plans for Daniel. It would make sense that he'd been furious that night I'd brought him the laptop. He'd probably been scheming some way to protect me and he just hadn't told me because. . .

Because you're a fucking idiot. I remembered too clearly how Aubrie had looked at me before lifting me and tossing me into the air, the iron corkscrew stinging in my shoulder. He'd meant to protect himself, avoid guilt by association.

It had been easy to bond with him over being half-Faerie recruits at the Consilium. The organization had been like a shitty boyfriend—charming us into hooking up with empty promises, then merely tolerating our presence once we did. Aubrie'd hated them as much as he'd hated the Court, going on outside the office about eradicating the old orders and building something new. It had seemed hypothetical, like a dark game we played to keep from being bored at work.

Not *always*. I felt the letter opener in my hand, that cold laptop shoved underneath my coat.

Maybe mixing Faerie and human DNA was just a bad idea. Maybe those mages who'd thought up the incantation had been onto something. If I asked Daniel to paint me with the magic words, take away my power and make me normal, would it be better?

Probably only if I got a lobotomy too.

I couldn't lay the blame on my Faerie blood. I couldn't say it was all from my human side either. It was all me: Judith Sylvia Waldron.

The windshield blurred and I hit the wiper button. They groaned across the dry glass. *Damn it.* I reached up with the back of one hand and wiped the tears away.

Daniel woke with a start at the sound. He sat upright, taking a deep breath as if to reorient himself, then rubbed his face with one hand and turned to the dark window. "Where are we?"

"Mexico, obviously."

"Turned the map upside down?"

"The *map* fell asleep." I glanced over again to find him still looking shaken and guessed, "Nightmare?"

"No." Too quick.

"You wake up that fast from a *good* dream?"

"Let's get something to eat," he said, as we passed the next white road sign advertising twenty-four-hour restaurants at the upcoming travel stop. Deflecting my question as usual, at least he'd read my mind about food.

Six in the morning, according to the clock on the dash. My back still ached from the fight with Mei. Sitting stiff and upright in the car for hours hadn't improved it. I pulled off into the travel stop and parked the car.

When Daniel disappeared into the men's room, I zeroed in on a guy checking out a wall of maps between the restrooms. I sauntered up beside him, pretending to study the twists and tangles of colour-coded roads. From the corner of my eye, I caught a bulge in the right back pocket of his jeans.

I turned and walked halfway around so my back was to him. Then I stumbled one step backwards like I'd jumped out of someone's way. I bumped against him, letting my fingers dart into the pocket and whip the wallet out. I tucked it into my own back pocket as I turned around. "Geez, sorry."

"Yeah." He just gave me a tired half-nod and then turned back to study the map, oblivious to the weight I'd lifted from him.

In the safety of a closed stall in the ladies' room, I opened the wallet and liberated the cash. Thirty dollars. I tucked that into the front pocket of my jeans and left the wallet in the bathroom.

One of the vending machines had single packages of aspirin. I bought two and took them with some water from the drinking fountain. The aches in my body stayed distant but ever-present.

Finding only Tim Horton's open this early, I walked over to join Daniel in the short line. "Breakfast is on me." I said, letting the cash peek out of my jeans pocket.

"I figured you'd come through sooner or later."

As we sat down at a table near the back window, digging into our meal, I asked, "Why Niagara Falls? Seems like a weird place to have to perform a spell."

"Aubrie needs a massive amount of natural energy to merge the spheres." When my blank look told him he needed to go further, Daniel said, "Most spells can work off energy produced by the earth, the air, living things. Small stuff. A spell this big needs something equally huge to feed off."

"And Niagara Falls can give it enough natural energy?"

"Do you know how much water goes over those falls in an hour?"

"They didn't cover that in our grade eight field trip. Okay, they probably did, but obviously I wasn't taking notes for future Faerie spells."

"It's one of the best sources of natural energy in North America."

"Too bad we can't just shut the thing off."

"The energy is built up there, in the place itself. I'm not sure stopping the flow of water would affect it right away. Even if it would, that would probably take a government treaty."

"Or a really big cork." I sighed. "Let me guess—he has to do this world-merging at the stroke of midnight on the full moon or some typical bullshit?"

"Midnight on the half-moon." Daniel unwrapped one of the egg and cheese sandwiches we'd bought as part of my breakfast feast.

"Poetic." I rolled my eyes. Magic—never subtle. "So if he doesn't have the incantation or this Faerie book he needs, why high-tail it out of Montreal?"

"Maybe he found it—the grymoire."

"It's over here?" I crumpled up the wrapper from my own breakfast sandwich, tossing it at the nearest trashcan. Not dead centre, but it went in. "Why do they keep stashing their dangerous shit over here? First the incantation, then this book—"

"Other way around," Daniel corrected, "Book first, incantation later. I guess they figured no human would know what either was. We're a game reserve and a garbage dump."

I tried not to dwell on the bitterness in his voice.

Over his shoulder, the guy whose wallet I'd stolen settled into a booth with a phone to his ear. In one hand, he tapped the wallet someone must have retrieved from the ladies' room, lightened of cash. His eyes flickered to me and narrowed with recognition.

"We should go," I said. If I'd been thinking clearer, I wouldn't have let us stay this long.

Daniel, to his credit, didn't turn to follow my gaze. He gave me a knowing look but said nothing, letting me lead the way out of the building.

Outside at the gas station, he used some of Grace's cash to fill the car up, then plugged his phone in to charge in the centre console and took over driving.

I crawled into the back seat to stretch out and sleep but was thwarted by a child's car seat in the middle. I still felt wired. The Sandman wasn't visiting, as my mom used to say. The thought of some little guy standing over me sprinkling sand in my face made me think of pixies.

Traffic slowed as the highway widened. Closer runs of buildings signalled the outskirts of Toronto. Seven thirty: the start of morning rush hour on the 401. We crawled through the city at a pace slow enough that I caught Daniel texting at one point with his phone against the steering wheel.

I leaned forward and offered, "I can do that," fully expecting the derisive snort I got in return. Stupid to think he'd let me near his phone, his secrets. It was probably just Grace anyway.

As the sun rose higher, traffic eased and we followed the 401 to the QEW, curving south around the lake. I ended up dozing upright in the backseat until we stopped with a suddenness that told me we'd reached some sort of destination. My heart leapt into my throat, expecting to open my eyes to downtown Niagara Falls and Aubrie, but instead we sat in the parking lot of a one-story motel beside the highway.

"Where are we?" I asked, not acknowledging the relief that rushed through me as I draped my arms over the passenger seat from behind.

Daniel didn't answer, shoving the door open and heading to the office, apparently to get a room. I climbed out of the car and stretched my stiff body until he returned with a room key.

He brushed past me to retrieve a nylon tool bag from the trunk. He hadn't brought any luggage, so whatever it was had already been stored in the car.

I followed him to a generic, dingy motel room. The bag gave a metallic clank when he set it on the table beside the double bed. Iron, had to be. No surprise Grace would have a bag of iron tools in the trunk of her car, given the battleaxe in her closet. She must have told Daniel about it after kicking me out of her place.

"What are we doing here?" I asked.

"Waiting."

"For what?"

"Information." He pulled a pillow out from underneath the bed's flowered bedspread and set it up against the headboard, then stretched out upright against it and busied himself with his phone again. Settling in for a long wait, then.

Fine. I needed a nap anyway. I flopped onto the mattress beside him. I kept my distance, but I stretched out on my back, letting my muscles relax against the lumpy mattress. I kept my gaze on the ceiling to avoid the startled look Daniel threw me.

It probably took all his resolve not to hurl himself off the bed to avoid being so close to me, but after a minute he settled back against the headboard.

"Tell me about the Consilium," I said.

"Why?"

"When I was kid, my mom read me poetry to bore me to sleep. I thought history might work the same way."

That won me a laugh. I thought I might not get anything else, but Daniel gave in. "What do you want to know?"

"Who started it? Why? When?" I had no idea how long the Consilium been around protecting the human world against Faeries. I'd been sent on a couple of missions, mostly stealing stuff I didn't bother to ask about: books, papers, talismans—talismen?—the usual magic garbage. I'd gone on recon: watching the Faeries, digging up holes where they could pass through to our world. And I'd trained, learned how to fight and use my gravitational advantages in new ways that surpassed my high school gymnastics lessons.

I'd been good at the fighting part. Too bad I'd never really gotten to use it until I turned traitor.

"It was a secret sect in Ancient Rome," Daniel said. "It might have been earlier than that, somewhere else, but Romans kept the better records. Gracie could tell you more than me. She's the history buff."

"How do you not know?" The question was out before I could bite it back. "How do you just join up with something like that without knowing?"

He was silent a moment, then, "You tell me."

Touché. I'd had a proclivity for fist-fights and nothing else exciting to do. Daniel at least had a family excuse. Alan hadn't been somebody you could easily refuse.

"The fight's been going on since back in old Rome then?" I asked, to steer us back to the safer story. "Or earlier, in the non-record keeping parts of the world?"

"Apparently." He sounded reluctant, but his tone evened out as he recalled neutral information: "There were periods—hundreds of years—of inactivity. Stalemate. Then sudden resurgence during World War I. And the Consilium started tracking the Antagonist portals and working out how to close them."

"Did somebody figure it out?"

"Short of dynamiting whatever natural element is anchoring the portal, no."

"Yeah, I remember we once closed a tree portal by blowing it up. Kinda fun."

"It's pointless. Antagonists can make new ones, and we can't really convince governments to let us go around destroying thousands of random places all over the world." Daniel paused, as if remembering. "Not that it matters now."

"It doesn't. But that's a relief, right? One less thing to worry about?"

His silence told me it wasn't, not as far as he was concerned. Despite his repeated insistence that the Consilium was gone, he'd still slipped and said 'we' when he talked about them. *Still fighting the good fight.*

I gazed at his profile as he studied the blank TV screen across the room. He'd lost weight since March—not a lot, but enough to make his face more angular than I remembered. Or was that just the shadow of stubble on his cheeks and bruises under his eyes? I'd always known him clean-shaven—clean-cut, in fact, upstanding. Normal.

Too normal to have been part of the Consilium, really—or to have grown up the son of somebody like Alan Cain. I obviously hadn't known him at all. I hadn't tried. He'd just been collateral damage with an apartment nicer than mine.

A flash of shame made it hard to breathe for a moment.

"What?" Daniel seemed to realize how long I'd been staring at him, annoyance in his voice as he looked over at me.

Without thinking I sat up and leaned over, planting my hands on the mattress on either side of him. I closed the distance between us and pressed my lips against his. The stubble on his cheeks was rough against my face, but otherwise kissing him was just like I remembered.

Daniel tensed, jerking back. His eyes met mine, startled and searching, and I expected him to shove me away. Instead, he took my face in both hands and kissed me back with an intensity that made me melt into him.

I swung my leg over his to put me squarely in his lap. Heat fused through my body as his arms snaked around my back to push my t-shirt up. My skin ached in the patterns his fingers brushed.

I had to break contact to tug my t-shirt over my head and fling my bra somewhere to my right, then I attacked his shirt, desperate to feel his warm skin against mine.

In a hurried tumble of limbs, we got the rest of our clothes off without sacrificing much face-to-face time. Daniel gripped my hips with both hands and steered me to the other side of the bed.

I let him press me down on my back, pinning me against the mattress. I writhed up to meet his body, tangling my fingers into his hair to pull his lips back to mine. No gravity tricks this time. No games.

28

MEI CHEWED ON THE inside of her lower lip, staring through the car windshield at the rundown motel. She'd found the place online and from the safety of her Montreal apartment, the seedy one-story building along the highway outside of St. Catharines had seemed distant enough from Niagara to be safe.

Sitting in the parking lot in her hired car, the roar of the highway traffic competing with her racing heart to fill her ears, it felt uncomfortably close to Aubrie's new headquarters.

"This the place you meant?" Her driver turned around in his seat to look at her, as if thinking her hesitation had to do with incorrect directions.

"Yes." Mei nodded. "You'll wait?"

"You paid for the whole day. I'll be here." He held up his phone to show her a half-finished crossword puzzle.

She hesitated before pushing the car door open, scanning the quiet parking lot as she climbed out. In the noon sunlight, nothing moved. Only two other cars sat in the lot with them, one a black hatchback with Quebec plates.

Daniel had texted a couple hours ago to tell her he'd arrived and given her a room number. Securing her purse on one shoulder and holding the strap tightly to keep it from swaying too much with its precious cargo, she headed toward the row of rooms.

With each step, she kept an eye out for motion. She'd seen Jasper on her flight and he'd seen her too. From the look he'd given her when their eyes met, he held the fight in the restaurant against her. He couldn't know she'd hit him on purpose, but at least he resented the accidental clumsiness. Luckily, it meant he hadn't tried to catch her at the airport to share a car or anything ridiculous like that.

Still, Aubrie would know she was headed his way before long. He might start looking for her if she didn't turn up in Niagara soon. She didn't have time to waste.

Rather than knock when she found the right door, she turned the knob. It opened, unlocked, to admit her.

Someone scrambled upright from a chair near the door, making her tense for a fight. She relaxed, recognizing Jude.

The other woman didn't seem as ready to see her, wide-eyed in surprise but shifting into a fighting stance. Her hair was wet and she radiated a tense, nervous energy.

"Down, girl," Mei said, unable to bite back her disdain. Ignoring the glare that earned her, she looked to Daniel, sitting on the edge of the bed near the headboard. His hair was damp too. Condensation beaded on the walls outside the poorly-ventilated bathroom. The room smelled like cheap shampoo. "I didn't think you'd really bring her."

"Do you want her to leave?" Daniel ignored the startled look Jude turned on him.

Mei couldn't take any pleasure in it. "I don't care. I've had a tiring flight. I go first, not negotiable."

He got to his feet without argument, waiting while she reached into her purse. She extracted a long, narrow paintbrush and the bottle of the ink she'd mixed up the previous night. Rather than risking putting it in her carry-on, she'd brought it the whole way in her purse, passing it off as high-end moisturizer when one of the agents had pulled it out at the airport security checkpoint.

Daniel accepted the ink and the brush, lifting the bottle to study the dark green liquid. His gaze moved past it to her. "Are you sure you want to do this?"

"What would make you think otherwise?" As if she hadn't dreamed about this opportunity every day of her life.

"It could kill you."

"It's not meant to kill. Besides, I imagine you'll get what you want even if it does, so don't pretend to be concerned with my welfare now."

She set her purse aside next to the TV, then flung the flowered bedspread from the mattress, leaving it in a heap on the floor and exposing the starchy white sheets. Still facing the bed, she unbuttoned her pale purple silk blouse. "Paint it on my back," she said, discarding the blouse to one side of the bed, then unhooking her bra. She lay down on her stomach. "And make it big."

Pillowing her head in her arms, she swallowed the terror that surged up through her chest. She didn't know for certain that the incantation would work and the terrible potential outcomes danced through her mind. It might kill her, like Daniel had said. It might do worse. But the most gnawing fear came from literally leaving her back exposed to potential enemies. Daniel needed her—that counted for something. But Jude . . .

Mei darted a quick glance to the other woman. Jude didn't look intent on interfering. She looked more like she wanted to flee the room now that she'd realized what was going on.

Tensing when she felt Daniel's weight on the mattress beside her, Mei held her breath. She waited for the touch of the brush on her skin, aching to have it over with. The seconds passed like hours.

It tickled at first, the soft bristles moving the liquid across her back. The brushstrokes were long and careful, using the line of her spine like a guide to centre the foreign runes. He worked slowly, as if painting one letter crooked would screw up the whole spell.

It might. Mei clenched her jaw to stifle her impatience and let him go at his own pace. A distant scuffling noise had to be Jude bumping into the chair by the door, as if trying to move further away. Mei ignored it.

The ink felt cold on her skin in the room's AC. Pressure lifting from the bed beside her told her Daniel had finished. She waited. The liquid became icier, the cold morphing into stinging pain. It started to burn, working its way from the flesh on her back straight down into her chest. Spreading further, it flooded her legs and blossomed into her throat, climbing higher to wrap around her forehead like a vise.

Her muscles started to twitch in the familiar way that meant she was about to morph into her dragon-self. Fire surged into her throat, choking her. She buried her face in the sheets, fighting to swallow the flames.

Pain crawled through, inhabiting every vein in her body and stopping the transformation. The flames crackled and sizzled in the room around her. She gasped, lifting her head, but couldn't scream through a closed throat.

A new pattern of agony cut through her back. This time it pushed up from her body in sharp slashes like something trying to escape rather than the cold ink being pulled in. It hurt enough to sear the template of runes into her mind, lines and swirls she'd never seen before but in an instant knew by heart.

Then nothing. The heat and pain rushed out like a tide retreating.

Her lungs spasmed, reminding her to breathe. She sucked in air full of the citrus-scented detergent from the sheets. Her fingers ached. She'd torn holes through the fabric with her nails.

Turning her head was surprisingly difficult. Her muscles didn't want to respond, exhausted like she'd exerted them to their limits. The air felt heavy and charged around her, full of electricity.

Like surfacing in viscous liquid, she managed to prop herself up on her elbows. She expected the movement to hurt, but her body felt light, like she was floating. The more she moved, the more it came back under her control. She exhaled fully then drew another deep breath, shaking her head to clear her hair from her face.

"How do you feel?" Daniel asked from one side. He hadn't felt the fire, the heavy electricity swirling in the air around them moments ago. He couldn't have—not and still have spoken to her in the calm, cautious tone he used.

"I don't know." Mei forced her words out through a throat that, from the memory of the flame, should hurt. She couldn't get a glimpse of her back over her shoulder. Even without visual confirmation, she knew that the ink had been drawn in, absorbed, just like it was supposed to be.

Turning her head back, she saw Jude's face. Hovering near the window, the other woman's expression said that she *had* felt the magic in the room, and she rubbed her arms as if trying to warm up.

When she met Mei's eyes, her own widened in surprise. The look gave Mei enough of a jolt to shove herself off the bed. She flew into the bathroom and stared into her own eyes in the mirror.

Relief flooded her like a wave, knocking her legs from under her. She clutched the sink edge to keep herself upright, unable to look away from the reflection, even through the haze of tears. Turning her head at different angles, she searched for a hint of the golden gleam. It had gone, replaced by the most beautiful, *human* shade of brown she had ever seen.

29

I FORCED MY HEART to slow to a normal rate while Mei examined her reflection in the mirror of the tiny bathroom across the room. The weight of the magic had left me lightheaded. My skin prickled, then calmed, then prickled again, like it couldn't decide whether the dragon was still there or not. I'd tried to talk myself down out of the panic during the spell, but my body had freaked out on autopilot. I'd spent most of the time focused on staring out the window instead of watching the woman on the bed.

Daniel clearly hadn't sensed the same thing. He looked unnerved, like he knew something wasn't right but couldn't place it, then surprised at Mei's sudden dash to the bathroom. He'd set the paintbrush aside at some point while I hadn't been watching and now held his phone in one hand.

I opened my mouth to ask what he'd been doing with that, but Mei emerged from the bathroom. She cocked her head to the side, closing her eyes. Creases formed on her forehead as she tried to morph into a dragon. Nothing happened.

Relief blossomed across her face and she blinked rapidly as if dispelling tears.

Something shifted again in the pit of my stomach.

She came back into the room, folding an arm across her breasts as if just half-remembering modesty. Pulling on her discarded bra from the mattress, she reached for her shirt.

I watched to see if her hands were shaking as she buttoned it, but I couldn't tell.

"Aubrie," she said, "is at the Queen Victoria Hotel in downtown Niagara Falls. Room 427. There are four bodyguards, *lesidhe*." Her voice sounded weak, but she squared her shoulders as if nothing was wrong.

Lesidhe. That one I remembered: a chameleon type of Faerie that blended into its surroundings, changing colours and patterns across their skin to go almost invisible if you weren't on the lookout for that third dimension of a body pressed against a wall. Perfect bodyguards.

Daniel recoiled at Mei's words, startled, as if he'd forgotten there was more to their bargain. While he hadn't been privy to the suffocating magic he'd just released, he still seemed to recognize Mei's reaction as weird. He looked to me, as if to see if her calm made sense from my view.

It didn't. Mei had just moved on like nothing had happened. If not for the weariness in her stance and the hint of strain on her face, I might have believed she hadn't felt anything at all from the mess of energy in the room a minute ago.

If she was dying, Mei wasn't going to let us in on it.

Daniel came to the same conclusion without my help, fixing on her explanation. "You said he was alone."

"This is as alone as he's going to be."

"And the bullshit about him expecting only you was another lie?"

Mei set her jaw. "He doesn't tell me when he changes his mind." She hesitated, then admitted, "Jasper was on my flight up here. I didn't realize they'd come up so fast."

"Which one is that?" Daniel didn't recognize the name. His assailants hadn't been polite enough to introduce themselves the way they had me.

"One of the pixies," I said, taking another peek out the window for the familiar punk.

"Whose *darling* girlfriend one of you killed." Mei could still manage sarcasm. She looked at me to as if to bestow the credit.

I pointed to Daniel. The vacuum had been his idea.

He fixed on the more pertinent concern. "So he could have followed you here?"

"He didn't," Mei said, voice sharp as if she resented the implication. "I'm not an idiot. He had no interest in following me, and believe me, I *checked*. He's gone straight down to Niagara."

"Then this was, what? A ruse to get me here too?"

Mei took a quick step back, nearly losing her balance. Still weak. She recovered in an instant, beyond Daniel's reach. "I gave you the information I had at the time."

"Your favourite refrain."

"Aubrie doesn't know you're here. You could still surprise him."

"*Surprise* him and his five bodyguards?" Daniel stared at her in amazement.

"Your lack of preparation and useful allies is not my fault," Mei shot back.

I glared at her. Seemed like they weren't sleeping together, though. Mei's showing up over and over at Daniel's apartments and then turning dragon in that diner to protect him really had been some kind of deal they'd struck to make her human. The realization cheered me a little in a way I didn't want to think too hard about.

"How many people does he have, total?" Daniel asked.

I jumped in, startled: "Wait, we're going to *believe* her answers now?"

Mei glanced at me, but when Daniel ignored my interruption, she answered him. "I don't know. Twenty, maybe thirty."

"And the book?"

"He hasn't got that stupid grymoire. He has rumours and hints, but he hasn't shared them because I don't care."

"Oh, for fuck's sake." I grabbed her arm, shoving her into the wall beside the door. Bracing an arm across her throat, I held it hard enough to keep her there without doing damage. "Paint her again," I told Daniel over my shoulder. "Put the dragon back."

Mei's dark eyes narrowed at me. "He can't," she said. "It doesn't work that way. Once it's gone, it's gone. My car's waiting."

She jabbed her spiked heel down on my toes. My flimsy, fake leather boot did nothing to blunt the pain. I jerked back, freeing her.

Grabbing her purse and jacket, Mei yanked the door open and flew through it.

I clutched my aching foot, glaring at Daniel across the room. "Thanks for the help! You could have pulled out some iron from that bag of tricks you brought from Grace's car!"

"She's human now." He sank down on the end of the bed without meeting my eyes.

"And hitting her with something heavy would probably still get us the truth."

"Why would she lie? If Aubrie merges the spheres, she's fucked." Daniel didn't sound like he quite believed it.

"Lying seems to be her default setting."

"Says the expert."

I wanted to be angry at that cheap shot, especially since we'd been getting along okay for the last few hours. Well, minus the awkward silence after we'd had sex, the drawn-out separate showers and another thirty minutes that had felt like years of avoiding each other in the tiny room before Mei had burst in.

I welcomed the cold sweeping through me, taking precedence over my other, more complicated feelings. What was at the root of Mei's break for humanity? She wanted it enough to take some uncertain magical cure? What did she know that I didn't?

I was out the door almost before I knew I'd gone after her.

Mei had one hand against the passenger side of a blue car in the parking lot, head bowed like the experience had caught up with her. The driver's side door hung open, but the driver hesitated from coming around the car to help her when he saw me.

"Why?" I demanded.

She half-turned. "I was tired."

"Of being a *dragon*?"

"Of being half a dragon."

"Bullshit."

"Your little gravity tricks," she said into the side of the car, "that power. Does it hurt?"

"What?" How would it hurt? "No."

"Of course not. You were lucky—you won the genetic jackpot. You didn't need glamour to hide anything, and you turn the world around yourself. Magic's great when you're lucky." Mei's half-smile reflected in the car window, her hand tensing so that her fingernails scraped the roof. "And it sucks when you're not."

"You were a *dragon*." I couldn't emphasize it hard enough, thinking of the awesome sight of her in the restaurant.

"And to be that, I turned myself inside out." A laugh shook her, a rattle in her lungs. "It hurt. Every time."

"A little pain seems worth it to me."

"Try it a few times and let me know." Mei dropped her hands to her sides, turning to face me. "Are you going to attack me?"

"Wouldn't be a fair fight. You're human now."

"Like that's ever stopped *you*." She pulled the back door of the car open, casting me a disdainful look before climbing inside.

Coward. I flipped off the car as it headed out of the parking lot. Giving up her power to be, what? Normal? Boring?

The thoughts I'd had driving across Ontario flooded back—that it might make me a better person if I let Daniel paint that incantation on me. Fuck it. Magic couldn't change us. Cutting out pieces of herself wouldn't make Mei better, even if it made her life easier. It wouldn't fix anything I'd done.

I headed back to the room, finding Daniel still sitting on the end of the bed, holding his phone in one hand but not looking at it.

"When are we leaving, then?" I shut the door behind me. "Should we just burst into Spence's hotel and take him down?"

"We're . . . what?" Daniel looked up in surprise. "No."

"I thought we came up here to take him out."

"We did, but—"

"Then what's the plan now? Try and paint him up? Because that could be pretty impossible."

"He's not alone." Daniel stood, speaking as if he needed to talk me down. "There are at least six of them and two of us."

"And the longer we wait, the worse those odds get!" I gestured to the door to remind him what else Mei had said. "Six looks good compared to thirty."

"It looks about the same to me." His voice sharpened.

I ignored it. "Maybe it's not what you planned, but we're here now! We have to get him before he gets us!"

"That's suicide."

"You're a pessimist."

"And you think you're a match for *six* of them?" he snapped. When I didn't contradict it, he shook his head and turned away. "Fine, *you* probably are. But I don't have magic fucking powers."

"Or a spine." A spark flared in my chest, sending heat through my limbs. "Typical. You're gunning for him until you actually have the chance to take him down. How very *Consilium*. I guess that's why you guys lost the war."

I spun around and made for the door, giving Daniel plenty of time to answer, to call me back.

He didn't.

Rage spilled over as I slammed the room door behind me. *I* hadn't gotten this close just to give up, to hunker down, hide and watch. I needed to do *something*. I needed to finally have this out with Aubrie.

I wished I'd thought to steal the car keys before storming out, but that thought dissipated when I caught sight of a familiar face in the car parked beside Grace's.

30

I HEADED TOWARD THE car where Zeb pressed himself lower in his seat, as if hoping not to be spotted. Tapping on the passenger-side window, I waved.

He looked at me, faced front for a moment as if he might ignore me, then gave in and rolled down the window.

"Hey!" I rested my elbows on the window, leaning in. "What are you doing here?"

"I, uh—"

"Want to give me a lift to Niagara?"

"To—" Zeb stared at me. "Where's Daniel?"

I thumbed over my shoulder toward the room, then reached inside to press the door lock button. Yanking the door open, I slid into the seat.

"Wait a minute!" Zeb protested.

Sitting in a car beside him gave me an unpleasant flashback to having my arms pinned over my head with duct tape, but if he tried that this time he'd find me a lot less malleable.

"Just drop me off," I said. "It won't take long. You can tell Danny you got stuck in traffic or something."

"He's not expecting me." He looked like he wished the words back as soon as he'd said them.

"Perfect." I put my seat belt on. "Let's go."

"Wait." Zeb studied my face, unable to ask his question. Finally, he sighed. "Look, is he okay?"

"Daniel? He's fine." I rolled my eyes at his uncertain expression and repeated, "He's *fine*." I ticked off on my fingers: "He's alive, he's conscious, and he's consciously chickening out."

Zeb continued to frown at me, fishing his phone out of the cup-holder. He dialed a number, putting it to his ear.

I sighed, unbuckling my seat belt and pushing the car door open. Loyal jackass.

"Hey," he said into the phone. "Hey, so, Grace sent me up after you." A pause, then, "Not far." He glanced sidelong at me. "An hour or so out, maybe. I'll give you a call when I get there."

I didn't realize I'd gotten my way until Zeb set the phone back in the cup-holder and shifted the car into gear.

Shutting the door, I re-buckled my seat belt, still startled that he hadn't ratted me out to Daniel. I couldn't help pointing out, "Like I *said*, he's fine. You're all so certain I'm going to hurt him again."

"That's because you have to say *again*." Zeb turned out of the parking lot and headed for the highway. "Where are we going?"

"Queen Victoria Hotel."

"Look it up." He gestured to the dashboard GPS screen.

I tapped on the screen, making it provide directions to downtown Niagara Falls.

"Why wouldn't Daniel drive you?" Zeb asked.

"Because he's a coward." I folded my arms, sinking down in my seat and trying to keep hold of my righteous indignation. Even I could hear that my tone lacked conviction.

Zeb gave a derisive response in what had to be French. I didn't know the word he used but I understood somebody calling bullshit on me.

"How would you know?" I snapped. "You weren't Consilium."

"He saved my life."

"From what?"

"A succubus." Zeb stared at the road.

"Damn." I'd never met one, but I'd heard enough nasty stories. "Where'd the thing find you?"

"At a bar." His expression told me it should have been obvious. "Elena. I should have known something was up because I'm not usually into women. But she had that Faerie thrall down, about to suck out my soul, or whatever it is they do—"

"Life force, I think?"

"Daniel and Olivier showed up and stopped her. She'd killed Olivier's brother and they were hunting her, I guess. You met Olivier at the warehouse—you punched him in the face. Aubrie's people killed him after you ran."

I didn't want to think about that. "What happened with your succubus?"

"By the time they got there, she'd gotten so deep in my head that I actually tried to save her, tried to *let* her kill me. She was all fangs and talons, but I didn't see it then." His expression said he didn't like revisiting the memory.

"She attacked them instead and they killed her," he said. "Then I got my mind back and wanted to know what the fuck happened, so I ended up here." He spread his hands on the steering wheel. "There you go. Almost murdered by a succubus. I don't recommend it."

"Could have been worse."

"See, that's *exactly* what Daniel said." Zeb watched me out of the corner of his eye as if awaiting an explosion of anger. "I think he still had a couple of broken ribs at the time, actually."

"Then he shouldn't have jumped into a fight." I didn't want to give Zeb the satisfaction of my shame, but I couldn't help sliding down a little in my seat. *Fighting the good fucking fight.*

"Your turn," Zeb said. "Where we going?"

I glanced out the window again, then had to admit: "Aubrie's there. At the hotel."

"Okay." He darted a glance in his rearview and started to change lanes back toward the right, intent on exiting and turning around.

"Hey!" I sat up straighter, gesturing for him to stay on the highway. "Look, you don't have to come in—you don't even have to wait for me! Just drop me off—please!"

The exit flew by. With a string of muttered expletives in French, Zeb let the car drift back into the left lane.

"You know he's the guy you're working *against*," I said. "You'd think you might be more eager to take him down."

Zeb snorted. "Is that what you're doing?"

"Somebody has to." I propped my boots against the dashboard, bristling when he laughed.

"I hope I never meet him face-to-face," he said. "You weren't in the warehouse that night he attacked. You didn't see what—" He stopped, clenched his jaw like it wasn't worth going on, and then finished, "You think Daniel's a coward for not going after him? I think you're a dumbass with a death wish."

That assessment sent an odd relief through me.

"Maybe," I said. "But we've got history."

31

By the time we reached Niagara Falls, I wanted to take Zeb's advice and turn around. Daniel was right: six of them might be more than I could handle. But I couldn't run. I'd come this far.

"There's the place." Zeb pointed through the windshield to a modern building with a lot of windows. We crept slowly along a busy street, the sidewalks packed with tourists.

"Pull around to the next block?" I didn't want Aubrie to see me coming if I could help it.

Tour buses blocked the entrance at the front of the hotel, so Zeb had to turn the corner anyway to idle at the curb. He frowned, tapping his fingers on the steering wheel. "This is a bad idea."

"Yeah, well, it's my bad idea." I shoved the door open without giving him a chance to continue.

I walked to the hotel with my head down, strode into the plush lobby and made a beeline for the elevator. The guy at the front desk looked up from his newspaper, but didn't greet me. As I waited for the elevator, I glanced at the clock behind his head. Just past two.

Up four floors, I headed down the hall, stopping at room 427. No chameleons blended into the wallpaper along the hall like Mei had warned. I knew what to look for: their bodies matched the colours of whatever they stood in front of perfectly—even their clothes changed—but they couldn't sink into the wall and lay flat.

I could have picked out the third dimension of a body pressed to the repeating wallpaper.

Turning to the door, my muscles itched to do something flashy, like directing the force of my gravity into a good kick that would knock it off its hinges. That would bring unwanted attention. Instead, I stood directly in front of the peephole, rapping my knuckles on the wood.

After a long pause, the deadbolt shot back. Aubrie didn't pull anything dumb like leaving the chain lock on. He faced me, door open, straight on.

My fury dissipated like a candle snuffed out. I ached for him to explain, put his arms around me and tell me the good reason he had for what he'd done to me. He must have had a plan he hadn't been able to tell me about—some way to get us out of the mess I'd put us in.

"Jude." He stepped back from the door to let me in, sounding pleased but not surprised. "It's good to see you."

"Can't say the same." A spark of anger tried to rally but it couldn't make my muscles move to punch him.

"I missed you." His tone seemed genuine. The words hurt.

"Shouldn't have thrown me off a balcony, I guess."

What looked like real regret moved across his face. No denial. No excuse. "Come in, will you?" he asked. "Let's not do this in the hallway."

Moving at his command came automatically, but he was right that I didn't want to hover in the hallway. I stepped inside, wary that he might try to grab me. A part of me that I hated still hoped it would be an embrace.

"I'm glad you came," he said.

"You shouldn't be." I jerked my chin toward the other side of the room. "I came to toss you out that window."

"I know." He flashed a brief smile. "But you haven't. Jude, I'm sorry."

A laugh and a sob mixed in my throat. He sounded sincere. I'd meant it too, more than I'd realized, blurting out those same words last night.

"Wow," I managed, "it really does suck to be on the other side of that."

Uncertainty slipped across Aubrie's face.

"I made a mistake," he said. "Hurting you, it was . . . a mistake. But you nearly compromised everything we'd been working for." He shook his head, drawing back. "It's my fault. I should have seen that conflict in you about Daniel. I should have been more careful with you."

"You mean you should have had him killed and those codes taken without telling me about it."

"In retrospect."

I stifled a bitter laugh at his honesty, but he wasn't wrong. If things had gone down that way, would I still be standing here, facing off with him, hating him? My doubt stung.

"You lied to me," I said, forcing myself away from that. "You never said smashing the worlds together was the endgame."

"Nothing's changed, Jude," he said. "My intent is the same as it's always been, the same as yours. There's an unknown wealth of power that they're keeping from us. We have a right to it. We're Faerie too. But they refuse to share because they find us *inferior*. This is the only way to force our claim."

I sucked in a breath to brace myself. "Getting our due was one thing. I didn't sign up to ruin both worlds."

"*Ruin* is a coward's take on what can be gained." Disdain crept across his face. "It's a refusal to see what we can *create* by bringing the worlds together. This world is dying by the day, cracking under the weight of humanity's short-sighted selfishness."

The venom in his voice startled me. "You think Faerie magic's going to clean up the oceans and turn the earth's temperature down a few degrees?"

"We have no idea what's possible. But the Faeries will stand back and do nothing unless we force their hand—unless we tie the fate of their world to ours."

"You throw humans and Faeries together with no warning and it will be a massacre," I said. "It's letting the tigers into the bunny cage! Humans are *prey*! This world doesn't even know that one exists! How are they supposed to fight back?"

"There will be casualties at first," Aubrie agreed, as if telling me it might rain. "It will take time to find a balance. But there's more to that power they're hiding than you know. There are spells to stop the Faeries, cripple them—magic there that can *defend* humans from their hunts and hunger. We just have to *get* to it."

"You want to let the Faeries in so you can use their magic against them?" It almost made sense. It almost sounded noble.

But he'd lied to me before. He'd tossed me aside as soon as I became inconvenient.

"How come you didn't have this wonderful, humanity-saving goal last winter when you told me we were grabbing magic they owed us?"

"I didn't think it would move you."

The answer rankled me, but he still wasn't wrong. "So, killing hundreds of people in two worlds three months ago was just a test run?"

"I didn't kill anyone." Aubrie recoiled. "I tried to remove the factions, invite some compromise—"

"We never talked about killing everybody."

"You feel guilty." He eyed me, surprised at the idea. "That war was between outdated, elite societies. The Court and the Consilium were bent on merely destroying each other, no matter the cost to anything around them. It had to end."

"You never told me we were *ending* them."

His voice sharpened. "Your pearl-clutching rings hollow given *you're* the one who murdered our Consilium director."

I loosened my fingers to keep my nails from digging into my palms. The about-face dodge, slapping the blame onto me when I raised a question, it felt too familiar now.

His words weren't convincing anymore. His plans had never been for us, for the rest of the half-Faeries living here, or to save humanity from supernatural predators. Aubrie wanted something for himself. He'd go through anyone to get it.

"Yeah, I killed Alan," I said. "But it wasn't for you. And you're not going to swing me back to thinking you're selfless. I've seen what happens when somebody doesn't get you what you want."

Aubrie moved closer. "Jude, you need to look past your anger to the importance of what we're doing."

"You want to sacrifice a bunch more people, mostly human people *you* find inferior, so you can get around the velvet rope and see what the magic club's like in the Faerie world. All this other garbage about fixing this world and defending humanity, it's just to blind everybody to your power grab."

"Who's gotten into your head?" He studied my face. "Are you parroting Miranda or Daniel now?"

Anger flared in my muscles. "Why do I have to be blindly following somebody?"

"That's what you do." Aubrie scowled down his nose at me, as if condescending to a five-year-old. The sudden sharpness made things much clearer—easier.

My fist hit his face while his found my stomach.

His blow sent me back into the wall, doubled over in pain. He had a supernatural driving force like a steel battering ram. The wall shook when I hit it.

A new man pulled himself out of the wall beside me. *Lesidhe.* A chameleon. I'd missed him blending into the white paint. I'd checked the hallway but not the room.

The door to an adjoining room slammed open. Two others bee-lined for me as I dodged the one who'd melted out of the wall next to me.

Only three. Where was the fourth Mei had warned about?

I went for the ceiling, bouncing off it to swing down onto the shoulders of the closest guy. My momentum yanked him down with me, both of us smashing into the other two to pull us into a pile on the floor.

One of the *lesidhe* gained his feet quicker than me. He reached down to grab me as I crawled out.

I rolled to one side, shooting to my hands and knees, diving through his legs.

The fourth caught me at the door, peeling away from the wall where he'd been hiding. A fist grasped my hair hard enough to yank me backwards and make me shriek. I grabbed the hand with both of mine as I dropped my gravity to make my body impossibly heavy.

It tugged him off-balance, breaking his grip on me. The floor creaked beneath us. I rushed to ease my power as I pulled away from him.

I tugged the door open, stumbling out into the hallway. A housekeeping cart sat there now, the employee herself standing behind it. She stared at me like a deer caught in headlights, halfway between lifting a cellphone to her ear. The fight had made some noise.

Behind her, the elevator was just closing. I ran to it, sticking my arm between the doors to make them jolt back open. Falling inside, I jabbed the button that made the doors slide shut. It didn't sound like I was being followed yet.

Safe in the elevator, I hunched over in pain and prodded my ribs for breaks. The ache didn't seem bad enough for that. Just bruised. I straightened up, pulling in a deep breath. For a guy who claimed to want me around, Aubrie'd hit hard.

I darted out the instant the doors opened to the lobby. Nobody waited for me there. I didn't stick around to see if that would change, dashing through the front doors into the sunlight. I dodged a car pulling to the curb, then slowed to a fast walk, making for the corner. A glance over my shoulder still showed no pursuers.

Not looking where I was going, I hit a person. I bounced back, mouth open to either swear or apologize, but stopped at a familiar pinched face ringed with blond hair.

The man's eyes widened. "Of course it'd be you."

It was the siren from the safehouse—somehow. I'd punched a wispy woman with long, blonde hair in the kitchen, and even though this figure looked like a taller man with a buzz cut, the eyes were the same. The air of disgusted menace was the same.

Soren the siren.

Before I could swing a fist, a different kind of siren made us both tense. Police cars turned down the block, lights flashing.

Soren almost yanked me off my feet as he tugged me further down the sidewalk, into the shadow of a tree. He shoved me onto a bench, perching beside me and craning his neck to watch two police cruisers pull up in front of the hotel. Four cops headed inside.

"Jude?"

I almost leapt into the siren's lap when the second, calmer voice said my name.

A woman stood beside the bench. She definitely hadn't been there a second ago when we'd arrived. Shifting colours of blue leached from the roots of her hair into the black strands.

"You're the messenger—Ilse." I recognized her from the sylph-vid. "How do you know—?"

"Let me tell the others it's off." She looked down the sidewalk to the flashing lights at the hotel entrance.

"No." Soren got to his feet, one hand extended to stop her. "It's not off. Just . . . just give me five minutes. I'll sing them to sleep."

"Aubrie and his people take too much of your energy." Ilse shook her head, black and blue curls swaying against her cheeks as she made a quick gesture with her hands, like drawing a letter in the air. "You won't be able to keep both them and the police under at the same time. We can't have more incidents visible to human eyes. The Mab's orders were clear. We're still cleaning up videos of the dragon in Montreal."

That seemed directed at me, but I wasn't about to apologize for Mei.

"The plan's still viable," Soren said. "I can knock out everybody in that lobby and—"

"No." Ilse's mild tone brooked no argument.

I turned to follow her eyes. Two police officers emerged from the hotel, scanning the area. Aubrie'd probably told them I'd attacked him. He'd spin it however he needed to keep himself out of the spotlight, same as always. Bitter anger buzzed in my chest.

"Jude, I believe it would be best if you came with us," Ilse said.

Hide with the Faeries who'd threatened to call the cops on me or run from the actual police ten metres away? I took a quick look around the area. Too bad I didn't remember what Zeb's car had looked like. Not that he'd probably stuck around.

I gestured for Ilse to lead on.

32

ILSE TOOK US DOWN a block before turning into an alley. Past a couple of dumpsters, she put a hand on a door that seemed to lead into the hotel's kitchen, then pulled it open to reveal the familiar tree wallpaper of the Faerie house the same way Miranda had at the hospital.

Soren stalked past me through the door. Ignoring his behaviour, Ilse gestured me inside with a polite smile.

As she closed the door behind us, it opened again, letting in Abe and a handful of unfamiliar people. The cowboy paused when he saw me. His eyes flickered to Ilse. "What went wrong?"

"You're looking at her." Soren nodded to me.

"Nice to see you again, darlin'." Abe stepped aside, letting three others brush past him. One headed upstairs and two turned right to go into the living room.

"There were six of you?" I asked, counting, "and you held off going after Aubrie? Why?"

Abe turned to Ilse for the answer.

She didn't falter. "There were four police officers, plus hotel staff and any other guests who came out to check. Jude's unanticipated arrival had already made Aubrie attentive, so, Soren's song wouldn't have worked as well. In addition, we didn't have anyone else to perform diffusion to help him."

"I could have dropped all of them *without* help," Soren put in.

"Does Aubrie have the grymoire?" Abe asked me. "Did you see it up there?"

Startled, I had to go with Mei's answer. I didn't trust the ex-dragon, but her disdain for the spellbook made me think she hadn't been lying on that count. "I don't know what it looks like, but from what I've heard, no."

"And your human?" Soren asked. "Did he go up there with you? Does Aubrie have him now?"

"No." The insinuation stung and I glared at him.

"There," Abe said, as if to placate the siren. "Aubrie's still lacking tools. We have time."

Soren rolled his eyes as slowly and obviously as he could, glaring at Abe then Ilse in turn. He gave me a hint of it for good measure as he stalked up the stairs. "Fucking diplomats."

Abe moved past me, lifting a hand to gesture me toward the empty kitchen. Ilse came with us.

Catching sight of the giant tree out the window over the sink as we reached the kitchen, I asked, "Does this place have the same backyard no matter what city you're in?"

"Always dusk," Abe agreed, glancing outside. "Wouldn't mind a different view."

"Especially for a place that moves all over the world. Rip-off." I ran a hand back through my hair, hanging loose around my shoulders then tried half-heartedly to twist it into a knot at the nape of my neck.

"Here." Ilse opened the nearest drawer, withdrawing something and offering it to me.

What was I supposed to say to the long, white satin ribbon in her hand? When I didn't take it, she prompted, "Shall I bind your hair back for you?"

"No . . . thank you?" The last two words came almost automatically in response to her bizarre offer. "Look, are you . . . okay?"

She'd spent a long time in that iron room, if I remembered right, and I'd felt shitty after spending just a couple of hours there.

"How kind of you to ask." She beamed. "I've fed well and am quite recovered, thank you."

The word *fed* made me tense but I didn't ask for details and she didn't offer any. "How do you know me?" I asked her, then glanced to Abe, demanding, "Did she watch *me* on some sylph video?"

The cowboy leaned back against the counter, lifting one finger to tilt his hat back on his head so I could see his face better. "What happened in Niagara?"

Dodging the question. "You act like I'm still working for you."

"Aren't you?"

"Haven't gotten a paycheque."

Abe reached into his back pocket, pulling out a wallet and withdrawing three twenties.

I hesitated before taking them. "This isn't twenty thousand dollars."

"You didn't get the spell we asked for."

"I'm not going to."

"Fair enough. 'Til you figure out where you want to stand, keep the money."

I stuffed the money into my pocket before he could reconsider.

He flashed a brief smile and prompted again, "Now, what happened in Niagara?" He must have been reading me because he added, "You all right?"

"Yeah." I didn't want to tell him that I'd gotten sidetracked in my revenge plan by expecting Aubrie to apologize, to explain, to make everything normal again instead of so much worse. "Aubrie gave me his usual bullshit about you guys hiding magic over there and how it's unfair that we don't have access." I slid my hands into my pockets. I hated turning the conversation over in my head. "He insinuated you could, like, fix the climate crisis or something. Can you?"

"Wouldn't know." Abe glanced to Ilse.

She frowned at him, then at me. "That's absurd."

I didn't totally believe her. Aubrie's voice in my head wouldn't let me. Consilium training didn't help either. *Faeries lie.*

Abe got my attention.

"Where's Daniel in all this? Thought you were running with him now." The words held no resentment. It looked like he wasn't holding that earlier escape against me.

"Stop trying to weasel information out of me."

"Jude, he's not safe out there. It won't be anything like his last visit."

"That's not going to convince Daniel," I said, "and I'm not going to fight him again."

"You're still trying to atone by letting him take a shot at you?"

That reminded me of Abe's earlier insinuation that Daniel could hurt me. Pieces fell into place. He could have, but he'd done the spell on somebody else instead. That's why he'd had his phone out during Mei's transformation. Whatever key the incantation had been meant to produce by using up her Faerie half must have actually appeared on her back.

"He already got the translation key for your stupid book," I said, flopping into a chair at the table.

"How?" Abe studied me harder, as if he'd missed something.

"Aubrie's dragon, Mei. Dragon no more. She let him paint it on her."

"She *let* him?" This came from a shocked Ilse.

"She insisted on it." The thought still made me uneasy.

Ilse blinked at the floor tile, looking like she might burst into furious tears. Her voice came out vehement, disgusted: "A *human* availing themselves to that kind of magic is . . . it's unnatural."

Abe didn't seem quite as concerned. "Where is he now?"

"Mei said Aubrie hasn't got the book." I tried to keep from refusing his question outright. "And the key's worthless unless he finds it. Does anyone know where it is?"

The cowboy sighed and looked away. "Your father hid it."

That answer settled on my shoulders like lead. The memory of the man in the photo with my teenage mother came back to me—a man I'd never met with a face I wished I'd never seen. A man who shared that face with a strange woman who'd paid my hospital bills, taken care of my comatose body, sheltered me, all without giving any decent explanation. A strange woman who was the last surviving heir to the Faerie dynasty.

"Never met the guy." I fought to keep my voice steady. "I don't even know his name."

"Joshua. Miranda's brother."

Having it confirmed didn't make me feel any better. "Does that make me a Faerie princess?"

"It's not really a title that we—" Ilse stopped when she saw my face. "Oh. That was a rhetorical question?"

"It was a joke," I said, chest tight again. "This is all a fucking joke."

Ilse started, "I assure you that it's—" but Abe put up a gentle hand to stop her.

I glared at him. "So that's why Miranda took care of me in the hospital. Because her brother took something you think I have."

"You underestimate her," he said.

"Keeps me from being disappointed." I felt jittery, too big for my skin. I wanted to grab the door handle and dart outside. Run.

Instead, I demanded, "So why can't you ask *him* where it is? He's dead?"

"Disappeared about fifteen years ago." The cowboy took his hat off and held it in his hands in a weird gesture of something like respect for my father's memory. "Can't think of anyplace he could be alive that we wouldn't find him."

"Too bad he hid your book first." I studied the wood grains in the table and the hairs on my arms. I hadn't cared about my father since turning ten years old and realizing life didn't work like the movies, where missing people turn up on your doorstep if you wish on enough twinkling stars. It wasn't worth starting again now.

"The book isn't large," Ilse said. "Hardcover." She sat down at the table beside me, an instant from grasping my hand. "One of my sources says it was bound in blue fabric. I have notes."

"I didn't even know the asshole's name," I told her, baffled. "I definitely didn't get any of his books. If he left anything, my mom burned it. Maybe she burned your grim-thing. Problem solved."

Ilse shook her head, making the blue in her hair dance under the kitchen light. "Something of such great power can't be destroyed that easily."

"Convenient that it can be *lost* so easily."

"It wasn't lost. I'm afraid he hid it."

"Why'd he bring it over here at all?"

"Seems he was looking for a way to close the portals between the worlds," Abe said.

I tensed.

"That's what the Consilium wanted to do." It couldn't be a coincidence.

The cowboy agreed. "And that's why Miranda sent Aubrie there to go double-agent."

"Wait, Miranda and *Aubrie*?" The thought didn't jibe. "No wonder there's no Faerie military force over here getting ready to take him out."

"*That* is uncharitable," Ilse said, an edge creeping into her mild tone again. "The Mab broke with Aubrie long ago. She doesn't condone this dangerous nonsense about merging the worlds—none of us do."

"Then why did she send you to steal the incantation?"

"To secure it against him."

"She's not the Mab everybody in her world wanted," Abe cut in. "Not everybody's ready to fall in line behind her, crown or not. So, methods to prevent this catastrophe have been a little unorthodox."

"Nobody in Faerieland's concerned about Aubrie merging the spheres?" I answered my own question: "Why would they be? They get more space and free run of a new world."

Ilse gave me a disapproving look I barely caught.

Abe sighed. "Aubrie hasn't got the book he needs. That's enough proof for some that there's no threat. And for others, well, he's part-human. They don't think he's dangerous."

"That's what he's pissed about," I said.

"It's what he's counting on," another voice said from the kitchen doorway.

33

I JUMPED WHEN ILSE leapt to her feet. Abe straightened up, removing his hat and holding it against his thigh.

"I didn't expect to find you here." Miranda faced me from the kitchen doorway, imposing and statuesque.

I stood more slowly than the other two. "You want me to leave?"

"Of course not."

"Of course not," I echoed her. "Otherwise you wouldn't have threatened me with that letter opener, to get you something you didn't even need."

Despite Abe's insistence that Miranda wasn't trying to use me to find hidden treasure, I added, "You didn't look out for me for those three coma months because I can climb walls or because I was in the Consilium, *Auntie*. You probably think I magically know the location of this book too!"

I gestured to Ilse, who averted her gaze.

Miranda's expression tinged with uncertainty. "The book? No."

"Then why?"

"Because you're our blood, human or not, and we can't lose any more of it."

Not a warm way to acknowledge our relation.

"So why didn't you tell me I was family?" I demanded. "I asked you before why you took care of me. That might have been a good time, rather than threatening me."

"It wasn't."

"Because you wanted me to fuck Daniel over again."

"Abe told me what happened with Soren." Miranda's gaze flickered over my shoulder to the cowboy and then back. "That wasn't my intent."

"Don't apologize to me," I said. "I'm not the one who got sliced up."

Miranda sharpened her tone to match my own. "Bring your human here, then. I'll issue a formal apology."

"Oh, yeah, Daniel'd love that. He's *super* into apologies lately."

We glared at each other, her vivid green eyes boring into me.

Without breaking her stare, Miranda lifted her chin. "Bring him here. I'll give you my word that he won't be hurt again."

Too simple a promise. Too easy. There was always a catch to a Faerie bargain. I couldn't help the sarcasm that rose to my voice. "Meaning you'll kill him painlessly?"

A flash of amusement crossed my aunt's features, flattening almost immediately into haughty disinterest. "The simplest remedy to my current situation is indeed to kill your friend and ensure that incantation is entirely lost to this world," she agreed. "Yet Abe's informed me that it's critical to you that Cain remain unharmed, so I am open to negotiation."

Something twisted in my gut. It felt hard to breathe. *Abe's informed me.*

"Since when do you give a shit what I want?" I shot a glare over my shoulder to add, "And Abe told you *what*?" Before the cowboy could offer a defence, I turned on him. "You asshole! Pretending you're trustworthy, that you're like me—oh, *we're both part-human, we should be friends.* Then you read my emotions and pass it all on so she knows how exactly to fuck with me, huh?"

"Jude," Abe started.

I turned my back to him, facing Miranda again. "What did he say? Let's hear it."

She studied my face as if she might not go on. Instead, she said, "When you woke up, we knew you'd want to run. We didn't have the resources to protect you at a distance. We had to keep you nearby."

"Telling me the actual truth wasn't an option?"

"You don't respond to what's in your best interest." Miranda's brow furrowed. "So Abe found something you would respond to."

"Daniel." I fought the heat rushing through my skin. "Guilt."

"Clearly it wasn't enough."

"So you pulled out the letter opener." The memory of it made me feel sick. The idea that she'd never meant to use it struck me even harder, cementing the anger in my blood. "Sending me to Daniel for information you knew he wouldn't give up wasn't just bullshit to find *him*, it was bullshit to manipulate me." I turned to put the guess to Abe. "What'd you do, sit in my hospital room while I came to and whisper names into my ear until you got the emotional reaction you wanted?"

The cowboy pressed his hat against his thigh and met my eyes, saying nothing.

"Fuck this." I shoved past Miranda to make for the front door. She had nothing over me. The letter opener was useless—she'd all but admitted she wouldn't use it against me. She couldn't keep me here.

Pressing a hand against the painted wood, I hissed, "Take me to the beach," and shoved it open.

I dashed down a set of concrete steps and found myself in the golden late afternoon sun on sand, waves crashing to my right. I looked back at the door I'd emerged from to find a small white clapboard building with green and red trim and what looked like a lifeguard chair rising beside it.

Kids splashed in the water near the shore, some of them swimming and jumping in the gentle waves while their parents basked on towels. The sand wasn't soft and white, but grey and rocky. A cool breeze blew in off the sparkling water, setting a familiar red and white flag flapping above the lifeguard seat. The city skyline rose in the distance beyond it.

Goddamn it, how was I back in Toronto?

Either the Faerie house had a twisted sense of humour or it had just taken me to the closest beach from our origin that had a building with a door it could use. *Should have specified.*

I stalked away from Lake Ontario, boots sinking heavily into the sand until I made it up onto the grass and a park trail. I glanced over my shoulder every few seconds to check for Faeries emerging from the lifeguard station, but nobody chased me.

I followed the trail to the nearest road, dodging around kids on scooters and families out for an afternoon walk. Why had I trusted Abe? He read emotions. He'd put me through this whole shitty reunion with Daniel for what? Just to keep me nearby for some nefarious purpose of his queen. My aunt. Who couldn't tell me what was going on because she'd already decided I was a fuck-up.

Not like she was wrong. But I should have known better than to trust her, or to trust Abe. *Faeries lie.* Everybody used you for what they needed. Not a new lesson, just one I couldn't make stick.

I trekked up through a park until I found a bus turnaround. Good, the house hadn't dumped me on the islands downtown. I wasn't in the mood to figure out a ferry, though at least that would have put me closer to an airport. With a whopping sixty dollars in my pocket, so never mind. I could talk myself onto a bus, not so much a plane.

Waiting at the stop alongside two families with strollers, I checked again over my shoulder to be certain the Faeries still hadn't followed. I had no real way to fight them if they did, but the fury pent up in my chest said I would try.

A bright pink flyer taped to the side of the bus shelter caught my eye. Car for sale. Price nowhere near the cash I had in my pocket. A blue one below it advertised a poetry slam. My eyes rolled automatically. My mom had always been nutty about poetry—the more melodramatic, the better. Sylvia Plath had been her favourite, the inspiration for my middle name. She'd had a whole book of depressing poems and she must have read me every line out of it fifty times before I was old enough to sneak out at night.

I could almost see her manicured pink nails opening that old book.

Shit. That book of poems, a thin hardback with a blue cover, had been a present from my father. Mom had admitted that once under the heavy influence of vodka and denied it every other time I asked.

Another exhausting weight settled on my shoulders.

34

"You planning to stay here?" Zeb took a dubious look around the motel room from the chair he'd sprawled in by the door.

"No," Daniel said, then amended, "I don't know."

"We can ditch the rental and take your sister's car." Zeb hesitated, propping his feet onto the bed in the same position Jude had held earlier. "Or maybe it's better to ditch her car and take the rental. They're both traceable."

Daniel hardly heard the deliberation. "He's here for a reason."

"You mean Aubrie?"

"Yes." He'd been thinking about it since Jude's departure, but he hadn't come to any satisfactory answers. Why would Aubrie have come here without the book? He couldn't perform his spell without it, and he wasn't any safer from the Court, no matter what Mei thought. So Aubrie either had the book or knew where it was.

Zeb broke back into his thoughts. "I took Jude to Niagara Falls."

"You did what?" Daniel jerked his head up to stare at his friend. He didn't think he could have heard wrong.

"I was in the parking lot here and she came storming out. I think she was going to steal Grace's car, but she saw me first. She's . . . persistent." Zeb shifted in the chair, moving his feet from the bed to the floor to lean forward.

"I assumed somebody should know what she was up to, right?"

"So you just drove her down to Niagara? To the Queen Victoria Hotel?"

"Yeah."

"And when you called me?"

"Checking that she hadn't, like, left you in pieces somewhere." Zeb winced, recognizing his lack of tact too late.

That reminder still stung. "Well, thanks."

"*Crisse*, I don't know if she has that mind control shit down like Elena did. You didn't want her around in the first place, then *whatever* went down after the museum, and then you're driving up here with her alone. Seemed like that thrall they do."

The word brought Daniel a flash of Jude pressed against him on the bed, tugging his shirt up. It dissolved into a flood of self-contempt that leached into his sharp rebuke: "It's not—Jude can't *thrall*."

"That's what we all say, man."

The frustration in Zeb's tone made him regret snapping. He wasn't mad at Zeb. Jude had played them both. That was his own fault. He'd known better than to bring her along, but he'd been weak. He hadn't wanted to make that drive by himself, spring a potential trap and get so close to Aubrie without backup. Maybe he'd taken Mei's sarcastic quip about a bodyguard too seriously.

Jude was neither of those things. Last winter, she'd used him as a cover, propped their relationship up as a facade against the Consilium to hide her true motives from prying eyes. Last night, he'd just been somebody with easy access to a car.

And this morning . . . probably just trying to win him over so that he'd run straight into a nest of Antagonists for her. He shouldn't have kissed her, shouldn't have given into her persuasion, but he'd wanted the distraction too much, the momentary dip back into his naive past-self.

Daniel took a breath to ease the knot that had tightened in his chest. He made his tone even again to prompt for the rest of his friend's story. "So you took her to Niagara."

"To the hotel, yeah. She went inside. I kept an eye on the door, called Grace." Zeb's expression turned guilty again at that admission. "She'd told me to follow Jude if you guys parted."

"You work for my sister now?"

"She's the only one telling me shit anymore."

"Telling you I'm enthralled and sending you to spy on me."

"As someone who's *been* enthralled, fuck you." Zeb glared. Then his shoulders slumped. "I should have told you first thing about why she sent me."

"I know my sister. It wasn't hard to guess." Daniel sighed. "I'm sorry. I'm being an asshole."

Zeb inclined his head to grant that, sinking back into his chair. "You keep me in the loop from now on, we'll call it even."

"I'll work on it." Daniel couldn't bring himself to make an empty promise.

Zeb gave him a dubious look but seemed to accept the answer anyway. He lifted the curtain over his shoulder to glance outside, as if turning his thoughts back to the debate on which car to take when they left.

Daniel pulled up a browser on his phone to search for breaking news about a recent attack or murder in Niagara Falls. Part of him still suspected Jude had gone into that hotel looking to get back into Aubrie's good graces, but she *had* seemed intent on revenge. Still, he had to proceed as though Aubrie were still a threat until he knew otherwise for certain.

"Whoa, nice." Zeb pushed the curtain back to see better. "Don't see too many hats like that this far north."

"What?" Daniel froze.

"This guy out here has an actual cowboy hat. What do they call those, something gallon . . . ?"

"Close the curtains." Daniel shoved his phone into his back pocket and went for the tool bag from Gracie's car. He unzipped it and pulled out the contents: a flashlight—heavy but too short to be an effective weapon, a telescoping lug wrench—steel, as well as a handful of chemical road flares, and finally a rusted cast-iron, open-ended wrench.

"Every time I think it can't get weirder." Zeb stared at the assortment and stood up without argument.

In the bathroom, Daniel pried the window screen out of the frame. He hadn't considered the Court coming after him again, although he should have. He'd been more focused on Aubrie and the grymoire. He remembered the man in the cowboy hat from Jude's description, though he couldn't bring up a name. An empath and a healer, and the silhouette who'd rescued him from the siren with the knife in the basement of that house. That in itself didn't make the cowboy trustworthy.

He grabbed a flare and the lug wrench, then passed Zeb the cast-iron wrench and gestured for him crawl out through the open window first. The smaller man complied, stepping up onto the closed toilet to hoist himself through and dropping into the narrow walkway between buildings.

Knocking came at the front door, making Daniel turn and crane his neck to see that the chain lock wasn't attached. At least Zeb had dead-bolted the door behind him when he'd arrived ten minutes earlier.

A shout from outside made him whirl back around to the window. He climbed onto the toilet to peer out.

In the narrow walkway between buildings, a familiar, spiky-haired man in a leather jacket had Zeb pressed against the wall. The pixie from the restaurant in Montreal. How—?

The pixie stepped back, meeting Daniel's eyes with a sharp-toothed grin as he released his captive and revealed a bloody switchblade.

Zeb crumpled to the sidewalk, groaning. The wrench clanged against the cement and the pixie kicked it away with his boot before bursting into a cascade of glitter. It drew together to swarm like a hoard of angry bees straight up at the window.

Daniel jerked back, slipping off his perch. He managed to stay upright as he hit the floor, stumbling into the wall. He dropped the lug wrench, opting for the road flare instead. Yanking the cap off, he struck it against the tip of the flare and ignited it. He thrust it at the sparkling cloud, forcing the glitter to split around the spitting flame.

In the other room, the front door shook and slammed open. Someone shouted. Daniel couldn't discern the sound fast enough to translate the words—a command or a spell in the Antagonist language.

He lowered the flare when the pixie laughed.

"Your pronunciation's shit." The spiky-haired creature floated beside the window in a shimmering form. His head left a glimmering trail in the air as he looked from Daniel to the newcomer in the cowboy hat, who now stood in the bathroom doorway. Finally, he bared his undulating teeth, growling in what was probably meant to be a warning. It sounded more like frustration. Rather than materializing and attacking, he came apart again and spiralled out the window.

Daniel stared at the place where he'd been. He shook himself out of the daze, turning the flare on the cowboy, who raised his hands in surrender.

"Not here to fight," the newcomer said, nodding to the window where the pixie had disappeared, "all evidence to the contrary."

"Prove it." Daniel moved away from him, back to the window. It wasn't enough space to feel safe, but he had no choice. He tossed the flare into the porcelain sink, then stepped onto the toilet again and pushed himself through the window.

He landed hard enough on one ankle to make it ache, but forgot the pain seeing Zeb slumped against the wall.

His friend had one hand pressed loosely to the left of his stomach, against a blossom of red on his blue shirt.

"*Tabarnak*," Zeb wheezed, blinking to focus on Daniel. Not in enough pain to swear in Spanish or else in too much to risk his *abuela*'s warning.

Daniel pushed Zeb's hand more tightly against the wound in his side, holding it there as best he could while juggling his cell in the other hand to dial 9-1-1. Unbidden, his mind drew up unwelcome images of the bodies at the warehouse, Gregory and Marc.

"9-1-1, what's your emergency?"

"My friend's hurt—he's been stabbed."

"Okay. Where are you?"

"Behind the Valu-Lodge. Off highway . . . " What the hell road had they driven in on? He ought to remember. He'd been driving.

"I know the place," the dispatcher said. "I'm sending an ambulance. Is your friend conscious? Can he speak to you?"

"Yes. He's awake." Daniel pressed harder on Zeb's hand, trying to stop the flow of blood.

"Where is he injured?"

"He—" Daniel tensed, breaking off as a shadow fell over them.

The cowboy stood at the mouth of the walkway between the buildings. He approached, hands still held out in surrender.

"I can help," he said. "You remember me? Abe." He seemed to read an affirmative and repeated, "I can help him."

Daniel hesitated, frozen, then forced his muscles to loosen. He slid to one side, allowing the cowboy to kneel beside him.

The other man lifted Zeb's hand and spread the hole in his t-shirt carefully to check the wound. "That's 9-1-1?" He nodded to Daniel's phone, where the dispatcher was still trying to get Daniel's attention. "Stay on with 'em. It took me an hour to heal you."

Had it only been an hour in that basement? The pain had blurred into an incoherent chaos that his mind wouldn't let him dredge back up in detail, but the agony of healing had seemed to go on forever.

"Sir? Hey!" The dispatcher on the phone got his attention again. "Is someone else there with you? Are you in a secure location?"

"No. Yes." Daniel didn't know which answer made more sense.

"You said your friend was stabbed. Did you see who stabbed him? Is that person still nearby?"

"No. We're—" The word *safe* didn't seem to apply. "—alone."

Abe had both hands over Zeb's wound. He remained frozen like a statue, head bowed.

"Who's this guy?" Zeb's voice came out weak. He struggled to focus on Daniel through half-lidded eyes. Then he hissed in pain, lifting both arms to try and shove Abe away. They fell to his sides as the sound from his throat turned to a low moan.

On the phone against Daniel's ear, the dispatcher said something else. Daniel fought to pay attention. "What?"

"Can you tell me what happened?"

"No. I don't know. I didn't see it." The lies came easily. It sent a flood of calm through him.

Beside him, the cowboy relaxed, tilting an ear back at the sound of distant sirens. He looked once more to his hands, covered in blood. "Not enough time," he said, "but I've got a few of the internal bits knitting back together."

"Bits?" Zeb echoed the word, panting in exertion. His eyes moved from the cowboy to Daniel, no longer fully focused.

Getting up, Abe started to brush the blood from his hands, then stopped before wiping it on his jeans.

"I hear the ambulance," Daniel told the dispatcher. "Thanks." He hung up and shoved his phone into his back pocket, wanting both hands free to fight if it came to that.

The cast-iron wrench was too far away, down the alley where the pixie had kicked it.

"He's got a good chance." Abe nodded down at Zeb, then toward the end of the walkway, where the sirens had grown louder. "They'll scoop him up, finish patching the wound. You need to come with me."

"The hell I do."

"I give you my word you'll be safe. No spells, nothing funny. Won't see Soren again." The cowboy eyed him as if he might continue in the same vein, then came to another conclusion when red flashing lights shone through from the front parking lot onto the wall behind them. "Fine," he said. "You want to go with him to the hospital? We'll go to the hospital."

"*You* are not coming with us."

"Don't see as you've got much of a choice."

Daniel didn't have the patience to call the Antagonist's bluff with Zeb bleeding on the ground. He moved to flag the paramedics down through the window as they peered into the motel room.

35

"AFTER THE STUNNING AMOUNT of forethought it took to slip into the trunk of the car that dropped Jude off, you managed to find Daniel nearby and you *ran*?" Aubrie summed up the clipped story he'd dragged out of Jasper.

The pixie rested his forehead against the hotel room window. He looked winded, eyes fixed but unfocused on the street four stories below. Getting the twenty kilometres back from St. Catharines without a car, in powder-form, had likely been more taxing than his ride there.

"I told you, some Court bastards showed up." Jasper didn't turn his head, voice sullen.

"How many?"

"Enough."

Aubrie's annoyance piqued at the evasive answer. The pair of pixies had always been an effective team, but Jasper solo proved significantly less so. He'd been dour, unmotivated and snappish since Pru's death.

Digging his fingers into the smaller man's shoulder, Aubrie exerted half the force of his strength to show his displeasure. "Enough that now *the Court* has the incantation?"

Jasper sank down before him, trying unsuccessfully to twist out of the grip. "I'm sorry! Goddamn it, let go! It was one! There was one goddamn cowboy there!"

Aubrie loosened his hand, letting the pixie crawl to the other side of the window.

Jasper straightened, rolling his shoulder with some difficulty. "I didn't know what he could do. He tried to pull me together with a spell, make me solid."

"Tried?"

"Didn't take. Knocked me back a little is all." The pixie shrugged, brushing off his leather jacket. "Guess he didn't speak the language well enough."

"So, you ran from one Court operative who couldn't even command a full spell, and a human? Yes, clearly you were out-matched."

Jasper glowered. "If the Court's got your human, what's it matter? You found that asshole who can sniff out the Mab's house. Cain'll be easier to find if he's there."

"He'll be dead, and the incantation lost." Though Jasper's information gave Aubrie hope. Daniel had thus far proven annoyingly lucky. Against just Abe—the only person associated with Miranda's Court that fit the description 'cowboy'—there was a good chance he'd escaped.

Why would Miranda have sent someone so useless as the healer after her incantation? She'd never been stupid, nor merciful.

Jasper's phone beeped as the pixie arranged his hair spikes in the window's reflection. He pulled it from his pocket and glanced at the screen. "My buddy's downstairs," he said. "The shapeshifter."

Aubrie'd forgotten he'd asked Jasper to recruit the man. It almost didn't matter now, after this latest debacle. Still, best to proceed as if the Court hadn't intruded on the chase and the incantation were still reachable. "Can he shift sympathetically?"

"You're looking for somebody *nice*?"

Holding himself in check at the pixie's ignorance, Aubrie asked, "Can he take a form by simply *seeing* the intended target? Amateur shapeshifters work contagious spells. They need personal belongings to start, like blood or hair."

"He just looks at you and changes."

"Bring him up, then."

Once the pixie had slunk out the door, Aubrie's eyes wandered to the imprint in the wall where Jude had struck it earlier that afternoon. She'd been worth ten of Jasper, back when she'd been loyal.

He rested a hand on the back of the desk chair. He should have handled her visit better, made her stay and hear him out until she fully understood. Seeing her face-to-face again had reminded him how much he liked having her around. She had a certain bluntness that he'd always appreciated.

How was it that even *she* wouldn't hear him out, wouldn't try to understand what he wanted? He'd expected it from Miranda, even from Daniel—they were already set against him for other petty reasons—but he'd always had a rapport with Jude.

She was angry that he'd nearly killed her. She did have a right to that. It had been a mistake, a rash moment of anger. He regretted it. Jude held grudges, to her detriment. She would come around.

A quick rap on the door brought the arrival of Jasper's friend. The pixie didn't bother introducing them, knowing well enough to just get out. His friend looked like a ghost, white skin and white hair, clothes hanging off his skeletal body.

A blank canvas. Hasn't really got a form of his own. Aubrie took up the chair at the desk.

"How close do you need to be to duplicate the form?" he asked, propping one elbow on the desk and resting his chin against his hand.

"It's not just about taking on a form, it's taking on the persona." The shapeshifter's voice belied a confidence that his stance did not. "Forms I can do from memory—give me a photo and a voicemail message. Personal details require some familiarity."

"We're short on time. This target is gullible. Show me something."

The man morphed, shrinking.

Aubrie faced Jasper. The shapeshifter had mimicked the pixie perfectly, down to the leather jacket torn on one sleeve, the uneven spikes of hair Jasper spent so much time on, and the slouch: shoulders and neck thrust forward at an angle that always looked painful to hold for so long.

"He doesn't like it when I mirror him. Sometimes I do it to mess with him." The quick, sharp voice and the vicious grin that accompanied it were both Jasper's.

A sharp tap at the door interrupted them. Aubrie nearly snapped when the real Jasper stuck his head in without waiting for a response. He stopped at the uncharacteristic shaken expression on the pixie's face.

"Mei's here." Jasper stepped aside.

She stood behind him, her gaze on the floor, then lifted her head.

Aubrie caught his breath when he met her eyes.

"Get out." He included both the shapeshifter and Jasper in the command. They scrambled out, leaving him alone with Mei.

"What happened?" he asked. Heat flooded his limbs as he laid out the chain of events without being told. "The incantation. Daniel used it on you." He could barely move, frozen with rage. "Where is he? I'll tear him apart!" He should have killed the boy after Jude failed to do so. He should have annihilated the entire family.

"It was *my* choice!" Mei's sharp voice cut through his rage. "I went to him!"

Aubrie stared at her, struggling to make sense of the words. A new rage surged through him. He closed a hand around her wrist, yanking her toward him.

"You did this," he said. "You *chose* this?"

"Yes!" Mei tried to free herself from his grasp and failed. "I don't want any part of this anymore—" her voice caught but she managed to finish, "—or you."

"You useless, selfish—" He couldn't find a word strong enough. He wrapped his other hand around her slender throat.

"Wait!" Mei lifted her shoulders as if that might dislodge his fingers. "I have the key."

Aubrie eased his grip. The strain on her face told him the toll the incantation had taken. She'd changed: pale and ill, only on her feet by sheer will. The conversion she'd undergone was probably killing her anyway.

She tried again to look calm, twisting her wrist in his hand to make him release her. "I felt it on my skin when it appeared," she said. "I can still feel it. It burns." She made a face that was probably meant to be a self-deprecating smile but came out a grimace. "I don't even know the goddamn runes but I could write them from memory now. I'll write them for you."

"You're no longer trustworthy. Why should I believe you?"

"I didn't have to come here. I want to go home." Mei took a shaky step back, her eyes fixed on his face. "I don't want to have to run from you."

"Why would you let him do this to you?" Aubrie tightened his jaw when he heard his voice break at the question. "Just to get away from me?"

"To get away from the dragon."

"I don't understand." Disappointment flooded him, the initial rage replaced by disgust. She'd thrown away the most precious part of herself like it was nothing. How had he never seen her true face?

"I didn't think you would." Mei sighed. "But I've gotten all of us what we want. You and Daniel can have this useless goddamn key and keep fighting over a book that *doesn't exist*, and I never have to hear about it again."

Her sarcasm seemed almost comical, so desperate and terrified.

"And when I do find this book you don't believe in—when I merge the spheres?" Aubrie prompted. "You're human now. You're nothing. You won't have your old life then. You won't survive."

"I'll take my chances," she said.

She didn't believe in him. Maybe she never had. She'd never liked his plan for remaking the world and she'd never been shy in her disdain for having his attention away from her, but she'd always been by his side.

Lying. Not a dragon, a snake. Holding onto someone more powerful for her own survival until she could find a way she thought was out. Another twinge of revulsion ran through him at her new vulnerability, at her dull brown eyes.

Mei drew a deep breath, still trembling. "Do we have a deal, Spencer? I give you the key and you let me go home?"

"You'll give it to me," Aubrie agreed, "and you'll stay until we know it works."

"That book doesn't exist!" Mei snapped. "Your *old friend* made it up to fuck with you!"

"If it doesn't exist, why would our current Mab be seeking it too?"

"Because she's as stupid as you are!"

Aubrie hit her before he realized he'd done it. He hadn't closed his fist, rendering the blow lighter than it could have been. It was still enough to make her stumble back, collapsing in a heap at the end of the bed.

She shoved herself up to struggle to her feet, then fell still, sprawling on the carpet.

He knelt beside her. Brushing the hair from her face and neck, he checked her pulse. Steady. Her breaths came more or less steadily too. Gingerly, he parted her eyelids to check one pupil. Her brown iris brought another rush of disgust, making him jerk his hand back as if he'd been burned.

He stepped over her to summon Jasper and the four *lesidhe* from the hallway.

36

MY SKIN PRICKLED DURING the bus ride northwest from Toronto to my hometown of Hartsville. No familiar faces seemed to be shadowing me, though I didn't know every minion Miranda or Aubrie had at their disposal. Maybe it was a coincidence. There were other Faeries walking around the world, after all. I could have ended up on a bus with a stranger who pinged off my supernatural alarm system. Still, that didn't exactly fit my luck lately.

From the bus station on Main Street, I grabbed a cab out to the Happy Hills Manufactured Home Park. My goosebumps fell off quickly as soon as the car pulled away from the station. The cab cost under twenty dollars and brought me into my mom's gravel driveway beside her beat-up sedan just before ten.

Lights on in the trailer said Mom was home. She didn't go in for any of that Astro-Turf shit, or even a welcome mat. Some of our neighbours had wind-propelled plastic flowers and trimmed gardens in front of their homes, but my mom's lawn only got cut because the park's riding mower came by weekly.

I'd been hoping she might be out at the bar, so I could just slip in, take the book and head back, but it must have been a drink-at-home-with-the-neighbours night. Still, I told the driver to wait, climbing the single steep step to the aluminum screen door. The door stood open in the summer air, but only the tinny sound of the TV came through. Maybe a drink-at-home-alone night, then.

I knocked and waited. The sofa springs creaked and a figure shuffled into view. The outside light flickered to life, making me blink to adjust my eyes to the sudden glow over my head.

"Jude?" A face squinted at me through the screen.

"Hi, Mom."

She almost knocked me off the step pushing the screen door open. Instead, she caught me, hugging me tight enough to press the breath out of my lungs.

"God, you're a sight for sore eyes!" She let me go, holding the screen door open to invite me in, then peered over my shoulder. "That your cab?"

"Yeah, but—"

"I'll get it." Her words didn't carry the judgment I'd been expecting. She grabbed her purse from the hook beside the door and slipped past me to pay the driver.

He drove off, stranding me.

The inside of the trailer hadn't changed in the nine months since I'd been back to visit. We entered the rectangle at the centre, into the combo living room and kitchen. One bedroom stood on either end, with the bathroom tucked snugly into the master bedroom. Well, it would have been two bedrooms, but my mom had thrown out my twin bed and replaced it with an exercise bike. For my last visit, I'd slept on the lumpy sofa that greeted us.

The TV chattered away. Beside it, a cigarette burned in an ashtray. A half-empty bottle of apple Schnapps sat by the sink.

"You should have called." Mom shooed me over to the sofa.

"Didn't have time." I flopped down.

She dropped into the threadbare armchair beside the TV, brushing something invisible off her jeans. "There's beer in the fridge."

"Great."

"How'd you get here?"

"Bus."

"You didn't need to take a cab, you know. I'd have come to get you." She glanced toward the window. "Car's on the fritz, but I could have borrowed Mike's. You remember Mike, from next door?"

"Nope." I tried to keep from tapping my hands on my knees.

She grabbed two cold bottles from the fridge, opening them and handing me one. Her bleached hair had been pulled back into a ponytail, but most had fallen out around her face. She'd put on too much eye make-up, as usual. It reminded me of the younger cheerleader version of her that I'd seen in the photo the night before.

She sized me up with odd, mostly sober affection. "What happened to your face?" she asked.

I touched one of the scabs across my cheeks. *Dragon's tails are sharper than they look.* "I fell off a bike."

"You bike?" She gave me a dubious look.

"Not anymore."

"Where've you been?"

"Montreal, mostly."

"No shit. How is it?"

"Big." I took a swig of my beer. "French."

"Always wanted to go there." She sounded wistful, but it faded. "Are you staying the night?"

"No. I mean, there's no room. It's fine."

"I'll make room." She dared me to challenge her. Why did she want me to stay? "You can have the bed," she added. "I'll sleep on the sofa."

"No, really . . ."

"I'll put on clean sheets, sweetie." Mom held up her hands to stop me, one still wrapped around the beer bottle.

"I'm sure I've slept on worse ones."

"Still got that mouth."

"Nobody's smacked it off me yet."

She rolled her eyes as if not remembering her favourite threat from my teenage years.

"So, what, you just came to get some cash outta me and you'll be on your way?" Her voice turned bitter.

"I don't need cash."

"Oh, no?"

"If you want me to stay the night, I'll stay." It wasn't worth the fight, and it wasn't like I had anywhere else to go.

I stood up. "Where are the sheets?"

"I'll do it." She stood too, heading for the bedroom to pull a set of sheets out of the plastic box under the bed.

Swallowing my impatience with another swig of beer, I scanned the living room for the familiar binding of that old book. Just paperbacks and knickknacks on the little bookshelf—Mom had never liked to hang onto stuff for long, taking a load to the thrift store and bringing new crap home at least monthly my whole life. But the Sylvia Plath book had stuck around, a fixture. It couldn't be gone now.

"Hey, Mom? Remember that book of poems you used to read to me? Have you still got it?"

"Of course I do. It's over here by the bed." She gestured to the bedside table I could see when I stretched my neck to peer into the bedroom. It held a box of tissues, a water glass, and a hardbound book. The blue of the cover had faded from what I remembered, but the scrawled gold writing on the spine was the same.

I walked in beside her to pick it up, the weight familiar in my hands. Seeing the script on the cover was like looking back through a mirror or a dream, something not quite real. So much had happened since I'd last held this book in smaller hands. Was it really a Faerie spellbook? I flipped it open, scanning the contents page. All in English, all poems.

"My dad gave this to you, didn't he?" I asked.

"Christ." Mom slammed her hands down on the new sheets, making them flutter around her arms as they settled. "I tried so hard, you know. And I guess I just wasn't good enough because you've still gotta go out and find that bastard—"

"I'm not looking for him." I shut the book, setting it back on the table.

"Well, don't," she said, voice tight and sharp. "He's not a good man, Jude. He's not worth finding."

"I don't want to find him, Mom. I told you. Just . . . we never talked about him." I couldn't tell her he was dead anyway. Then I'd have to tell her how I knew. 'The Faeries told me' wasn't going to fly, even if she'd been drinking.

"What was there to talk about?" She bent down to tuck the corner of the sheets under the mattress, stopping to give the window a far-off look. "It wasn't a great romance, okay? I didn't picture myself marrying him or any of that nonsense. It was just a good time. My girlfriends were jealous."

I nodded toward the hardcover on the bedside table to steer us back into safer territory. "When did he give you the book?"

"He sent that after he took off. A couple years." Her voice hardened.

"After he ruined your life, huh?"

"Jude." She gave me a weary look that I didn't understand. She'd said that to my face more times than I could count.

"So why'd you keep the book?" I asked. "You hated his guts by then, right?"

Her eyes took on the distant look again as she frowned. "I guess I just didn't want to throw it away." She glanced at the book. "I went for Sylvia Plath when we read a few of her poems junior year. I checked her collected works out of the library a dozen times. She's just got . . . a hell of a way with words, you know? And Josh used to tease me, say I was going morbid."

It gave me a jolt when she said his name aloud. "I'd have dumped it," I said. "Or burned it. Anything an asshole like that sent me."

She only shrugged, looking oddly dreamy again. A *spell*. There had to be something on this book that made my mother keep it.

Retrieving her beer from the bedside table, she said, "I don't like it when you disappear."

"I didn't disappear."

"Before last night, I hadn't heard from you in nine months. What do you call it?"

"Well, I was in a coma for three of those."

She seemed to think I was joking. "Doesn't explain the other six."

"I've been busy. With . . . life stuff."

Mom had always been able to catch me in a lie when she tried. She didn't seem to have the energy tonight, sighing. "You want something to eat?"

"What have you got?"

The answer pleased her. She headed out into the kitchen to open the fridge. The TV kept yammering away at low volume. "I've got some cold cuts. I could make us sandwiches."

"That sounds great." I retrieved my beer from atop the fridge and stood out of the way while Mom bustled around the kitchen space, placing turkey, cheese and lettuce on slices of wheat bread. She handed me one and we ate in silence for a few minutes.

Finally, she sighed as if she'd been holding the question in. "Were you really in a coma?"

"Yes." I wished I'd lied when she looked stricken.

"Nobody called me."

"I didn't have any say in that." Miranda had probably kept them from calling her, keeping my profile low while I was out.

"Are you all right now?"

"I'm fine." I hesitated at her expression. "For real, Mom. I'm fine."

"What happened?"

"Car accident."

Her eyes flickered to my beer and she reached for it. "You shouldn't be drinking after that."

"Oh, I definitely should." I lifted it out of her reach. "It's not like this is the first drink I've had since leaving the hospital."

"Jude." She stared at me with wide eyes.

"Hold the motherly anxiety, okay? I've actually had a really long day, and I'd really like to go to sleep."

Mom frowned, her expression saying that she wanted to press, but instead she backed off. "Okay, sweetie."

Getting into the bedroom and shutting the door felt like a relief. The light stayed on outside but the TV volume got lower. I leaned back against the door, wishing I hadn't come. But I couldn't leave my mother sitting on this bomb. If it even was a bomb, a mystical spellbook, and not just a bunch of stupid poems.

I made a face at the book on the bedside table. Remembering the unpleasant feeling that had followed me on the bus, I peered through the window curtains. Nobody stood outside in the dark. My skin stayed calm.

I still stuffed the book under my pillow before shutting off the light.

37

Daniel eyed Abe, two chairs away in the surgery waiting room. The cowboy pretended not to notice, flipping through a magazine. He'd taken off his hat and left it on the empty seat beside him. He hadn't spoken in hours, shadowing Daniel without argument from the waiting room to the hospital cafeteria to the lobby and then back to the waiting room.

Upon reaching the hospital, Daniel had made up a story about an attempted mugging, one he hadn't seen but had heard. Abe had contributed to the lie by naming himself a concerned bystander only when asked directly by the police detectives who'd shown up.

Now Daniel wanted nothing more than to get some sleep, but he didn't dare with the cowboy around. He didn't want to leave until he'd seen Zeb awake and, apart from Abe, no one had paid him much attention. The hospital wasn't a half-bad place to hide, if being tailed by a silent Antagonist now counted as hiding. Still, he couldn't make the mistake of relaxing, thinking that the cowboy wouldn't call in his more powerful companions in at any moment.

Abe's calm turning of a magazine page broke Daniel's last nerve.

"This is starting to get creepy," he said.

"*Starting* to?" the cowboy chuckled. "Sets your threshold for 'creepy' pretty high. Can't say I'm surprised, though."

"What do you want?"

"If we're blue-skying here, we'd all be better off if you just forgot that key in your head, but I'm going to settle for making sure Aubrie doesn't get his hands on it." Abe shut the magazine. "Hospital was a good choice. He won't check for you here. Wouldn't occur to him that you'd look after a peon."

"Zeb's not a *peon*." The archaic word grated. It felt too much like a term his father would have used—and meant.

"Exactly." Abe nodded. "Friends aren't really something Aubrie traffics in."

Daniel flinched when his phone rang. The screen displayed Gracie's number but he hesitated before answering. He'd called her earlier to tell her what had happened with Zeb and promised to keep her updated, but he hadn't done so with Abe around.

Abe stood and moved several chairs further away, as if it were possible to find a spot in the small room where he couldn't overhear.

Not knowing what to make of that, Daniel put the phone to his ear anyway. "Hey."

"Any news?" Gracie asked.

"He came out of surgery an hour ago. He'll be all right."

"God, I wish I'd never sent him down there."

"That's pointless."

"Maybe. I can't help it."

"Well, don't tell me about it, then." It was too late for regrets or guilt, and if his sister lapsed into it, Daniel would give into the nagging voices at the edge of his own mind. *You're in over your head. You're no leader. You can't even protect your own people. Never could.*

Rather than return an equally spiteful comment, Gracie said: "Are you still at the hospital?"

"So far, there's no reason to go anywhere else." Daniel didn't tell her about Abe's presence. She couldn't do anything about it.

"Which leads me to question the brilliant decision that got you down there."

"Mei said Aubrie had a mage after me in Montreal." He didn't mention the rest of the information Mei had given him, since it had turned out to be useless.

"Then I'm guessing that's what broke into my house after you left last night." Gracie paused. "A mage. Huh."

"What?" Daniel jerked upright, stunned by his sister's offhanded tone. "Grace—"

"We fought," Gracie said, "I won. She's dead."

"How?"

"I got her with the axe and then I stabbed her."

"A *mage*?"

"It was lucky. She was strong, powerful. She tossed me around a little. A lot." She finally began to sound shaken, recounting it.

"Are you all right?" That should have been his first question. "Riley?"

"We're *fine*." Gracie said the word with a heavy dose of irony, then admitted, "I'm a little bruised, but it could have been worse. Riley didn't see anything. He was asleep upstairs."

Daniel slumped forward, rubbing his eyes with his free hand. The idea that he'd led something so dangerous to his sister and nephew made it hard to draw a breath. "I'm sorry," he said.

"It's not your fault. We both knew what we were getting into."

The hell we did. They'd been so overconfident, assuming they could step into the void left by the Consilium and pick up the guttering torch of this uphill battle themselves.

"I didn't tell you last night because I didn't want you coming back," Gracie went on without giving him time to argue. "In case there were more. Are there more?"

"Mei only mentioned one. One mage, anyway." Daniel glanced to the door as a nurse stuck her head in, apparently looking for someone else. "I thought it would follow me," he added. "I never meant for it to turn up at your place."

THE FLAWS OF GRAVITY

"If it's gone, then come back, okay? We'll figure something out. We always do." She hissed another sigh. "Riley's crying—I have to go. I'll call you in the morning and we'll go from there, okay? Be careful."

Daniel ended the call without a similar admonition to his sister. She didn't need the reminder. She'd dispatched a mage. He'd put her in the position to have to do that.

I shouldn't have read that incantation. I should have stayed out of it. Let the Consilium die. Or never joined in the first place. Told Alan to go fuck himself ten years ago.

Right. In what universe would he have done any of that?

Walking away three months ago hadn't been a choice he could have made. What else would he have done? At twenty-eight, he'd never held a job that could reasonably be explained on a resumé. He'd barely eked out a college degree, more interested in Consilium research than regular coursework.

So he'd driven himself—and Gracie—straight back into the fray, because he should have died in Toronto. He should have been there at the office with the others when the Court attacked. He had to have some purpose, had to do something to make it up to them.

But he was failing. He didn't have the resources, knowledge or experience to keep the people around him safe. He could barely think to do so running for his own life.

Driving the point home, Abe got to his feet. The cowboy moved one chair away from him, stretching his long legs out. He laid his head back against the wall. "Ought to get some sleep," he said.

Daniel stared at him in amazement. "What do you think the likelihood of that is, with you here?"

"Up to you." Abe placed his hat over his eyes to block the overhead lights, folding his arms across his chest and settling in.

From under the hat, he added, "I don't get the idea you're gonna try to shake me tonight, but you should know we've got your blood. Scraped it off that basement floor. Means we can track you anywhere now with a simple spell." He paused, as if to let it sink in. "Didn't want to bring it up, but it seemed relevant."

Daniel didn't have the capacity to be horrified the way he knew he should be. The day had numbed him. "Then why are you here?"

" 'Cause I'm no good at spells. Easier to keep an eye in person."

38

"THIS IS IT? YOU'RE certain?" Aubrie studied the plain bungalow across the street.

"Yes." The man in the driver's seat of the car—the *houle* from the casino had initially introduced him as Sam—stared through the windshield at the house, face drawn in concentration.

"Kind of a shitty palace," Jasper remarked from the backseat.

"How can you tell?" Aubrie looked to Sam. The blue house sat only a few kilometres from his hotel in Niagara, fitting in among the others on the residential street. With the morning sun still low on he horizon, nothing stirred in the neighbourhood.

"It doesn't belong here. We wouldn't see it normally, but I called it up."

"Can anyone inside tell you've called it?"

"No." Sam shook his head. "Unlikely."

"And how do we get in?"

"Just walk in. It should stay put here as long as the front door's open."

Unlikely. Should stay put. The edge of uncertainty gave Aubrie pause. He glanced over his shoulder to the car parked behind them at the curb. Five others waited there for his signal. He could send them in with Jasper and Sam, remain outside in case something went wrong. It was an unnecessary risk, with no guarantee that the house held anything he needed. But he wanted to see Miranda's face.

She thought she had him on the run. She thought he wouldn't play offence.

"How many people have you seen?" he asked. Sam had watched the house for the last twelve hours.

"Ten distinct, coming and going," the other man answered. "But there's a back door too."

"So, we don't know how many are in there now." Jasper sounded cautious.

"More than there will be when we leave." Aubrie pulled his phone from his pocket to call the driver of the second car.

"Yes." The woman answered in one ring.

"We're going in. The front door has to stay open. Sam will stay with it. I want one person to each room. Neutralize anyone you find and bring out any book you see. If there's anyone human in there, he comes with you." Might as well cover all the bases, while they were here. "Relay all that to the others. No exceptions."

"Yes, sir." The woman hung up.

The eight of them met at the end of the sidewalk. Sam and Jasper went first. As promised, Sam only had to turn the front doorknob and it swung open for him.

The others rushed in behind, Aubrie coming last. The front hallway stood empty, the house quiet, apart from the footsteps of his invading faction. The woman from the other car and three others hurried up the stairs. Jasper led another toward the back of the house.

Noise of a scuffle came from the second floor. The driver of the second car tumbled down the stairs, face bleeding from what looked like fingernail scratches.

Aubrie sprinted up past her, coming face-to-face with Miranda in the upstairs hallway.

"Get out!" The Mab flew at him, hitting hard enough to knock him into the wall. Wrapping both hands around his throat, she dug sharp fingernails into his skin. "How dare you come here?"

Aubrie shoved her away as easily as if he'd brushed dust from his shirtfront.

Before Miranda could round on him again, the woman she'd just tossed down the stairs raced back up at them, as if intent on jumping back into the fray.

Miranda caught her as she reached them. Rather than sending the woman sprawling back to the bottom, the Mab slammed her into the wallpaper, one hand tight against her skull. She kept her vivid green eyes fixed on Aubrie's, pressing down hard enough to produce an audible crack, the same way he might have done with his own power.

The woman slid into a heap against the wall, blood trickling from the indentation beneath her hair.

"Does that make us even?" Aubrie asked, unable to hold back a smile at the pain in Miranda's eyes.

"Not by half. You probably didn't even know this sad creature's name."

"Whereas the members of the Faerie Court who exiled you were such close friends of yours," he returned.

Rather than flying into the incandescent rage he expected, Miranda took a deep breath and seemed to pull herself together. She gave him a pitying look. "If you're here for the grymoire, you've got some lousy information. Joshua hid it from both of us, John."

Having her use his real first name rankled him. She'd always used it when she wanted to remind him of his mother, point out everything he'd lost—missed out on—by being born half-human.

She seized on his inattention to spring at him again. Grabbing his hair with one hand, she clawed at his eyes with the other as she grew heavier to press him against the wall.

With the dead woman fresh on his mind, Aubrie shoved her away before she could pin him. He used enough force that she flew backwards.

She changed course in mid-air, falling up rather than down and settled against the ceiling above the stairs, glaring down at him.

Her effortless manipulation of gravity gave Aubrie a sudden flash. He'd watched Miranda bend the same laws of gravity Jude did for years but the connection had never struck him. The pale, lithe creature before him now moved with more grace, spinning the world around her with barely a whisper. It made Jude's motions seem almost clumsy by comparison, but there *was* a comparison.

Why had Miranda had wasted her dwindling royal resources to protect a comatose half-human woman? It couldn't be a coincidence that she and Jude had the same ability, even though he'd heard there were plenty of Faeries who did.

"Jude's yours," he said.

The disdainful glower Miranda returned from the ceiling told him he'd missed his protégée's connection to the new Mab by half a step. Miranda's predilections didn't run toward humans, or very regularly toward men for that matter. "Joshua's daughter, then."

He should have recognized it sooner. He'd known Joshua for years, up until the bastard had stolen the grymoire meant to help them all and disappeared with it. Jude didn't look like her father, but then, Aubrie didn't actually know what Joshua or Miranda looked like when they weren't using enough glamour to bestow a human face.

If Joshua had a human family hidden in this world, it was a spot worth checking for the grymoire. Most Faeries wouldn't consider humans worthy of protecting something of such great power—Aubrie's own mother had been so disgusted with him that she'd abandoned him to retreat into the safety of the Faerie realm alone. Yet Joshua had had a perverse enough sense of humour to consider the human world a decent hiding spot.

The house shifted under Aubrie's feet, making him brace himself.

Miranda chose that moment to fly from the ceiling. This time she contorted herself, knocking him back into the wall again. With her hands on his collar and her knees against his ribs, the hall spun around him as if he were lying on the floor, her weight pressing down on him. Her green eyes glittered in the shadow of the hallway and sharp fingernails brushed his throat again.

He shoved her aside and struggled to his feet. Rather than pulling himself upright, the motion caused him to slam into the floor face-first. He'd tried to haul his body upright from an already-vertical position, forgetting under the hypnotic effect of her eyes that he still stood against the wall.

Before he could curl his hands and knees under himself to stand, his stomach lurched and his body jerked upwards. He hit the ceiling hard on his back, plaster dust flaking off around him. It was really the ceiling this time—he could tell by the position of the stairs behind Miranda.

She stood below him, one hand extended to hold him in place. Becoming the Mab had strengthened her powers—as far as he knew, she'd never been able to manipulate someone else's gravity before. The force squeezed him against the ceiling so hard that the breath was pressed from his lungs.

Beyond the fury in her eyes, Miranda's face was creased, strained. Her hand trembled as she kept it pointed toward him and the pressure on his body eased just enough that he could snatch a breath. She wasn't practised with this power. She couldn't hold him for long.

"How easily you've embraced crown and country again," he huffed, keeping his eyes on the stairs to stay oriented as he tensed his muscles. "Last year you'd have danced a jig to poison the world that exiled you."

She inclined her head as if in agreement and the room seemed to tilt with her. "Now I know better."

"Now you own it. No wonder you'd rather keep it to yourself." He channelled all of his power into peeling away from the ceiling. It fought to hold him, tugging at his skin like Velcro, but he tore through it. The floor whirled to one side beneath him and then rushed up too fast.

Miranda jerked back as he crashed down, but this time he'd anticipated the jarring impact. He shoved himself upright, staggering to one side to keep his balance and avoid her as she launched forward. He caught the back of her collar with one hand, and before she could make herself heavier or fight back, swung her toward the banister, smashing the side of her face into it.

The house groaned around them. Aubrie had to release Miranda in order to catch himself against the wall. Her limp body folded and slid down the first few stairs. When she stopped, she lay still but her back rose and fell with breath. Before he could snatch her back up, the stairs lifted like a wave, throwing him inches into the air.

He found himself in a heap on the floor in the front hall, body aching from a painful tumble down the stairs. At the door, Sam fought with a blonde woman—losing control of the house. Someone grasped Aubrie's shoulder, then his arm, helping him up in a frenzy. His vision blurred but he made out the distinctive spikes of Jasper's hair.

"Come on," Jasper muttered, tugging him toward the still-open front door.

Aubrie put his weight on the pixie's shoulder, testing his legs to make sure nothing was broken before Jasper dragged him out of the house.

The front door slammed shut. The house was gone.

Shaking Jasper off, Aubrie moved to the end of the walkway. He reached out to pass a hand through the space where the house had been. Nothing but air in an empty suburban lot.

He turned, keeping it slow so as not to overwhelm his spinning head, and counted his people as they loaded books into the car trunks. Only missing three: Sam, the woman Miranda had killed on the stairs and one other. Not a perfect victory, but a decisive one.

His muscles replayed the memory of smashing Miranda's head into the banister. If she wasn't dead, she would be soon. The ever-present whisper in his past, campaigning against him and reminding the rest of their colleagues that he couldn't be trusted. *Put him out. Cut him loose. He's not one of us.*

The Mab. The most powerful of his enemies—the only one who had presented a real threat. Yet he'd dispatched her easily.

Jasper flipped open one of the books on the pile, shaking it. "It's blank." He tried another. "This one too."

"It doesn't matter." Aubrie barely heard him. Nothing could dispel the morning's triumph. "We've accomplished what we came for."

39

I WOKE TO SUNLIGHT streaming through the flimsy curtains and a dull ache in my ribs that turned into a sharp one when I moved. I yanked my t-shirt up to check the spot where Aubrie had hit me yesterday, finding an unpleasant purple bruise. It hurt less once I'd sat up and stretched a little.

With a sigh I regretted after it twinged my ribs, I pulled the book from under my pillow, then flipped it open to run my fingers over the type on one of the pages. How did the key work? Did you whisper some spell to the book and watch the words blur and rearrange on the page? Did you paint more runes onto it and watch it shed Sylvia Plath like a snake's skin?

It didn't matter. I wasn't going to see it work. But I did have to get it out of here.

Listening for sounds of my mother stirring, I re-dressed to leave. The alarm clock on the night table said it was just after seven.

In the living room, Mom had curled up on the sofa, an old wool Bay blanket we'd inherited from her aunt crumpled over her lower body.

I tucked the book under one arm, grabbing the cordless phone receiver from the wall as I slipped out the front door. Shutting it behind me, I sat on the stoop and dialed the taxi company whose number I'd memorized at fifteen. They hadn't changed it. Thanks to Mom's generosity with last night's cab, I still had about forty dollars to get back to the station and hop a bus back to Toronto.

The taxi dispatch said it'd be twenty minutes. I hung up, tilting my face up to the sun. In the daylight, the lawn of the trailer looked just like I remembered it. I could have been a teenager again, waiting outside on the stoop because I'd gotten home too late and Mom had locked me out.

I crept back inside to replace the phone. Should I wake her and say goodbye? Seemed easier not to. I snagged a magnetic pen and shopping list paper from the side of the fridge, jotting a quick note that I left by the sink. *Took the book. Sorry.*

True to the dispatcher's word, the cab showed up in twenty minutes. It dropped me at the tiny bus station on Main Street. The next bus left for Toronto at nine, so I bought a coffee, a bottle of water and a bagel at a cafe down the street. I stuffed two sugar packets into my pocket but skipped the non-dairy creamer cups before heading back to the station. After finishing the bagel in my uncomfortable plastic chair, I slid the book into the brown paper bag it had come in.

Someone sat down beside me. I side-eyed her, doing a double-take at the polite smile and black curls with blue roots. Ilse.

"In the future, I'd advise using the house to travel," she said. "That bus ride yesterday was interminable." Frowning at the ticket in my hand, she added, "Now you're planning to repeat the experience?"

"That was you on the bus, giving me goosebumps the whole way? I didn't see you."

"That's correct." The words answered both questions.

"What, you poofed into pixie dust and hovered in a seat for two hours?"

"I'm not a pixie." Ilse looked offended. "Your former colleagues would have classified me as a sprite."

"My bad. You poofed into sprite dust, then?"

"Water, in fact."

"You spent *two hours* hanging out as a puddle on the floor of the bus?" I asked, to cover my shudder at the realization. "Did you hide in my mom's sink all night too?"

"Of course not. I kept a respectful distance outside. I'm not spying, I—" She stopped, eyes fixed on the brown paper bag on my lap. "What's that?"

"A book. To read on the bus." I added, maybe too defensively, "I read books."

"Is it—?"

"No."

She studied my face like she couldn't figure out why I would deceive her, but didn't quite believe me all the same.

"May I see it?" she asked.

"No." To distract her from my blunt refusal, I added, "Why'd you follow me? Did Miranda put you up to it?"

"If you mean did she send me, no, she did not. I came of my own accord." Ilse continued her explanation without prompting, making her my current favourite person. "You were angry. I wanted to make sure you didn't do anything rash."

"Like what? Run back to Aubrie?"

She inclined her head as if to grant that had been a possibility. "Your mother's house was . . . not where I'd have predicted."

"Glad I'm not predictable," I muttered. "Why do you talk like you know me?"

"I've . . . studied you. No, *studied* is the wrong word—"

"Investigated? Researched? Stalked?"

She frowned but didn't correct me. "You're Miranda's only remaining family."

Something in the way she said my aunt's name struck me, making me remember how she'd addressed the sylph at the warehouse, that wistful longing in her voice. "Are you and her like . . . an item?"

Ilse blinked. "Item?"

"Together. In a relationship. Screwing." I ticked off the synonyms on my fingers.

"Yes."

I hadn't expected such a ready answer. Thinking of how Miranda had barely acknowledged Ilse's presence in the kitchen yesterday, I couldn't help but return, "Did *she* get the memo?"

The sprite's blank look reminded me that it wasn't important.

"Never mind," I said. "Look, can I *order* you to leave me alone?" I was royalty now too, after all.

"My orders come from the Mab." Despite what she'd just told me, Ilse said the title in her usual mild tone, which only made it clearer that she wouldn't budge.

But now I knew she was a water sprite. I had a half-remembered idea of what might distract her.

I waited through two announcements about boarding for my bus. When the final announcement came over the loudspeaker, I dug into my pocket and pulled out one of the sugar packets I'd taken with my coffee. I ripped it open, emptying it onto the floor with a flourish.

Ilse stared at the sugar granules I'd poured out onto the floor. "Someone will have to clean that up."

So sprites weren't compelled to count sugar. Great. But they were compelled to count *something*—I remembered that much from the required Consilium reading I'd skimmed.

I only had one other option. I reached into the bag in my lap, pulling out the wax paper wrapper that had been around my bagel. As I got to my feet, I let it fall open and spill poppy seeds across the scuffed tile floor.

Ilse jerked back, startled. She lifted her chin and parted her lips like she'd caught a scent. Narrowed violet eyes snapped to me for an instant before she was on her knees, pawing through the sugar to find the sprinkle of black seeds.

I darted past the station agent, who'd come out of his booth to see what I'd tossed all over the floor, and hustled outside to the bus. The driver was just about to shut the door, but I flashed my ticket and he let me on.

For the first fifteen minutes of the ride, I waited for Ilse to burst into the empty seat beside me, fuming. When my skin remained calm and no angry sprite appeared, I relaxed, resting my head against the window and hugging the book in its paper bag armour to my chest. Seemed unlikely that magical house could jump a Faerie onto a moving vehicle, but I stayed vigilant.

After the bus pulled into Toronto, I caught a commuter train to Hamilton and used the rest of the cash in my pockets on a hefty tip for the reluctant cab driver who agreed to take me the forty minutes to the motel in St. Catharines. Daniel might not still be there, but it was the only lead I had. Dumping the book with him seemed safest, because I definitely didn't want the damn thing.

The cab dropped me off in the parking lot. Grace's car was parked in the same spot in front of the motel office. Would it work to just leave the book outside the door to the room where I'd left Daniel and run?

No, I had to put it in his hands.

Bracing myself, I crossed the parking lot to knock on the door. No one answered. I knocked again, double-checking the black car in the lot over my shoulder. I didn't have a great memory for cars, but the hatchback had Quebec plates. A green sedan beside it looked familiar, probably the one Zeb had been driving when I'd hijacked him yesterday.

"Hey!" I called. "I know you're pissed, but I've got something . . . I need to give you something, okay?" I shifted the book in its brown paper sack against my ribs, taking another quick glance for any onlookers.

The motel seemed quiet and deserted. A cleaning cart sat outside the room at the far end, with no housekeeping nearby.

Anxiety buzzed in my chest when I still didn't get an answer. Maybe he'd gone out. But where, without a car? The motel squatted beside a highway access road, surrounded by other cheap motels. No restaurants in walking distance.

The door opened, interrupting my speculation and making me jump as I spun back to face it. Startled at the semi-familiar woman facing me, I asked, "Grace?"

Daniel's sister studied me like she didn't remember who I was.

"Hi," she said, voice about two shades warmer than last night.

"Hey. Um . . . is Daniel here?" Something felt wrong.

"He's not."

I didn't believe her, though I wasn't sure why. "Can I come in?"

She stepped back, pushing the door open wider to let me in.

I took a small step in, just enough to see the room and make sure she'd told the truth. No one else inside. The bathroom door hung open, broadcasting its emptiness too.

"Satisfied?" Grace asked.

"I—" My words caught in my throat at the electricity pricking my skin now that I stood close to her. The nylon bag from the car trunk sat open and empty on the bed, a flashlight and two road flares beside it. Whatever else had been in there had been taken.

I pulled the paper-bag-clad book back under my arm.

Her eyes went to it. Without warning, she grabbed my shoulder, all but flinging me into the room.

The door slammed behind me as I hit the bed, fighting to keep my grip on the paper bag as the bruise on my ribs made me catch my breath. I spun gravity without thinking, pushing my feet off the floor and falling onto the ceiling.

"Huh." The other woman cocked her head to look up at me.

I crouched above her, upside down. "You're not Grace."

"And you're not important." She leaned back against the door, one hand on the knob. "How about you just get out of here, save us both a lot of trouble?"

She had to be waiting for Daniel. Car keys gleamed on the table by the door. "Who are you?" I asked.

"Going to make this hard, then?" The person wearing Grace's face rolled her eyes. She surged upwards, legs extending like rubber. Standing suddenly a whole metre taller, she grabbed the back of my neck, tossing me to the floor like a doll.

I landed hard on the carpet, the book digging into my aching ribs. Rolling over, I kicked her with both feet as she stooped down to grab me. I staggered upright, snatching the car keys from the table and swinging them as a weapon to force her from the door.

Her form shrank as she dodged me, face melting away to turn her into a pale, unfamiliar man. Had to be a shapeshifter, maybe a higher class of chameleon.

He lunged, grabbing the front of my t-shirt and launching me backwards. I hit the floor hard enough to knock my breath out. He fell on top of me, hands sliding around my throat and squeezing.

I gasped, letting go of the book and the keys to wrap my hands around his and force them away. My body spasmed, trying to throw him off and pull in air, but he wrapped his legs around mine to hold me still.

My lungs burned. Fighting the panic, I inverted my gravity with enough force to send us flying up.

His fingers loosened as I slammed him into the ceiling.

I couldn't hold us there in my current state, and we landed back on the floor in a heap. Kicking him off me, I found the paper bag with the book in it, scrambling back as I sucked in air. My throat throbbed where his hands had been. Nearly losing myself in a painful fit of coughing, I snatched the plastic fob of the car keys and struggled to my feet, weaving toward the door.

Outside, I half-jogged despite being unable to draw a full breath. Grace's black hatchback unlocked as soon I had the key fob close enough. I slid into the driver's seat, engaging the automatic locks and jabbing the ignition button.

The shapeshifter banged into the passenger-side window, yanking on the door handle.

I slammed the car into reverse. Peeling back and shifting into drive, the body next to the car disappeared.

He reappeared in the backseat. Must have shapeshifted into something tiny enough to slip inside through a crack in the door.

I jerked the wheel to the left to throw him against the child seat in the back, but his hand found my hair and yanked. The car flew up onto the sidewalk, aimed at the motel office. I got hold of the wheel and put us back on the parking lot asphalt, almost side-swiping another car parked at the end of the lot as I used the swerve to force him off me.

The black spots in my vision made it hard to stay on the right side of the road as we swung out of the lot. My throat ached as if his hands were still wrapped around it.

The shapeshifter surged over the seat again. "Stop the car!"

"Nope!" I veered into the oncoming traffic and then back in an effort to throw him back. A car horn blared as another driver narrowly avoided us.

I took another turn fast enough to do Zeb proud, but didn't correct in time. We jolted to a stop with a crunch of metal.

The air bag exploded, catching me before I went through the steering column. Blinking and coughing on the dust, my ears rang as I batted the bag, trying to flatten it. I pinched my eyes shut to dispel the stinging pain, then opened them again. Over the deflating air bag, through a cracked windshield, the smashed trunk of the parked car I'd plowed into didn't spin dizzily to one side like everything had been doing before.

From my left, someone pounded on the window. The locked door handle clicked as a person outside tugged on it.

Keeping my head back against the headrest, I shifted my gaze sideways to an unfamiliar man tapping on the window.

"Hey! Hey, are you okay? Can you unlock the door?"

Fingers twitched against my thigh.

My adrenaline surged. I slapped the shapeshifter's hand away then strained to the automatic lock button. The door opened, letting in cool air. I couldn't suck it into my lungs fast enough. Shoving myself sideways, I fell out of the car.

A distant voice started, "Hey, no! Wait, I don't think you should—"

40

WHEN I COULD OPEN my eyes again and focus them, I was back in the hospital. Well, *a* hospital. Dressed in a scratchy gown, planted securely in a bed made around me, at least I could draw a deep breath, even though my lungs protested. My throat throbbed with a distant, dull pain. The ceiling spun above me at the speed of a carnival carousel, but no dark spots intruded.

Visions trickled back in: Grace's body elongating into the shapeshifter, the fingers like a vise around my throat, the jarring stop of the car as I crashed it. All of it seemed slow-motion and distant.

Hospital drugs. Awesome.

The door opened, making me turn my head with some difficulty. I blinked at the dark-haired figure. What the hell was Daniel doing here?

"You're awake," he said, letting the door slide closed behind him.

"What the fuck?" I tried to say. It came out as an inaudible croak. That sent the jolt of memory through me, making me rub my arm to jump-start the goosebumps that would tell me he wasn't who he looked like.

Nothing.

He watched me, puzzled.

I swallowed hard enough to make me shudder at the pain in my throat, forcing out raspy words. "Shapeshifter at the motel."

"That's what made you crash Gracie's car?"

"How do you know?" Alarm flared through me again. I pinched my arm for good measure. Had the accident knocked out my internal Faerie detector somehow?

Daniel moved closer and caught my hand, keeping me from digging fingernails into my skin. "What the hell are you trying to do?"

"Your sister wasn't . . . her. Maybe you're not you." I had to take a couple second's breather. "Prove it."

"The police called Gracie about the car. She called me." He seemed to realize he still had my hand and hurried to set it back against the rough blanket. His aversion to touching me seemed on brand, but it wasn't enough.

"Where'd we meet?" I hissed. If he gave the easy answer and said the Consilium, he was lying. We'd known each other in passing at the office for a couple of years before we'd really come face-to-face.

He regarded me with the same uncertainty, then seemed to accept that I was serious. "At a bar."

"And?"

"And . . . ? And I pulled you out of a fight you were about to lose."

"Bullshit," I huffed.

"No, you were definitely about to get your ass kicked." He continued as if he thought he still had to prove himself, or at the very least, prove me wrong. "You slammed a boot into my knee when I grabbed you, then told me it was my own goddamn fault for getting in your way and took off. Then you showed up at my place the next night with a bottle of very cheap tequila, ostensibly to apologize. We finished half of it watching a Leafs game."

The memory and his take on it made me fight not to smile.

"Who won?" I managed.

Daniel sighed. "We didn't actually watch the end of the game."

We definitely hadn't. He'd been a curiosity at that point. I'd wanted to suss out whether a son of Alan Cain's could

THE FLAWS OF GRAVITY

actually be so chivalrous or if he'd jumped into the fight to keep me from revealing my powers to a bar full of civilians. Inviting myself into his apartment and into his bed hadn't answered that question but I'd stopped caring. Because I'd liked him.

My throat tightened, but it wasn't the same pain I'd woken up with. Fuck me, I wanted to apologize again. I wanted to explain myself, better this time. But I didn't have a better explanation, even if I could even get the words out through my bruised windpipe. It would just be more lies. I'd liked Daniel, but not enough to trust him. Now he knew that. Nothing I could do or say would ever be enough to wipe that out.

"Why you here?" I had to ration my words against the pain. My voice sounded dull, stilted by the new lump in my throat.

Daniel didn't notice. He'd turned toward the door, as if only half-hearing the question. "Abe's outside lying to your nurse and—"

"Abe?" What the hell day was it? Had I been asleep another three months? Had Daniel and Abe joined up and stopped Aubrie and now everything was fixed?

No. Daniel had on the same t-shirt and jeans he'd been wearing when I'd left him at the motel . . . what, yesterday? I'd left him, I'd gone to Aubrie. I'd run into Soren, gone to the Faerie house, run out and to . . .

Mom's.

The book.

I shot upright again, opening my mouth to tell the story. The sudden motion sent a crack of agony through my stomach, breaking through the fuzzy warmth of the painkillers. I slumped back against the pillow, catching my breath. Talking was no good. I scanned the room. Writing might be okay. I gestured to a dry erase pen clipped to the whiteboard on the wall.

It took a frustratingly long time for Daniel to understand my impatient flailing, but finally he retrieved the pen.

Book in car, I scrawled on my left palm, penmanship loose from an inability to keep a good grip with fingers that felt numb.

He read it off my hand as I held it up. "What book?"

I scribbled furiously on my skin again: *Grimthing.*

"You found the grymoire?" He sounded stunned. "Where?"

Hartsville. I'd started to to run out of skin. The blunt tip of the dry erase marker made it hard to write small. The ink bled into my skin, blurring the letters. Had to stick to relevant information. I jotted the shortest scribble that might get the whole story across on the back of my hand: *shapeshifter @ motel waiting for u attakd me in G's car left book car where?*

Daniel took a moment to make sense of the mess, then answered, "An impound lot."

"I knew it." Another voice came from the other side of my bed, making me flinch.

Ilse. I hadn't heard her come in. From the expression on Daniel's face, he hadn't either. Glad it wasn't just me and the drugs.

"I just *knew* you had the grymoire in that bag this morning," Ilse said. "You could have told me, Jude. I wasn't going to harm you."

Agree to disagree. Not that my poppy seed ruse had made any difference in the end, apart from probably pissing her off. If Ilse could even *be* pissed off.

She tilted her head to read my hand before I could think to stick it under the sheets and hide it. "What's the type of car?"

When I didn't answer fast enough, she fixed me with her steady violet gaze. "Jude, Aubrie hired the shapeshifter who attacked you. The man came in from the accident with you, but he disappeared from this hospital an hour ago. He knew about the book, yes? Please *tell me* what kind of car so I can get it first."

"Black hatchback." My words slipped out in a painful whisper.

"And there's an identifier on it." At my blank look, she held her hands up to form a rectangle. "It denotes a location. A *province*?"

A license plate. "Quebec."

"Yes. Thank you." Nodding, she patted me on the shoulder. "I'll find the car." She disappeared.

The door opened again as Abe stepped inside. He turned to gaze out as if something had slipped past him. Looking to me and Daniel, he asked, "Where's Ilse off to so fast?"

I sank back against my pillow, exhausted. Maybe I could pass out until all of my visitors went away and saved the world without me.

Daniel didn't answer Abe either, moving away from the cowboy in a way that said they weren't hanging out as friends.

Apparently not taking offence to our silence, Abe shut the door. "Heard you had an adventure," he told me, crossing the room to stand by my bed. He set a paper shopping bag at the end of it. "How you feeling?"

I let him read the answer from my glare.

He removed his hat, setting it aside on my bedside table. The fluorescent lights gleamed off his bare head. He reached for my neck.

When I pulled away, he gave me a disappointed look.

Grudgingly, I held still, letting him run a finger around my throat, over the painful bruises. The ache felt distant, reaching me a few seconds after it should have. It still hit hard enough when it came.

Putting a hand around the front of my neck, Abe placed his fingers in an unpleasant mimic of the shapeshifter's grip.

I twitched at the warmth of his skin against mine. It grew warmer, twinging then starting to burn. Tears pricked the corners of my eyes. My own voice startled me, popping out instead of rasping silence. "Ow!"

"You're a tough gal," Abe said, not giving me time to grab a breath before he'd put a hand on either side of my stomach through my flimsy gown. The fire it started in my mid-section made me choke.

Yet when he stepped back, my head felt shockingly clear. "Hey, what happened to the drugs?" My voice still came out scratchy as I put my fingers against my head. Could he do hangovers, too?

Rather than thank him, I challenged, "So, I guess you're here to heal me up and trick me into doing something nefarious for the Faeries again?"

"Only one of the two, darlin'." He sighed, retrieving his hat from the table.

"How'd you find me?"

"Hiding out here with your—" Abe turned to look for Daniel.

We realized at the same moment that he'd slipped out while Abe had been healing me.

"Damn it." Abe slapped his hat against his thigh. "I'd hoped he'd realized what was in his best interest."

"Yeah, he did, and went after Ilse," I said. "She's gone to get the book."

"What book?"

"The one you guys are all looking for. I found it at my mom's. I think I did." I brushed my hair back from my face, still revelling in the feeling of drawing a deep, painless breath. "I guess Ilse's jogging my memory yesterday with her notes actually worked. It made me remember this book of poetry my dad gave my mom."

Abe's eyebrows shot up, expression somewhere between impressed and annoyed. "You shouldn't have gone alone."

"And you shouldn't have manipulated me. Are there cops outside?" I peered around him toward the door.

He shook his head. "They'll probably be looking to talk to you, but I figure the doctors told them you wouldn't be talking for a few days. Doctors probably also told them you wouldn't be going anywhere. You ready to get out of here?"

"With you?"

"Have you got somewhere else to go?"

"Lots of places. Anywhere I goddamn please."

He caught my tone. "I understand you're angry, darlin'. I do."

"Great read. Super empathic."

"I'm sorry. But, Jude, things are . . . things are difficult right now." He glanced toward the window, admitting, "Aubrie attacked the house."

"The magic house?" The thought gave me a jolt.

"He's got more powerful people than we'd anticipated." Abe shook his head, glossing over the details in a strained voice. "Miranda was injured. Some others took her across through the portal. The healers on the other side . . . well, they'll do a damn sight better than I can."

"She'll be okay, though?" I pressed.

He inclined his head toward me in a way that was not quite a nod. "Prognosis was better, last I heard."

I bit my tongue. *Better than what?*

"Okay," I said, shoving the starched blanket off my legs. "Let's get out of here. Where are my clothes?"

"Ilse conjured you some fresh ones." Abe passed me the paper bag from the end of my bed.

"How long was I out this time?"

"Most of the day. It's about seven."

My boots sat at the end of the bed. I dumped out the contents of the bag he'd handed me. Ilse had brought a neatly folded pair of jeans, clean underwear, socks, a bra and a blue t-shirt that would have matched the roots of her hair perfectly. The last thing to fall out of the bag was a white ribbon.

No hard feelings about the poppy seeds, then.

41

DANIEL FOUND THE ADDRESS for the impound lot using his phone in the hospital elevator. As he mapped the route via bus, an irritating regret tugged at him for leaving Jude in her drugged haze with the cowboy's hand around her throat. The new Mab's cohort had never hurt her before though. Leaving their house, he'd been the one with the scars—Jude hadn't had even a scratch. It seemed unlikely she was in any danger.

He shouldn't have cared if she was—she'd conspired with the Court to start with. She'd made her choices a hundred times over.

That didn't stop the nagging unease. What the hell had she been doing back at the motel? Had she gone there just to get Gracie's car? No—she'd found her way all the way to her mother's place and then boomeranged back to the motel on her own. Why steal a car just to get the last twenty kilometres after all that?

The ten-minute bus ride let him turn his thoughts from that puzzling mess to more immediate problems. He'd swiped a metal butter knife and some packets of salt and pepper from a cart of hospital meal trays while an orderly's back was turned, but hadn't found any better weapons. Going after the book unarmed like this bordered on suicidal, but he couldn't waste the opportunity. He just hoped he'd beat Ilse and any friends she brought with her to finding it.

A brisk two-block walk brought him to a chain-link fence wrapped around a lot of empty cars. As he reached the corner in search of an entrance to the lot, a screech of metal from his left made him stop short.

Two men sprinted toward him, fleeing something. The gate to the impound lot hung askew behind them, the metal in the centre torn open like a train had burst through it. A blond man and what looked like a very motivated cloud of mist followed in pursuit.

Right place, then.

The man in the lead carried a crowbar and had something else blue tucked tightly under his arm. Daniel waited until he had reached the corner of the fence then swung out and tackled him.

They hit the pavement hard together and rolled, the other man taking the brunt of the fall in one shoulder. As they came to rest in a heap on the ground, Daniel threw a punch. His opponent blocked it and managed to return a cuff to the side of his head that made his vision blur. A high-pitched ring started in his ear.

Over it, he heard the scrape of the crowbar against the cement. As the man above him hefted it into one hand, raising his arm to swing, Daniel tugged the butter knife from his back pocket. He jammed it into his adversary's armpit, using all of his force to thrust the dull blade through the soft spot of flesh.

The man howled, dropping the crowbar.

Daniel kicked him off and swung a fist again, snapping the other man's head back. His opponent collapsed against the curb, then turned with difficulty onto his stomach as if he meant to crawl away. Instead, he fell still, panting.

Daniel snatched the thin, blue hardback book that had fallen to the sidewalk. Staggering to his feet, he faced the cloud of mist.

It shaped itself into a human form, then solidified into Ilse.

She kept her distance, a metre away. Disdain crept across her features as she eyed him, but her stance didn't indicate an immediate attack.

Daniel crouched to grab the crowbar his earlier adversary had dropped, tucking the book under his arm to take it in both hands.

"That will only make things worse," Ilse warned. Her expression remained haughty but her gaze darted to her partner, as if she didn't want to draw his attention.

The blond man straddled the remaining book thief, pummelling him against the sidewalk. The sound of Ilse's voice made his head jerk up. Leaving his previous quarry bloodied and unconscious on the sidewalk, he glared at Daniel. "You?"

The word came out as a derisive laugh.

A terrifying familiarity pressed the breath from Daniel's lungs. He didn't recognize the man but his memory screamed at him to run. It was the siren from the basement. She had a different form now but it was still her. The face was too similar to the one in the shadows, the lips forming the same twisted grin that had parted to reveal sharp, glittering teeth before a smaller, feminine hand had jammed a blade into his ribs . . .

Daniel took a step back without meaning to, raising the crowbar.

The siren tilted his head up, making a show of sniffing the air before his smile widened. "Steel," he remarked, eyeing the weapon. "Not quite good enough. As usual."

"Feels heavy enough," Daniel spat back.

Car tires squealed down the street, making them both turn. A white sedan swung around the corner. It had no lights or sirens but barrelled straight toward them, bumping up over the lip of the curb and coming to a sudden stop.

The doors swung open. Two figures leapt out. One man started making a constant motion with his hands, shooting something off his palm with the speed of bullets.

Whatever it was smashed into the pavement with force, chipping the cement.

Daniel scrambled back against the chain-link fence, keeping the book pressed tightly under his arm.

The hail of tiny missiles stopped. Readying himself to run, his eye caught on something lodged in the concrete near his foot. He couldn't help yanking it out to examine it. The smooth, white oblong piece looked like bone.

The shard jerked from his fingers. All of the other projectiles pulled themselves from the pavement, returning in a swarm to their caster, whose right hand hung limp and deflated at his side like an empty glove. He gathered the projectiles back in his left hand.

The man could shoot bones from his hands like bullets. It wasn't a magical ability Daniel had heard of, nor one he wanted to tangle with. He still couldn't help the fascination that seeped through him at the logistics of the idea.

A second round of shots jolted him out of it. The Antagonist aimed the bulk of the barrage at the two figures in the street. The blond siren already lay face-down on the ground. Blood gleamed on the asphalt. Ilse materialized over him with a cry of pain, slapping a hand over her bicep as one of the shards clipped her.

Sprays of water shot from the sewer grates on both side of the street. Another surge erupted from a manhole under the white car, spinning the vehicle sideways into the two men and knocking them off their feet.

Still on hands and knees, bowed over her partner, Ilse hissed in exertion, fingers digging into the asphalt. Ripples ran through her body and she shimmered, no longer solid. Her eyes fixed on the two men with the car as she lurched to her feet.

The sight of her made Daniel dizzy. Her glamour had chipped away so that her hair became a raging ocean around her head. Her eyes glowed pale blue. The same terror that had smothered him when the cowboy had started to heal him pressed in again. The air around him felt alien, unfamiliar. Instinct told him to cower, cover his head and pray that the massive power passed him by.

He forced himself to fix on the solid, steady lines of pavement under his feet, sprinting away from the lot. He expected to hear bone shards drumming into the pavement behind him—or have them tear into his back—but he focused on putting one foot in front of the other at a pace he wouldn't be able to sustain for long.

A deafening metallic pop from behind him made him skid to a stop and spin around. Even from a block away a spout of water was visible gushing into the air. A red fire hydrant fell from the sky. He couldn't see where it landed, but the distant, wet crunch it made probably meant it had hit flesh.

He kept running.

42

I SLIPPED OUT OF the hospital room with Abe, following him down the hall to what looked like a locked supply closet.

Taking a quick glance to make sure we weren't observed, he pushed the door open to reveal the familiar Faerie house.

I balked. "You can just get here through any door?"

"Most doors." He stepped back to let me inside.

"How?" My next question caught in my throat upon seeing the dark trail of liquid running across the hardwood floor of the hallway. My muscles tensed in anticipation of a fight.

Abe closed the door behind us and pushed past me, ducking into the living room.

Ilse knelt beside another figure stretched out on the floor. Blood pooled on the carpet under his buzzed blond hair. Soren. Pressing rhythmically on his chest, the water sprite applied CPR one-handed. Her left arm hung useless at her side. When she moved, it caught the light and shimmered to let me see right through the spot where her bicep should have been.

"Let me." Abe pushed her gently aside.

Ilse lifted her head in surprise as if she hadn't heard us come in. She resisted my attempt to help her to the sofa for a moment, then consented to let me lead her away from Soren.

"What happened?" I asked.

"We went to the impound but Aubrie's men were there already." Her voice turned a shade more disdainful. "They shot at us with bone fragments."

"With—" I didn't have the patience to imagine that. "Damn."

Abe sat back on his heels, shoulders slumping as he lifted bloody hands from Soren's body.

The siren still wasn't breathing.

"Why are you stopping?" I asked.

"He's dead." Abe removed his hat, setting it aside.

"For a few minutes." The finality in his voice sent a chill through me. "People come out of that all the time."

Abe got to his feet. "Death creates a psychic void. If I try to establish a connection, it's too likely I'll get pulled in."

I opened my mouth to argue, but I didn't have one to make. I hadn't killed Soren. I hadn't even liked him. It still felt shitty to stand here, useless, in a magical house, and let him be dead.

Abe lowered himself down beside Ilse on the sofa, taking her wounded arm in his hands. He lifted it, making her cringe in pain as he healed the injury. It seemed quick compared to his time spent fixing me up in the hospital.

"Cain's son has the grymoire," Ilse said, rolling her healed shoulder forward to test it, adding, "At least I hope he does."

"He took it from you?" Abe looked surprised.

"He took it from Aubrie's man." She cast him a cool look that faded quickly. "And escaped while they attacked us." Her eyes flickered to the siren's body and away, then she got to her feet. "With the half-moon tonight, it's imperative that—"

"Tonight?" My voice cracked. "What the hell? Why didn't anyone *tell* me that?"

Abe and Ilse's matching startled expressions reminded me that it wasn't the most important question, but goddamn it, did they think I regularly consulted lunar charts? How come nobody had mentioned this critical deadline?

Because I'd gotten pissed off and split yesterday before they could. Because nobody had expected me to wander off to Mom's and unearth the stupid spellbook.

"Find Daniel before Aubrie does," Abe told Ilse. "I have to try and speak to Miranda."

"Why?" I'd never seen him ask for orders before.

"She can send troops through the portal."

"Troops? Like Faerie troops? Fuck no!" The Consilium part of me I hadn't known still existed rose up to balk at what sounded too much like an invasion. I tailed him to the hallway to demand, "You think she's even well enough to give orders?"

"I need to try."

"Because she's the Mab? If she's so powerful, why hasn't she already just killed Aubrie?"

"The bulk of her power's in her world," Abe said. "The only way she can wield the entire force here is if the boundaries cross."

"So, if Aubrie does his spell, she can take him out. She's a . . . whatsit—fail-safe."

"Jude, if the worlds merge, there's no way to undo it." He took a step away from me, putting out a placating hand. "Let me see what we're working with."

Right, let him call up my injured aunt in Faerieland and ask *her* what to do from a world away. I didn't need orders.

Leaving him heading upstairs, I swung back into the living room to grill Ilse. "Can you find out where Daniel is, like Abe said?"

She blinked, composing herself to consider my question. "Yes."

"How?"

"I could use his blood."

"What—? Oh. You have that from when you guys . . ." I didn't bother to finish.

Ilse brought her eyes up to meet mine as if she expected a reprimand.

"So, you've got some kind of blood tracking spell?" I asked. "Or is there just a pixie holed up somewhere waiting to be taken out?"

"It shouldn't take long." Polite evasion, so very Ilse.

"And how long's Abe going to take?"

"If the Mab's conscious, he'll speak to her through a mirror upstairs."

"And if she's not? Does he know what '*midnight tonight*' means?" I *really* hadn't planned to be the one rushing in and shutting off the ticking bomb three seconds before it blew.

"Yes, Jude. We're aware." Ilse frowned at me.

"Sorry." Being blunt with her made me feel like a brute, especially after taking advantage of her with the poppy seeds that morning.

Ilse went to do her blood thing and I retreated to the empty kitchen so I didn't have to stare at Soren's body.

What must have been fifteen or twenty minutes passed. I started to get antsy, tapping my foot against the tile and stopping each time I realized I was doing it. The house had no clocks, and even if it had, who knew what time zone they'd be in? Not the one I needed.

"Did you find him?" I pounced on Ilse as soon as she appeared in the doorway.

"Yes." She'd written down the name, address and room number of a hotel in precise, calligraphic script.

"And he's . . . alive?" The question slipped out without permission.

"The tracking wouldn't work if he weren't."

"Then I'll go get him."

"Wait." Ilse trailed me into the front hall. She put a hand against the front door as I pulled it open. "Give us time, Jude. Wait and see what the Mab has to say."

"*The Mab*'s not here," I snapped. "She's laid up in a Faerie hospital bed, a world away. And, as you all neglected to tell me, time isn't something we've got."

43

DANIEL SET THE STOLEN crowbar within easy reach on the desk. After jumping back onto a bus, he'd found his way to a new hotel room. He didn't feel any safer. Being in motion had been better, but not practical long-term.

Opening the cover of the small, blue book titled *Collected Poems of Sylvia Plath*, he thumbed through the pages. All poems, all in English. Maybe it was the wrong book. Jude had seemed certain, and Aubrie and the Mab had sent people after it, but they could be all mistaken.

It's glamoured. Daniel tapped his fingers on the pages, trying to remember anything that would help him dispel it. He recited a simple spell he'd learned at the Consilium. The book didn't change.

If I'm going through this for a book of poetry . . .

With no other recourse, he called Gracie.

She answered after one ring, relief tinging her voice. "What's going on?"

"I might have the grymoire."

"Shit. Tell me you're at least at the airport."

"There aren't any flights out tonight. Did your research say anything about diffusing the book's glamour?"

"The book's glamoured?"

"If it's the right one, it's disguised as a collection of poetry," Daniel said. "In English."

"I guess that makes sense, but where'd you get it?" Gracie asked. "What makes you think it's the grymoire?"

"Jude found it. She thinks it's right."

"And we trust *her* judgment now because . . . ?" When she didn't get an answer, Gracie relented and asked, "Where'd she find it? Mystical cave?"

"Rural Ontario."

"My second guess. And she doesn't know how to change it?"

"Not that she mentioned. But she wasn't talking much after crashing your car."

"Don't remind me." Gracie's dour tone was accompanied by the clicking of a keyboard. "There should be unique symbols on each page," she relayed, "and some will correspond to the translation key you've got. You turn down the bottom corner of the page with the corresponding symbol, in order, and the book translates itself."

"There aren't any symbols." Daniel skimmed the pages. "If it's glamoured, they're hidden too."

"That's your area of expertise, not mine," Gracie said.

Daniel held in a sigh. He would hardly call researching Antagonist spells and dabbling in a few defences against glamour *expertise*. "There should be a specific part of the book that needs to be destroyed," he said. One of the older Consilium researchers in the Magics department had told him that. *A glamour's like a cover thrown over something. Taking it off requires finding the loose thread and pulling. Antagonists can do this like blinking; it's harder for us.* "Maybe a specific page which, torn out, tears off the glamour too."

His fingers slid over something sharp on the back of the book. He turned it over to find shrapnel buried in the cover: a tiny piece of something white. It looked like a small shard of bone—the same thing the Antagonist at the impound lot had been shooting. He pried it out from where it had bored into the hard cover. It should have torn into the back pages of the book, but the paper there remained pristine and undamaged.

A glimmer from the corner of his eye made him turn his head. A fine, sparkling mist flooded through the crack under the door. The mist formed into a human shape, re-materializing not a foot away into a short, leather-jacket-clad man: the one who'd stabbed Zeb.

Daniel snatched the crowbar but didn't have time to swing it before the pixie laid a hand flat, blowing a heavy cloud of sparkling dust. He struggled to stay on his feet as the dust stung his eyes, but his knees gave out without permission. He hooked one arm over the end of the mattress. The room swam around him. Everything had a fuzzy outline.

The pixie retrieved the weapon, then slammed a heel down on the phone Daniel had dropped on the carpet. Once he'd crushed the screen with a boot, he turned and went back to the door, unlocking it and swinging it open so that two other men could enter.

"I'd have broken it down," Aubrie said as he stepped inside from the hallway and closed the door, "but no use causing a scene." He picked up the tiny white shard that had been buried in the book, tossing it to the other man beside the door. The other man palmed it, as if returning it to its proper place.

"You weren't wrong about the page." Aubrie's words indicated that he'd heard at least part of Daniel's phone conversation from outside the room. He lifted the blue book off the desk, holding it gingerly in both hands. Flipping it open, he grabbed the edge of the first page and tugged on it hard enough that it should have torn.

The page held fast, making a snapping sound. "The trick is—" Aubrie sounded pleased. "—only one *will* tear out. You *have* found the right book." He took two steps closer, crouching down to put his face closer to Daniel's. "I appreciate it, though I doubt that means much to you."

Daniel tried to shove himself upright, but the pixie pounced, driving him back down toward the floor. The smaller man wrestled him to his stomach, pinning his arms with more strength than Daniel would have expected. A sharp pain when the pixie twisted his arm sent a crack through the haze still clouding his mind, letting him remember some of his training. *Pain clears the effects at the onset.* He shifted to make the pixie tighten his grip. That stab of pain brought the room back into startling clarity.

Lifting his left shoulder to throw the pixie off, Daniel swung the smaller man into the side of the bed. Free, he shot up, jamming an elbow into the pixie's face to keep him down.

Aubrie caught him by the throat before he could get further. "No," he said. "I didn't think my gratitude would be enough."

"Why this spell?" Daniel managed. "You already destroyed the Consilium and the Court. Merging the spheres now gets you what?"

"Well, I didn't expect *that*." Aubrie smiled. "Threats, perhaps, insistence that you'd *stop me*, even some pathetic attack. Not the attempt to *reason* with me." He gave a short laugh. "Your father would be ashamed of you."

"That wouldn't have been much of a stretch for him," Daniel shot back.

"Commiseration," Aubrie said, as if it completed the list. "You're better off begging." With what seemed like little effort, he tossed Daniel backwards, across the room and into the far wall.

Daniel hit hard with one shoulder, collapsing to the floor. The sudden motion seemed to reactivate the last vestiges of the pixie dust. The room tilted sideways and then righted itself as he fought to stop the spinning in his vision.

As if down a tunnel, Aubrie spoke: "Stay here, Jasper. Make sure he keeps breathing until you hear from me."

"He killed Pru!" Jasper brandished a switchblade that flashed in the overhead lights.

"And once I know for certain that the key I have unlocks this book, you can settle that. Until then, wait to hear from me." Aubrie and the third man disappeared out the door, leaving Daniel with the pixie.

Aubrie had a key? Daniel fought to focus on the repeating pattern in the carpet, digging his fingernails into his palm to make it hurt and clear his head. How could Aubrie already have the translation key to unlock the grymoire?

Mei.

The realization hit with sickening certainty. He'd been an idiot to trust her—but that was just par for the course these days.

He had to get the book back before Aubrie took it to her and translated it. He shoved himself off the floor, going for the crowbar the pixie had tossed onto the bed.

Jasper burst into a cloud of glitter. Flickering between dust and solid, he circled Daniel and slashed at him with the knife. He moved too quickly to inflict deep cuts, but there was no way to avoid him.

Daniel crouched, covering his head with his hands until Jasper had given up the immediate attack. As soon as the pixie solidified, he launched himself forward, knocking the smaller man down.

Jasper exploded into glitter before hitting the floor, leaving Daniel batting at the dust from his hands and knees to keep it out of his eyes. The room was too small a place to get an advantage over an enemy who could blink in and out of solid form at will. He hauled himself to his feet, then raced through the shimmering cloud to reach the door.

Yanking it open, he plowed into somebody directly outside.

44

POISED TO TAP ON the hotel room door, I tensed at muffled noise from inside. It sounded like a fight. I shifted to one foot, intent on kicking down the door with a little extra boost from my gravity.

Before I could try it, the door opened and Daniel ran right into me. The collision bounced us both backwards: me into the opposite side of the hallway and him against the wall beside the door he'd escaped.

The door slammed open again, putting me squarely in Jasper's glare. The pixie snarled when he recognized me and charged.

Daniel caught him with a punch just as he cleared the doorway, hitting hard enough to send the spiky-haired man stumbling back into the room. Something flew from Jasper's hand and landed with a soft thud just inside the door.

I propelled myself forward before either the door closed or Jasper recovered, plowing into him just inside the doorway. I'd meant to knock him to the floor and tackle him, but I hit the carpet hard on my hands and knees, solo. A wave of glittering dust gusted up past me as his body dissipated and slipped from my grip. I dodged sideways to avoid him, knowing that he'd reformed behind me, but his boot caught my shoulder-blade, slamming me to the carpet again.

His fingers raked my scalp and he yanked me up by my hair hard enough to make me howl. Before I could get my bearings to reverse my gravity and tug him off-balance, he grunted and faltered, releasing me.

Daniel had gotten Jasper's attention with a knife—probably one the pixie had dropped when he'd been decked a second ago. From Daniel's stance, he'd tried to stab Jasper in the back but had been thwarted by the other man's heavy leather jacket.

As Jasper turned, Daniel struck again. This time he buried the blade in the side of the pixie's neck, then yanked it out to take a third swing.

Jasper reeled to one side. Blood gushed down his throat and he struggled to keep his footing. He hissed something unintelligible. Swaying on his feet, it seemed like he couldn't decide whether to dive at Daniel for the knife or past him for the door.

Instead, he dissolved into glitter. The cloud wove across the room toward the door, which must have fallen shut behind us. It hovered there, then started to stream down toward the crack at the floor.

It lost its shape with a sudden jerk. The gleaming pieces floated apart, drifting to the ground like snow. They flickered and disappeared on their way down.

I caught my breath as my shoulder blade and scalp remembered to start throbbing in unison.

Daniel approached the spot where the cloud had fallen apart and tapped the carpet with the toe of his shoe. He looked ready to jump back, but nothing sprang up in response.

I couldn't even see the glitter anymore as I got to my feet and joined him. "Good riddance to a bad hair-do."

Daniel slumped to the side, bracing a shoulder against the wall. Bleeding gashes crossed his arms and chest. Another ran down the side of his face.

But he wasn't dead or being tortured by Aubrie. Relief surged through my muscles, trying to get me to throw my arms around him. I couldn't bring myself to do that, so I blurted out, "You look like hell."

He gave me a reproachful look. "Glad you got your voice back."

I couldn't help but grin. "Abe healed me. Back in fighting form."

"Good, because Aubrie's got the book." No mirth there.

"How?" I stared at him. "And how are you alive? Did he take the key from you somehow?"

"Mei has it too." Daniel dropped the switchblade on the desk and wiped the blood from his hand on his jeans. That hadn't turned to glitter with the pixie. "She must."

"Goddamn it." Should have laid out the ex-dragon after her transformation at the motel in St. Catharines. Well, better late than never. "Okay, Niagara it is." I turned toward the door.

He caught my wrist. "You're not going alone."

"Oh, *now* you want to come along?" The sarcasm came instinctively, to make him angry, make him let go of me.

He sighed, shaking his head. "I should have gone with you the first time."

"No, you were right." I countered before I could stop myself. "I shouldn't have gone at all. I just got some bruised ribs and screwed up a Court plan to take Aubrie out. This could have all been over already if they'd done their thing. I wanted to fuck him up myself."

"Still want to do that?"

"More than ever."

"Then let's go."

My relief at finding Daniel alive morphed into something sharper in my stomach. Aubrie had the book, and according to Mei, he had twenty to thirty people with him. Half-Faerie people, with magic powers. Daniel had been right the first time: this had always been a suicide mission. I couldn't let him come with me.

I stopped him before he could brush past me toward the door. "You're bleeding."

"They're not deep."

"Still." I took a quick inventory of the room around us. There was a bathroom near the front door that couldn't have any windows in it. "You can't go out like that. Somebody's going to call the cops."

"It's not that bad." He rubbed away a trickle of red from the side of his face, then examined the amount of fresh blood staining his hand.

I snagged the fancy Hotel Services binder from the desk, pulling him toward the bathroom. Trying to keep my movements as calm as possible, I switched on the light in the tiny room as if to see his injuries better, then ran the tap.

As Daniel followed me reluctantly across the threshold, I waved the binder. "You clean up. I'll find a cab company in here."

I slipped past him, back out into the room, then pushed the door shut behind me. The bathroom was small enough that the door opened out into the room. Two good kicks had the binder wedged underneath it to hold it shut.

"Jude!" Daniel tried the knob. "Open the goddamn door!"

"Nope." I gave the wedge another kick with my heel to make sure it was tight, taking a step back. I snatched the switchblade from the desk. After checking that the room's door locked behind me, I hurried out of the hotel.

A block down and around the corner, I started scouting for a ride to downtown Niagara. I could have used the Faerie safehouse, but Abe and Ilse might try to stop me. Maybe they could even make it lock me in. I didn't have time to follow the Mab's orders.

I found an old sedan, sea green with one blue door, hopefully too rusted out to have a working alarm. Searching the street for something to put through the window, a broken piece of thick metal wire gleamed up instead from the gutter. It took some gravity force to form into a hook, but then I slid it between the window and the door, jimmying the lock open. Inside the car, I smashed the ignition with my boot, knocking away the plastic to leave a slit for the metal wire.

The old junker came to life easily: a little jiggling, a turn, and the engine purred to life. And Mom had called my friends useless.

I followed the road signs to Niagara Falls in the dark. The quiet highway gave my brain too much time to find reasonable objections to my spontaneous plan. I turned the radio up.

I couldn't remember how Zeb had gotten us to Aubrie's hotel, but by following the downtown exits, I landed on a familiar street with a familiar hotel. Less tourists at this hour, but a handful seemed to be stumbling back to their hotels from either the bars, the casino or the Falls.

Ditching the car in the first legal-looking spot I found, I did an automatic, hasty wipe of my fingerprints with my heart tapping against my ribs.

I went straight through the deserted lobby to the mirrored elevator and up to the fourth floor. I checked for the hidden forms of chameleons against the wallpaper, but like last time, nothing stood out. They'd all hidden in the adjoining room before, so I readied myself for a repeat performance.

I pounded on the door to 427, half-expecting a stranger.

Aubrie opened the door, not even having the decency to look surprised.

"You're a cocky bastard," I said. "Same room."

"No use moving my suitcases." He stepped back to invite me into the room, but I didn't move.

"Where's my book? I want it back!" I held my muscles in check rather than leaping on him. Maybe I could work this, catch him off-guard. He'd wanted me on his side last time. Pretending for a second would hurt less than running right into his fist. "My mother gave it to me."

He flashed a wan smile. "Yes, I remember how devoted you are to your mom."

"I just don't want to see her huddling in some half-Faerie world."

"I'm not planning the end of the world. Just the opposite." *Bingo*. He sounded like he still thought I might jump back on his bandwagon.

"But you don't know *what* it'll be," I countered. "Maybe we should wait a while and do some more research. There's a half-moon, like, twice a month."

Aubrie sighed. "You used to be more open-minded."

"You mean obedient." I spun to land a high-kick to his chest.

Without time to steel himself, he stumbled back into the room.

I followed, ducking him as he bounced back to rush me. I let my hands propel me into a somersault past him.

He caught me as I climbed to my feet, backhanding me hard enough to send me into my old impression in the far wall from our last fight. He pinned me there with a hand around my throat.

"You're still a pathetic, deluded little girl if you actually think no one's pulling your strings now," he said. "Your aunt Miranda—"

"Not working for Auntie." I moved my foot to stomp on his with the full force of my gravity, readying to tug myself away when he let go.

"But you're still her heir."

The word stopped me short. It hadn't occurred to me what it might mean to have the Mab as my aunt.

Aubrie seized on my moment of surprise, twisting my arm in his vise-grip to yank me off my feet. I hit the floor hard on my back, the air knocked out of my lungs.

The room spun above me but I rolled to one side to escape him, then let myself fall up. I miscalculated my own force and hit the ceiling almost as hard as I'd hit the floor. At least, on my back up here, I was out of his reach.

The book sat perched on the desk by the window, the faded blue cover the same as it had looked in my mom's place.

I turned back onto my stomach and pushed myself to my hands and knees. Before I could dive for the book, the door to the adjoining room opened, letting in one of Aubrie's hulking bodyguards.

The goon was tall enough to bat me across the ceiling without jumping, knocking me backwards like a volleyball into the seam where it met the wall. I lost my grip on gravity and ended up sprawled across the pillows of the bed.

Scrambling upright off the end of the mattress, I came face-to-chest with the much bigger and broader *lesidhe*.

Before he could hit me, something struck him from behind. He grunted, falling to his knees and revealing Mei.

She'd emerged from the adjoining room too. Dressed in the same clothes as the last time I'd seen her, she grasped a barbell-shaped silver lamp without a shade. The bulb was broken and blood stained the metal.

Her eyes darted past me and she lifted the lamp again. Before she could swing it at me, another bodyguard grabbed her from behind. She shrieked in surprise, flinging the weapon forward. I dodged to the side, letting it thunk onto the floor beside my feet.

A hard sucker punch from my left knocked me down beside it. Above me, a fuzzy version of Aubrie held the blue book in one hand as my vision dipped. He stepped over me to head for the door.

I snatched the lamp from the floor beside me and shoved myself up to take a desperate swing. Before it could connect with the back of his knee, something yanked me backwards.

The first bodyguard had gotten to his hands and knees and grabbed me by the waistband of my jeans. He flipped me onto my back, angling to get a hand around my throat.

I kicked him in the balls, then kneed him in the stomach and rolled out from under him as he crashed down to the carpet. Another swift kick to his face once I'd gained my feet made him fall still.

Beyond him, the door to the adjoining room still hung open. Mei had gotten free of the second bodyguard somehow and brought him down. She toppled the flat screen TV onto his head. He didn't get up.

My room's door sat ajar where Aubrie had fled with the book. I threw it open and ducked into the hallway. Empty.

"You were supposed to hit Aubrie in the head with the lamp," Mei said from behind me.

I spun to find her shoving a cellphone into the tiny pocket of her pencil skirt.

"And you were supposed to *not* give the asshole the translation key to the world-ending spellbook!" I took a breather against the doorjamb, keeping an eye on the hallway for hotel security.

"I thought he'd let me go if I told him." Chagrin crossed Mei's features. "I wanted my life back."

"Well, I'm sorry your shitty, selfish plan backfired on you."

"Like I could have anticipated *you'd* randomly find that goddamn book?" She glared at me, fingers clenching like she wanted to wring my neck.

"Do you know where he's going?"

"As close as he can get to the Falls."

I eyed her bare feet. I hadn't been here since I was a kid, and I didn't know exactly where we were in relation to the Falls, but we'd have to descend a hill to get down to the park that ran along the river. "I'm not carrying you."

45

EVERY CONCEIVABLE JOINT IN my body hurt as Mei and I hurried through the hotel lobby. Special emphasis weighed on the major areas: knees, hips, ankles. You'd think my ribs would be used to the dull ache, but it still vied for my attention.

Outside, Mei pulled out her cellphone. "You're alone?" she asked. "Where's Daniel?"

"I locked him in a hotel bathroom."

Her sharp laugh echoed off the buildings around us. She put her attention back on her phone to ignore the glower I sent her way, probably mapping our route.

I glanced up and down the street, looking for helpful signs. A handful of tourists trickled past us, probably coming home to their hotels after seeing the World-Ending Source of Natural Energy lit up at night.

I put my face to the sky, willing the magic Abe had used to knock into me and send me running toward the nearest special door.

Nothing.

Taking a deep breath, I tried again, waiting for some hint of the electricity in my skin to stir me. How had Abe done this? Did I need a running start?

The air stayed still.

"Come on!" I shouted at the sky.

Beside me, Mei's expression turned sour as she guessed my intentions. "Your Court friends aren't obliging tonight?"

"They're not my friends," I muttered.

"That's patently untrue." The sudden voice from my left almost made me jump out of my skin. Ilse materialized beside us.

"Fuck." Mei took a step back, raising her phone as if she might try to hit the sprite with it.

"It's okay." I put out a placating hand. "Ilse, Mei, Mei, Ilse. Ilse's a water sprite. Mei's newly human."

The two women eyed each other but neither objected.

"Aubrie's got the book and he's going to the Falls," I told Ilse.

"Yes, I know," she said.

"Where's everybody else?" I waited for her to tell me they'd already been through the battle, leaving her the last one standing.

"Abe said the cavalry's on the way." She frowned at the phrase she clearly didn't understand. "But right now you have my aid."

"I'll take it. Can you get us to the park?"

"Yes." Ilse gestured us back to the glass doors of the hotel lobby. When she pulled one open, despite the lobby sitting beyond the glass, we stepped into the empty front hall of the Faerie house.

Closing the door behind us, Ilse turned to put her hand against it. "Table Rock Welcome Centre," she said. She really did know where we were going, specifics and all.

We came out through a glass door from a dark, closed welcome centre and emerged onto a brick platform. The Falls roared ahead of us, mist glowing under the overhead lights. The open plaza was deserted. Even this late at night, I'd expected to find a few tourists milling around.

Electricity skittered across my skin. Something felt wrong.

Mei stopped short, brows furrowing in confusion as she stared at the empty space before us. She started to shake her head, taking a step back as if she meant to turn and retreat back into the locked building.

A foreign wave of uncertainty surged through me. *There's nothing worth seeing up there. We should go back.* I almost turned the way Mei had, but Ilse tugged on my arm.

"They're in there," she said, inclining her head toward the edge of the falls.

"In where?" As I got the words out, she vanished. That gave me the jolt I needed to shake myself out of the whispers pressing me away from the place. A sizzle of goosebumps passed over me as I followed her, making me shiver from my toes to my hairline.

One more step and I saw Ilse again, crouching behind the tall plants in a raised flower bed, as well as a scattered group of others beyond her—Aubrie's minions. I ducked behind her to keep from being seen. They'd glamoured the place.

Ahead of us, three people stood apart from the rest at measured intervals, holding up the wall of magic that infused human thoughts and kept anybody from wandering past the welcome centre into their ritual.

Aubrie stood at the far edge of the guardrail, just above the lip of the falls. He had the book tucked under his arm and his head tilted back as if absorbing that natural energy I'd been told about.

The Horseshoe Falls poured out behind him, curving from our side across the river to the American side. Coloured spotlights moved across the massive rush of water as it fell, pink melting into yellow into green and blue. The moon shone overhead, cut horizontally with one perfect half lit up, like a cartoon grin.

"Where's your cavalry?" I asked over Ilse's shoulder.

"Damn it. Abe must have gotten waylaid." Ilse craned her neck to look behind us, back toward where we'd lost Mei.

I marvelled that she had actually cursed, but her meaning hit me harder.

"We can't wait," I said, straightening up.

"What do you suggest?"

"Rush them on three?"

Ilse sighed, then to my surprise said: "Counting to three seems unnecessary."

She flashed into vapour that matched the mist visible in the overhead lights and flew toward the guards.

I dashed after her, using my power to give me extra lift as I jumped from our elevated position. Clearing their heads, I landed on my feet behind them, putting a hand down for balance. A glance over my shoulder showed one batting at Ilse's vapour and the other two turning on me.

A hand grabbed my arm. "I do miss the obedience."

Aubrie's condescending voice in my ear sent a crack of rage through me. I tried to jerk out of his grip.

Something slammed into the back of my head hard enough to make me see stars dance under the lights. I hit the bricks on my face.

Sucking in a breath, I pulled myself to my hands and knees. He'd hit me with the book, which he tucked gingerly back under his arm.

I snarled, springing at him, but he caught me by the wrist before I could do any damage. He tightened his fingers, then jerked his hand to one side, snapping the bone. Tears blurred my eyes without permission and the breath left my lungs as a wave of fire radiated up my arm.

Ilse's shimmery shape shot between us, her hands materializing to snatch the book. Aubrie dropped me to grab her throat, flinging her at the railing. His strength gave her enough lift to clear it and disappear over.

Still reeling from the broken wrist, I stared at the edge of the overlook from my spot on the concrete. Part of me expected to see a small hand come back up over, followed by a soaking Ilse.

Nothing.

I struggled to breathe through a closing throat. *She's a water sprite. She's made of water.* She could vaporize before hitting the river's surface, or the wall of rough rock along the way.

Another man grabbed me from behind, tugging me away from Aubrie toward the barrier at the edge of the falls. My muscles refused to rally, too drained to fight back. The guardrail stood only as high as my waist—a low stone wall with a metal rail on top of it. It'd be easy to heft me over it and into the river, just like Ilse. Easier than throwing me off that balcony in Toronto. Aubrie didn't even have to do it himself this time.

The man dumped me on the cement. He wore a uniform of some kind—maybe park police. Probably stolen. As I struggled to get to my feet, he pulled my arms above my head and zip-tied my wrists together around the top bar of the guardrail, anchoring me there.

I gasped as the tie tightened on my broken wrist. Over my shoulder, I got a glimpse through the railing. Our platform ran along the top of the gorge, and the edge dropped right off beside me, straight down into the water crashing over boulders far below. The ringing in my ears had turned into the roar of the falls. Looking down made me dizzy.

Aubrie crouched beside me. "You're curious what the new world will be like? Take a front-row seat."

46

DANIEL SAT WITH HIS back against the bathroom door, scanning the tiny room for what felt like the millionth time for anything he might have missed. Nothing presented as a useful tool for getting the door open.

He'd tried to force it by ramming his shoulder against it, then braced himself against the counter and kicked beneath the knob to pop it open. Using his fingers to push the wedge out from his side of the door hadn't worked either. The goddamn binder Jude had stuck there held fast.

How much time had passed since she'd left?

His cuts had scabbed over but still ached. He could just give up, wait until housekeeping found him in the morning. Jude wanted to handle this one? Let her. And if in the morning, there was some bizarre new world outside the window, then they could all just blame her.

Because that would make it better.

A muffled knock at the front door to the room made him jump. He stopped himself short of calling for help, getting up to put his ear to the bathroom door. The chance whoever was in the hallway would help him seemed about even with the chance they'd kill him.

"Mr. Cain? Daniel?" Abe's voice. "You there?"

Devoid of other options, Daniel replied, "Come in!"

"It's locked."

"I can't open it for you."

After a brief pause, Abe said, "All right, hold tight."

Daniel pressed his ear to the door again as if he might be able to make out the sounds of the cowboy breaking in. He couldn't fathom an easy way through the electronic lock. After another minute of silence, it seemed like the other man had left.

He gave the door another half-hearted kick. There wasn't enough room in the tiny bathroom for a running start to get any momentum to batter the door further.

Batter. The word struck him, and he turned to lift the heavy porcelain lid off the toilet tank. It would make a decent battering ram. He slammed it against the door.

It left a satisfying dent that told him it would probably work to smash through the wood. After two more hits, the door cracked.

He froze at the whir of the electronic lock from outside, then the creak of the room's front door opening.

"Ah, there it is." Abe's voice again. "On the desk. Think I'd forget my own head if it weren't screwed on tight. You need to come in, look around?"

"No, sir, I don't think that's necessary." Another voice, male.

"All right, then. Thanks for your help."

"You're welcome. Have a good night."

"Will do." The door shut. Silence. Another noise came from under the door as the cowboy struggled with the binder wedged so tightly beneath it. The door shook once, then opened.

Daniel lowered the porcelain tank lid to the floor, hesitant to give up the only weapon he had.

Abe straightened up, examining the binder.

"Had it stuck under there pretty good," he said.

"Who let you in?"

"Security guard." To Daniel's raised eyebrows, the cowboy added, "*Some* people respond to politeness."

"Some people don't know any better," Daniel shot back. "You used a spell?"

"Told you, I'm not very good at spells."

"So, he just didn't *notice* your knife?"

"Glamour's a different animal." Abe glanced at the hunting knife sheathed on his hip, realizing aloud, "You can see it. Huh. Must need more practice there too." He shrugged as if that didn't concern him, tapping the binder. "I assume this was Jude? Ingenuity, I'll give her that. Where is she?"

"She's gone to get the book from Aubrie." Daniel brushed past him into the room to see the clock and stopped short. It couldn't possibly be 11:52. He stepped over the cracked remains of his phone to snatch the crowbar off the bed.

Abe stood between him and the door. "Couldn't get an army through the portals on short notice, but I've got a handful of trained people who were already on this side. I know where Aubrie's going."

Daniel stopped, startled. "That's an invitation?"

"It is."

"Why?"

"Power in numbers. Diversity of skills. Need the cannon fodder. Take your pick." Abe shrugged.

"You have some way to get us there in under five minutes?"

"'Course I do." Abe turned and headed for the hallway.

Daniel followed, balking when the cowboy pulled open the door to the hotel stairwell. Instead of stairs, they faced into the foyer of a house. The place radiated a claustrophobic aura even through the open door, and something under that, sharp and acrid. He fought to quell a flicker of panic, swallowing bile. He hadn't seen this part of the house but he remembered the awful, unnatural feeling of the place well enough.

Voices came from inside.

Abe hesitated, glancing back, then stopped whatever he'd been about to say. He changed his mind again and spoke: "Don't tell 'em your name."

"Why would I—?"

"You wouldn't. So don't." The cowboy seemed to regret saying anything at all.

That probably meant whoever was inside would recognize his name, know him as Consilium, or worse, know his father. That would be what Abe was trying to avoid. The realization made Daniel hesitate.

But there was no other choice. He braced himself and followed the cowboy over the threshold.

A group of people stood beside the staircase in the foyer. Six unfriendly faces turned to meet them. Five men and a woman, though the giant ram's horns spiralling out of the sides of one man's head made Daniel rethink his initial classification.

"Cutting it close," one of them told Abe. His eyes flickered to Daniel then back to Abe to add, "Didn't find the little princess then?"

"She'd already gone," Abe said.

"So you brought another worthless human back in her place?"

Something sharp scratched Daniel's arm, along one of the scabbed-over knife wounds the pixie had left. He jerked away, spinning to see a man he hadn't noticed initially.

"Oh, I don't know." The man examined the dried blood on his finger, then licked it off with a long, black tongue. "Seems logical to bring provisions."

Abe's hand clamped on Daniel's wrist just long enough to keep him from raising his weapon at the creature. "This isn't the fight y'all want to have right now," he warned, then released Daniel, stepping between him and the others as they clustered closer. "We've wasted too much time already."

"We were waiting for you, boss," the black-tongued man returned.

Ignoring his snide tone, Abe looked to the one with the ram's horns, who now stood closest to the front door. "Get us to Niagara now."

47

I STRAINED AGAINST THE plastic tie, struggling to get to my feet. The bulk of Jasper's switchblade dug into my hip, but I couldn't contort my body into a shape that would force it out of my pocket into my grasping fingers. I could barely move my arms. The pressure on my injured wrist made my eyes fill with black spots.

Aubrie took a few steps toward the place closest to the lip of the falls, opening the book and flipping to a page he had marked.

The platform around us darkened. My heart surged into my throat. The overhead lights on poles illuminated our platform, but the coloured lights shining onto the rolling water had gone off. It was as good as a clock chiming down the fatal hour.

Aubrie's voice rose beyond the roar of water. He started a chant in what sounded like drawn-out sing-song gibberish. The sounds involved—chirps and trills that he strained on—seemed impossible to make with human vocal chords.

The air stirred, then the wind picked up with force, whipping my hair across my face. The scattered clouds overhead glowed as the lights from the cities in both countries bounced off them. The glow began to change colours, pale white turning into blue and green, then reddish. It looked like the lights that had been shining onto the falls had been turned back on and bled up into the sky.

The world felt wrong already, twisting like a knife in my chest. I tugged on the zip-tie with my good hand, tears stinging the corners of my eyes. The air pressed down, heavy and charged, a hundred times worse than when Daniel had painted the incantation on Mei's back in that crappy motel room. I held my breath, expecting a sharp tearing noise, waiting to watch the watercolour sky fall apart.

A small, dark object came flying from the steps to the welcome centre. It bounced off Aubrie's left arm, abruptly cutting off his chant.

Mei stood on the bottom step. She'd made it through the glamour.

Aubrie snatched her cellphone from the damp bricks. "I question your choice of weapon."

He crushed it in one fist as he straightened up, letting the pieces sprinkle back down to the ground. Meeting the eyes of his minions nearest her, he jerked his chin toward her.

She darted back up the shallow steps, disappearing into the shadows behind the raised garden beds. At least she'd drawn three of Aubrie's guys away. That just left twenty or so for me to take on while tied on the rail.

A cry of surprise came from the darkness. More voices followed, as what had to be Ilse's cavalry arrived.

Abe appeared first, then Daniel. A few others I didn't recognize were with them—the Mab's soldiers, maybe. Nine in all—ten with Mei—still less than half the followers Aubrie had.

Surprise flickered across Aubrie's face when he saw the new arrivals, replaced as quickly with a mix of anger and disdain. He kept the book open but didn't continue the spell, as if waiting for the noise to die down.

The thick charge in the air didn't ebb. The colours hung in the sky as if the spell were just patiently waiting too.

Aubrie's people surged forward, forming physical barriers around him to keep the new arrivals from reaching him. Abe's soldiers didn't hesitate, rushing right into the fray. They seemed to react faster, jump higher and hit harder than Aubrie's people. Full-blood Faeries.

In the pool of an overhead light, Mei leapt onto one woman's back, tearing at her face with sharp fingernails. When the woman bucked her off, she rolled back to her feet with grace I hadn't known she still had.

Beyond her, Daniel faced off with a taller man who seemed in the midst of turning into some kind of animal—a griffin, from the look of the tiny wings sprouting from his back and the hook of his nose partially changed into a bird's beak. The griffin's hands had morphed into wide, heavy paws with sharp talons and he tore Daniel's weapon away, flinging it back into the flower beds behind them. He buried the claws of his other paw in Daniel's shoulder, forcing him to his knees.

I turned gravity, bracing both boots against the stone below the rail, and tugged backwards with my good wrist. The plastic refused to snap. I put enough force into it to make my broken wrist take some of the pressure. The agonizing fire knocked me back to the concrete, huffing in pain.

A shriek and a gurgling howl from their direction got my attention. Daniel tossed something powdery into the griffin's eyes, giving himself time and leverage to twist his adversary's free paw and jam the deadly claws into the giant creature's own neck.

He crawled out from under the collapsed beast and saw me. When he reached the railing, he dropped down to examine the zip-tie around my arms. The closeness of his body sent an irritating relief through me, cut short when he pressed too hard on my injured wrist.

"Knife in my pocket," I hissed through clenched teeth.

He patted my hips to find Jasper's switchblade, then dug it from my pocket and opened it, reaching over my head to snap the zip-tie.

I breathed a sigh of relief when it broke. The blood flooded back into my hands, choking me off mid-"Thanks" with a gasp of pain when the tingle gave way to throbbing in my broken wrist. The agony made me double over, certain I was about to throw up.

Daniel jerked out of my way as I came within centimetres of ramming my head into his bleeding shoulder.

"More iron filings?" I rasped, focusing teary eyes on the furry, motionless hulk of the griffin beyond us.

"Pepper."

"*Why* are you carrying—?"

A roar of water cut me off. A wave rose over the guardrail, fighting the flow over the falls. As it came past the railing, it slimmed down into a narrow strip of water, a liquid snake, sliding through the fighting and sweeping Aubrie's people under.

Ilse!

She cleared a hole to Aubrie, who still had the book open. He'd put his head back, lips moving as he continued the spell.

Daniel tackled him first, knocking the spellbook from his hands. It bounced and slid along concrete slick with river water.

I dashed for it. One of Aubrie's people slammed into me before I reached it, sending us both tumbling to the concrete in a tangle of limbs that spewed fire through me from my wrist. I got upright before my assailant, hooking my good arm over the guardrail and kicking him in the face.

Aubrie's returning punch to Daniel sent him flying back into the shadows of the welcome centre flowerbeds. Abe and the sentient rush of water that was Ilse slammed into Aubrie a second later, toppling him. He kicked Abe off with only half his usual force, then seized on the moment the surge of water needed to turn back toward him and crawled, drenched, to his knees. He flipped the pages of the book, searching for something.

Throwing his head back, Aubrie shouted words I didn't recognize.

As soon as they left his lips, fatigue flooded through me. I crumpled, sinking to the pavement. Every other Faerie on the platform succumbed the same way. Abe faltered, pushing himself up from where he'd landed. Ilse's limp form rolled out of the wave as it splashed down on the concrete.

Aubrie'd knocked out his own people too. They all fell like dominoes.

Unaffected himself, he got to his feet, snatching the book from the ground and flipping through it to a page he'd marked. He lifted his face to the sky, ready to shout the rest of his sphere-merging spell to the half-moon.

Before he could, something flew out of the dark and slammed into his ribs, knocking the book from his hands. Metal clanged on the pavement, a crowbar hitting the ground as Aubrie doubled over. He bared his teeth in a hiss at Daniel, who had gotten to his feet again somehow in the flowerbed and flung the weapon.

Nice trick. The spell didn't work on humans.

Mei swept in, her bare feet skidding in a puddle Ilse had left on the concrete as she snatched the book from the ground.

Aubrie swung his arm and caught her by the hair, making her scream as he curled a fist into her scalp. Even hunched over in pain at his injured ribs, his stance said he had enough energy left to toss her over the guardrail and into the rushing water of the falls.

I summoned the bits of strength left in my heavy body, shoving myself forward with a grunt. I was half-human—this spell wasn't going to ground me either. I tapped into the non-magical part of me, the skin and bone and muscle bestowed by my human mother, probably sipping schnapps in front of her TV right now. That shitty line I'd quipped to the Consilium therapist that I'd seen printed on the page in Daniel's oven echoed in my head. "*All I got from her was her ability to drink anybody under the table. Probably not magic, huh?*" It mingled with the sights of Mei barefoot, throwing herself at creatures twice as powerful as her, or Daniel flinging that crowbar despite his mangled shoulder.

I didn't need my Faerie power to gain my feet. My muscles burned as I ground them against the spell but I got up. I took one half-staggering, half-flying step to hurl myself onto Aubrie's back.

He dropped Mei, spinning to dislodge me and stumbling both of us into the guardrail. Before he could pull away, I gripped the metal railing behind me with both hands. Pain exploded as I tightened the muscles in my broken wrist but I pushed off. The force of my Faerie power rushed through me in a scattered tumble, joining the simple human stubbornness in my bones to carry me over.

Aubrie flipped backwards with me, tearing my hair as he struggled to shove me away. For an instant, we were tangled together upside-down, perpendicular to the railing bar, then the thrust of my jump tipped us, swinging us like a pendulum over the guardrail.

The force of motion made the real world's gravity tear like claws through the fragile wisps I'd managed to build of my own. My fingers strained to hold the slippery metal bar as the fall put the weight of my body on my wrist. My howl of agony echoed off the rock walls around us.

A hand snapped around my forearm from above, then two more latched onto my broken wrist on the other side. Bright white stars exploded in my eyes.

Something heavier tugged on me from below. Fingers had my ankle in a vise grip. Without being told, my free leg slammed against whatever was dragging me down, struggling to free myself from the extra weight. The roar of the falls almost drowned out the ragged screaming in my ears.

All of my muscles tensed, and I kicked again.

Fingernails dug into my ankle, then the weight disappeared. I looked down to see Aubrie disappear into the misty darkness.

48

Two people hauled me back up over the railing. Dark, shimmering spots still filled my eyes as I collapsed between Daniel and Mei.

The spell must have died with Aubrie. Distant, blurry shapes moved nearby—the Faeries had picked themselves up, their energy returned. A flash of blue had to be Ilse's hair as she and the others Abe had brought herded Aubrie's remaining people toward the dark welcome centre.

Overhead, the sky had returned to reflecting yellow lights from the city. Whatever Aubrie had started was over. The worlds were still separate.

I realized with a start that somebody held my hand and jerked my chin toward Mei. She had my fingers pressed between both of hers as if to hold my arm still while as she studied my swollen wrist.

"Sorry about that," she said, meeting my eyes. She'd been the one who grabbed my wrist to haul me up, then. Daniel's must have been the hand on my other arm.

"Water under the, you know, waterfall." My voice came out cracked and tears filled my eyes at the sheer effort of speaking.

When Mei raised an eyebrow, I added, "I know it's 'under the bridge', but there's a waterfall *right there*."

"Hilarious." Her flat tone said she was already done humouring me.

"Are you all right?" Daniel sat against the wall beside me, not looking much better than I felt. The left side of his face had flushed red, probably where Aubrie had clocked him and sent him flying. A scary amount of blood stained his shoulder and he grimaced when he tried to move it.

"Just another day at the office." I tried to haul myself up using my good hand, but my legs wobbled like rubber and I couldn't.

Daniel wrapped his uninjured arm around my waist to pull me to my feet and keep me from toppling over. The warmth of his body made my muscles want to melt. It took all of my resolve to straighten my spine so he'd let me go.

I caught Mei staring over the edge to the gorge. I knew the look on her face. An ache started in my chest that I tried not to feel. Aubrie didn't deserve it, from either of us.

"You fought," I said too loudly, snapping her attention away. "Human."

"Ten years of jujitsu." She brushed blood off her neck from the spot where Aubrie had torn her hair. "I always wanted an alternative to the dragon."

"Guess you've got one."

"Oh, no. This was my last . . . whatever this was." She indicated the platform behind her, then her eyes darted over my shoulder, making me aware that Daniel no longer stood beside me. I turned to find him kneeling next to the railing.

He got to his feet when he realized we were watching, keeping his injured arm tight to his chest.

An exasperated look that I didn't understand crossed Mei's face, then her expression settled back into vague disinterest. "We should be scarce, before the victors get hungry." She darted a glance at our immediate surroundings, as if making sure nobody was sneaking up to grab her. "I'm finding a phone, calling a cab and an ambulance, then taking whichever comes first."

Without waiting to see if we'd join her, she turned on her heel to stride across the platform toward the stairs. So much for that blossoming friendship.

"You should probably take the ambulance," I told Daniel, jerking my chin in her direction. The Faeries hadn't noticed him yet, but Mei was right—they would.

"What about you?" he returned.

"Oh, didn't you hear? I'm a Faerie princess. I'm set."

He snorted as if I'd made a joke. "No kidding." When I didn't say anything further, his expression changed but his tone remained dry. "Congratulations, then."

"Hand to God—the Mab's my aunt," I said, holding up the appropriate palm as I cradled my broken wrist against my chest. "How do you think I found that book at my mom's place? My father—Miranda's brother—stashed it there."

Daniel still looked unconvinced. Couldn't exactly blame him for doubting me but it still annoyed me after all we'd been through. Like I'd bother making this shit up?

When I didn't recant, he finally said, "Enjoy the tiara, then."

The mocking in his voice made it a challenge.

"I will *rock* the fucking tiara," I snapped. My fatigued muscles twitched as he left, readying me to go to his aid if anyone's head so much as swivelled toward him. All of the Faeries looked busy subduing Aubrie's people. None of them paid attention to the human slipping past them.

Swallowing the persistent urge to follow him, I started when Abe approached from my other side.

The cowboy tipped his hat back to look me over. "What's this about a tiara?" he asked. "You joining the Court?"

"I only told Daniel that so he'd leave." I rolled my shoulders and shook out my emotions like a dusty rug so he wouldn't read them. "I assume I have you to thank for him being here at all."

"Seemed prudent to recruit every warm body with a weapon."

"Wouldn't have hurt, though, if he'd gotten killed and rid you of that pesky incantation in his head, huh?"

Abe jerked back as if I'd bitten him, but he looked more annoyed than offended.

As a peace offering, I lifted my broken wrist. "Can you fix this?"

The cowboy frowned, as if refraining from rolling his eyes, but eased his fingers around it.

I clenched my teeth together to keep from groaning at the burning sensation of the healing. It wasn't as bad this time as the pain of having it snapped.

When he'd finished, I touched my face, wincing as my fingers slid over swollen, painful spots. None of my other injuries seemed urgent enough to ask Abe to heal. I could deal with them myself.

Ilse appeared beside him, having finished up with the group near the welcome centre.

"What took you so long with the water?" I demanded.

"It's a rather tricky spell," she said.

"I was beginning to think . . . "

"Well, I didn't mean to worry you." Something about her tone told me she was teasing me. Ilse teased the same way she did everything else: politely.

"Can you walk, Jude?" Abe asked.

"I can square dance if you want me to, Cowboy." My legs still felt weak, but I could hold myself up. I needed a long, hot shower, a lot of sleep and food. "What say we go back to the house and you whip me up some flapjacks?"

He grinned. "That could probably be arranged."

While we'd been talking, Ilse had moved past us, scanning the ground. "Did you see where the grymoire landed?"

I looked to the spot where Aubrie would have dropped the book.

Empty.

Things pieced together in my head with surprising speed: Daniel crouched beside me, the way he'd kept his injured arm pressed against his chest. The flash of annoyance across Mei's face. She must have seen him hide the book under his shirt. What the hell was wrong with him? Stealing the grymoire didn't exactly bode well for disappearing off Miranda's radar.

On the other hand, *I* didn't want the thing, and I sure as hell wasn't taking it back to Mom. I didn't really want the Court to have it either. Who knew what other dangerous shit was in there? At least Daniel would destroy it. It still pissed me off that he'd snuck it out under my nose, but I'd kind of had that coming.

"It went over," I answered Ilse. "I kicked it off the edge. Sorry."

Abe gave me a half-smile that made me wonder how quickly he'd seen through my lie. Instead of calling me out, he shrugged. "There's another copy."

I gaped. "There's a *what*?"

"On the other side of the portal. In the palace library."

"Your father only imposed it onto that book." Ilse frowned, standing on tiptoe to look over the edge of the guard rail as if she might catch sight of the tiny blue book bobbing on the river's surface in the dark. "The original is safe. But the copy . . ."

"It's gone," Abe said.

Ilse landed heavily on her heels, then looked from him to me. Her lips pressed into a thin line. "I see." She lifted her chin in the direction of the bridge. "I should go. The Mab will want to know it's finished."

"She's okay?" Relief flooded me. It hadn't really occurred to me until now, but if Miranda died, it bumped me up in line to be freaky Faerie royalty. No thanks.

"She's recovering." Genuine relief coloured Ilse's voice and I remembered her vested interest in the Mab's well-being. *You're Miranda's only family.*

"Aubrie said I'm her heir," I said. "That's . . . for real?"

Ilse nodded. "As the closest female relative, yes."

"You'd think she might have protected me a little more." I touched a painful spot on my ribs.

"Not like you make it easy," Abe said. He hesitated then admitted, "She had concerns about an heir who's part human."

"Though others didn't." Ilse gave Abe a quick smile before she headed off, avoiding the scowl he sent in her direction.

"So you like me, huh?" I asked.

"Aubrie was right about one thing," Abe said. "Us less-than-Faerie folk need to look out for each other."

"Thanks." I leaned back against the railing, nodding to the rest of the Court Faeries. "But this doesn't mean I'm on your team."

"I get it. Any port in a storm."

"What—you're a pirate now? Don't cowboys have sayings?"

"Stick around long enough, darlin', I may think one up." Abe rested his arms on the railing, watching at the dark water rush over the edge of the falls.

"Stick around?" I snorted, surveying the platform again. "For the cleanup and the paperwork?"

"Not worn out on running alone yet?"

I sighed, turning to the city lights up the hill. "I'm working on it."

Acknowledgements

Going more or less chronologically in this expression of gratitude, my first "thank you" goes to my parents, Harry and Margee, who believed in my writing from the start, somewhere in my early years. (This was indicative of their habitual encouragement, which ensured I had no family drama or simmering resentment from which to draw inspiration, thus developing my imagination by force.) Thank you too, Mom, for editing this story chapter-by-chapter with no judgment back in its early incarnation when it was a terrible mess.

Thanks to my sister Ronnie, who has been reading my various stories for thirty years and used to give me notes after lights-out even when she would have preferred to go to sleep. (Don't feel sorry for her—she got back-rubs out of the deal.) Also to my sister Coco, and my twin-sister-from-an-entirely-other-set-of-parents, Kelli, for letting me bouncing ideas off of them at various points. And to my brother-in-law, Stu, who needed something to read on the train and thus became one of my earliest male readers. And to Michelle, one of my first (if not *the* first) critique partners.

Thanks, Carmen (my BFF), and Emily (my big sister), both wonderful people and early readers of this book who provided helpful advice and suggestions on scenes that probably don't exist anymore (and some that do—I swear!) Thank you also to my more recent beta readers Meredith and Samia, for being so supportive and optimistic about the book even as they pointed out plot-holes. Same for my critique friends on the SFF Writers Workshop, in particular Robyn and Boz, who stuck with me through each chapter I posted.

Big thanks to my editor Julie Kay-Wallace, whose keen eye and thorough analysis pushed me to problem-solve (more than I would have preferred) and make the story so much stronger.

Finally, thank you to my partner, Jonathan, for your love and support. I promise never to ask you to read my book again.

Stephanie Caye lives in Montreal with her partner and two furry supernatural beings disguised as cats.